A
COMPLICATED
KINDNESS

MIRIAM TOEWS

FABER & FABER

First published by Alfred A. Knopf Canada in 2004

First published in the UK in 2004
by Faber & Faber Limited
Bloomsbury House,
74–77 Great Russell Street
London WC1B 3DA

This paperback edition first published in 2018

Printed and bound by CPI Group (UK) Ltd, Croydon, CR0 4YY

A CIP record for this book
is available from the British Library

ISBN 978– 0–571–34100–9

MIX
Paper from
responsible sources
FSC® C020471

2 4 6 8 10 9 7 5 3 1

To Marj

ONE

≈

I live with my father, Ray Nickel, in that low brick bungalow out on highway number twelve. Blue shutters, brown door, one shattered window. Nothing great. The furniture keeps disappearing, though. That keeps things interesting.

Half of our family, the better-looking half, is missing. Ray and I get up in the morning and move through our various activities until it's time to go to bed. Every single night around ten o'clock Ray tells me that he's hitting the hay. Along the way to his bedroom he'll stop in the front hallway and place notes on top of his shoes to remind him of the things he has to do the next day. We enjoy staring at the Northern Lights together. I told him, verbatim, what Mr. Quiring told us in class. About how those lights work. He thought Mr. Quiring had some interesting points. He's always been mildly interested in Mr. Quiring's opinions, probably because he's also a teacher.

I have assignments to complete. That's the word, *complete*. I've got a problem with endings. Mr. Quiring has told me that essays and stories generally come, organically, to a preordained ending that is quite out of the writer's control. He says we will know it when it happens, the ending. I don't know about that. I feel that there are so many to choose from. I'm already anticipating failure. That much I've learned to do. But

then what the hell will it matter to me while I'm snapping tiny
necks and chucking feathery corpses onto a conveyor belt in a
dimly lit cinder-block slaughterhouse on the edge of a town not
of this world. Most of the kids from around here will end up
working at Happy Family Farms, where local chickens go to
meet their maker. I'm sixteen now, young to be on the verge of
graduating from high school, and only months away from
taking my place on the assembly line of death.

One of my recurring memories of my mother, Trudie
Nickel, has to do with the killing of fowl. She and I were
standing in this farmyard watching Carson and his dad chop
heads off chickens. You'd know Carson if you saw him. Carson
Enns. Arm-farter in the back row. President of the Pervert Club.
Says he's got a kid in Pansy, a small town south of here. Troubled
boy, but that's no wonder considering he used to be The
Snowmobile Suit Killer. I was eight and Trudie was about thirty-
five. She was wearing a red wool coat and moon boots. The ends
of her hair were frozen because she hadn't been able to find the
blow-dryer that morning. Look, she'd said. She grabbed a strand
of hair and bent it like a straw. She'd given me her paisley scarf
to tie around my ears. I don't know exactly what we were doing
at Carson's place in the midst of all that carnage, it hadn't started
out that way I'm pretty sure, but I guess carnage has a way of
creeping up on you. Carson was my age and every time he
swung the axe he'd yell things at the chicken. He wanted it to
escape. Run, you stupid chicken! Carson, his dad would say. Just
his name and a slight anal shake of the head. He was doing his
best to nurture the killer in his son. It was around 4:30 in the
afternoon on a winter day and the light was fading into blue and
it was snowing horizontally and we were all standing under a
huge yellow yard light. Well, some of us were dying. And Carson
was doing this awful botch job on a chicken, hacking away at its
neck, not doing it right at all, whispering instructions on how to

escape. Fly away, idiot. Don't make me do this. Poor kid. By this time he'd unzipped the top half of his snowmobile suit so it kind of flapped around his waist like a skirt, slowing him down, and his dad saw him and came over and grabbed the semi-mutilated chicken out of Carson's little mittened hand and slapped it onto this wooden altar thing he used to do the killing and brought his axe down with incredible speed and accuracy and in less than a second had created a splattery painting in the snow and I was blown away by how the blood could land so fast and without a single sound and my mom gasped and said look, Nomi, it's a Jackson Pollock. Oh, it's beautiful. Oh, she said, cloths of heaven. That was something she said a lot. And Carson and I stood there staring at the blood on the snow and my mom said: Just like that. Who knew it could be so easy.

I don't know if she meant it's so easy to make art or it's so easy to kill a chicken or it's so easy to die. Every single one of those things strikes me as being difficult to do. I imagine that if she were here right now and I was asking her what she meant, she'd say what are you talking about and I'd say nothing and that would be the end of it.

It's only because she's gone that all those trivial little things from the past echo on and on and on. At dinner that night, after the slaughter at Carson's place, she asked us how we would feel if for some reason we were all in comas and had slept right through the summer months and had woken up around the middle of November, would we be angry that we had missed the warmth and beauty of the summer or happy that we had survived. Ray, who hates choosing, had asked her if we couldn't be both and she'd said no, she didn't think so.

Trudie doesn't live here any more. She left shortly after Tash, my older sister, left. Ray and I don't know where either one of them is. We do know that Tash left with Ian, who is Mr. Quiring's nephew. He's double-jointed and has a red Ford Econoline van. Trudie seems to have left alone.

Now my dad, you know what he says in the middle of those long evenings sitting in our house on the highway? He says: Say, Nomi, how about spinning a platter. Yeah, he uses those exact butt-clenching words. Which means he wants to listen to Anne Murray singing "Snowbird," again. Or my old Terry Jacks forty-five of "Seasons in the Sun." I used to play that song over and over in the dark when I was nine, the year I really became aware of my existence. What a riot. We have a ball. Recently, Ray's been using the word *stomach* as a verb a lot. And also the word *rally*. We rally and we stomach. Ray denied it when I pointed it out to him. He says we're having a good time and getting by. Why shouldn't he amend? He tells me that life is filled with promise but I think he means the promise of an ending because so far I haven't been able to put my finger on any other. If we could get out of this town things might be better but we can't because we're waiting for Trudie and Tash to come back. It's been three years so far. My period started the day after Trudie left which means I've bled thirty-six times since they've been gone.

This town is so severe. And silent. It makes me crazy, the silence. I wonder if a person can die from it. There's an invisible force that exerts a steady pressure on our words like a hand to an open, spurting wound. The town office building has a giant filing cabinet full of death certificates that say choked to death on his own anger or suffocated from unexpressed feelings of unhappiness. *Silentium.* The only thing you hear at night is semis barrelling down the highway carting drugged animals off to be attacked with knives. Do not make eye contact with those cows. People here just can't wait to die, it seems. It's the main event. The only reason we're not all snuffed at birth is because that would reduce our suffering by a lifetime. My guidance counsellor has suggested to me that I change my attitude about this place and learn to love it. But I do, I told her. Oh, that's rich, she said. That's rich.

We're Mennonites. As far as I know, we are the most embarrassing sub-sect of people to belong to if you're a teenager. Five hundred years ago in Europe a man named Menno Simons set off to do his own peculiar religious thing and he and his followers were beaten up and killed or forced to conform all over Holland, Poland and Russia until they, at least some of them, finally landed right here where I sit. Ironically, they named this place East Village, which, I have learned, is the name of the area in New York City that I would most love to inhabit. Others ran away to a giant dust bowl called the Chaco, in Paraguay, the hottest place in the world. My friend Lydia moved here from Paraguay and has told me stories about heat-induced madness. She had an uncle who regularly sat on an overturned feed bucket in the village square and screamed for his brain to be returned to him. At night it was easier to have a conversation with him. We are supposed to be cheerfully yearning for death and in the meantime, until that blessed day, our lives are meant to be facsimiles of death or at least the dying process.

A Mennonite telephone survey might consist of questions like, would you prefer to live or die a cruel death, and if you answer "live" the Menno doing the survey hangs up on *you*. Imagine the least well-adjusted kid in your school starting a breakaway clique of people whose manifesto includes a ban on the media, dancing, smoking, temperate climates, movies, drinking, rock 'n' roll, having sex for fun, swimming, make-up, jewellery, playing pool, going to cities, or staying up past nine o'clock. That was Menno all over. Thanks a lot, Menno.

There is also something annoying about a man who believes in complete humility naming a group of people after himself. And using his first name. Nominites. Hmm. Maybe after my sojourn at the slaughterhouse I'll start a people. At times I find myself imagining Menno as a delusional patient in an institute off some interstate in a pretty, wooded area. Shuffling off to Group, hoarding his meds. That I belong within the frightful fresco of this man's dream unnerves me. I wonder what exactly happened in Menno's world that made him turn his back on it. I wonder what a re-enactment of a typical day in the childhood life of Menno Simons would look like. I've heard of Tolkien and Ursula Le Guin and the guy who wrote *Watership Down,* that delightful allegory about rabbits. But I'm not a fan of fantasy. There's so much of that being crammed down our throats every day in this place. The mark of the beast? Streets paved in gold? Seven white horses? What? Fuck off. I dream of escaping into the *real* world. If I'm forced to read one more Narnia series book I'll kill myself. I would love to read the diary of a girl my age—a girl from the city. Or a textbook on urban planning. Or a New York City phone book. I would kill to own a New York City phone book.

Trudie always said her eyes were hazel, but in fact they're the same smoky green as Ray's. Trudie and Ray are second cousins. Which makes me and Tash not only sisters but also third cousins. There's no deep end in this town's gene pool. That sounds like a worn-out joke, but it's not to us. No, she said, they're hazel. I'm putting hazel on my passport. Look again. Tash and I looked and saw nothing that looked like hazel, no flecks, no dots, no threads, but we said okay, they're hazel, fine. And what do you need a passport for anyway, my sister had asked. Trudie said for identification. I think it made her feel adventurous to own a passport, to think she actually might one day get on a plane and fly away to a magical place with a temperate climate where people dance.

Mennos are discouraged from going to the city, forty miles down the road, but are encouraged to travel to the remotest corners of Third World countries with barrels full of Gideon Bibles and hairnets. Maybe that's where she is now—planting churches in the Congo, wearing a pretty floral ankle-length dress, rubber boots and a straw hat. But I doubt it. That's what The Mouth did with single older women who were probably gay but were called spinsters—sent them off to hot places with a shovel and a monthly allowance and a camera so they could come back every couple of years and set up a slide show in the church basement for all the little Mennos. At the end of the slide show the surliest guy from the village always comes around to see the light and starts wearing clothing and helps the white gay women with their good work in spite of threats and disapproval from his own people. Sometimes the missionaries are killed. But that's just how it has to be. There's usually a strange, simmering sub-plot in these slide shows that involves either running the witch doctor out of town or getting him to smile for the camera while holding up a copy of the New Testament, which means, praise the Lord, he's been saved. After the slide show we eat cheese and buns and maybe play a little hide-and-seek, with groping, in the foyer.

Anyway, I can't picture my mother as a missionary. I can see her doing other things like deep-sea diving or leading groups of tourists around places in Europe. Trudie was short for Gertrude, which she hated a little less when she found out about Gertrude Stein and all those cats in Paris. She had always wanted to see Paris. She used to sing all those old Jacques Brel songs with a thick French accent. She sang them up big, comically, but Tash told me it was a *façade*. She said Trudie was

punch-drunk crazy from the endless domestic grind-a-thon.
Said her back was up against the wall of an oppressive
patriarchal regime.

Trudie loved to read but mostly she read mysteries (even
though the current thing to say around here is: There are no
mysteries!) or books about the Holocaust. She loved to say
unreal. That's just unreal, she'd say about things that surprised
or disappointed or amazed her, and there were lots of those
things it seemed. She also enjoyed the word *wheeeeeee,* said with
gusto—a reaction to whatever little thing was turning her on.
We as a family in a little motorboat on big waves. We as a family
coasting down a hill with the car in neutral. We as a family
chopping down a Christmas tree. We as a family. Another thing
she said a lot, when she was reading, and didn't want to answer
whatever question we had interrupted her with, was:
Whaaaaaatttttt?? An incredibly drawn-out word with a lot of
vocal range from low to high to sustained high. She'd keep her
eyes on her book. Hey Mom, I'm going outside to pour some
gasoline over myself and light a match! Whaaaaaatttttt? Eyes
never leaving the page. I loved it.

My mother's dream was to go to the Holy Land. She was
very intrigued with Jews. There were none in our town. There
were no black people or Asians either. We all looked pretty
much the same, like a science fiction universe. My sister and I
went to school in the morning and my mom would stand in the
doorway in her nightgown and say goodbye, goodbye, I love
you, good luck, have fun, until we couldn't hear her any more,
like we were foreign sailors leaving a port of call after a fantastic
unreal night together, and we'd come home at four o'clock in
the afternoon and she'd still be in her nightgown, but on the
couch, with her finger as a marker in the book saying hello,
hello, how was your day? Don't tell me it's after four already. It
is, we'd say. What's there to eat? And my mom would sit up real

fast and say, usually, oh I sat up too fast, and we'd wait for five seconds for her to clear her head. She had bright red down-filled slippers that were almost perfectly ball-shaped. In one hour she'd have gotten dressed, gone to the grocery store, the Tomboy (who names grocery stores after gender anomalies?), bought stuff for supper, come home, made the food, and put it on the table, smiling, happy, warm and untroubled.

She was a whiz with Klik, that canned meat that looks like crushed human flesh and comes with a built-on key you twist around to open the tin. I wish I had harder facts about her, a complete picture with high tone definition, but she was hard to pin down.

There was something seething away inside of her, something fierce and unpredictable, like a saw in a birthday cake. She played content like Jack Nicholson played crazy in *One Flew Over the Cuckoo's Nest*, but Ray truly was content to sit at the head of the table in his suit and tie and joke around with his two relatively normal daughters and fun-loving wife who had hazel eyes and sexy nighties and a passport with a glamorous black-and-white photo of herself tucked away in the top drawer of her dresser.

The place Trudie travelled to most often was the church basement. The women have to spend a lot of time there. If they don't they go to hell. (Who're you gonna serve? Missionaries in Botswana, or Satan? That's right. Any questions? Didn't think so.) Their job was to sew clothing and blankets for the missionaries and send it all overseas in barrels. Trudie hated it. She got into trouble for throwing a couple of romance novels into a barrel headed for Nicaragua. She was supposed to do all sorts of stuff at church, cook for weddings and funerals, quilt, teach Sunday school and just generally get her ass in humble helping gear. They were always calling her and asking her if she could spare some time to help out. It wasn't really a question.

She'd go sometimes at the very last minute saying oh I should
go, I should go right now.

It didn't help that her brother was the Über-Schultz. It
was like being the sister of Moammar Gaddafi or Joseph Stalin.
You fall into line or you fall. My dad liked it when she went to
help but he also liked it when she didn't. It seemed like he could
never figure out which Trudie he loved the best, the docile
church basement lady in the moon boots or the rebellious chick
with the sexy lingerie. I imagine that both of those extremes
were just poses and that the real Trudie fell somewhere in
between. But that's the thing about this town—there's no room
for in between. You're in or you're out. You're good or you're
bad. Actually, very good or very bad. Or very good at being very
bad without being detected.

Two

~

People come to East Village from all over the world for a first-hand look at simple living. Most of the time Trudie refused even to acknowledge the fact that in the summer months we were on display as backward Jesus freaks. She'd wonder out loud what all these cars with American licence plates were doing in town. Faker, you do so know, Tash would say. Trudie hated thinking of herself as a citizen of the world's most non-progressive community. When the Queen came to visit our town years ago for a glimpse backwards in time, Trudie said she wasn't going to go. The Queen was half a block from our place and everyone in town was going and it was kind of a big deal to Ray for some reason and he had wanted Trudie to put on her dark blue dress and join him in the crowd but she said nah, she was going to stay at home and read. She said she wasn't going to stand there like an idiot just to be called a local yokel by the sneering British press. Or have a picture of her taken with the caption: Unidentified Mennonite Woman unmoved by Queen's visit to religious community. Please Trudie, said Ray, please accompany me. No, she said, take the girls. Which he did. And we met up with my mom's brother-in-law, who had a stepladder that his kids and me and Tash took turns climbing to get a really good view of the Queen and her entourage while the people behind us swore in the whimsical language of our people. It's hard to take offence when you're being called *upemmuhljefulle und siehn muhl blief ope,* or a *schlidunzich.*

On the way home we met up with my mom, who told us that she had seen the Queen after all. Trudie had been sitting on top of Kliewer's machine shop in her housecoat and Keds with a bunch of teenage boys and they'd had the best view in town. So, she said, are you happy now? I saw the Queen. She linked her arm through my dad's and dragged him home. Tash and I exchanged looks that meant something like: Is our mother crazy in a cool, fun way or has she now stepped over the line into disturbing crazy that we'd like to see stop? Ray didn't seem pleased or displeased, just confused. It was really typical of the way she'd do something for his sake but in her own vaguely defiant way. Half in the world, half out. She was like the funny kid in class who knows just how far to go with the sassing.

She hid her records in Tash's old toy box in the basement. One time when I was around ten, Tash called up The Mouth and told him she'd found one of Trudie's Kris Kristofferson eight-tracks and she was very afraid she was about to listen to it and The Mouth said okay, now, calm down, pray with me. Take the . . . item and put it in a paper bag. Staple the bag closed and bring it to me here, at the parsonage, and we will deal with it together. Satan is tempting you, do you know that? Yes, said Tash, he's such an awful . . . man. (What exactly was he again? A fallen angel?) She started to cry. It was all fake. She and her friends, who were listening to the whole thing, rolled around on the floor killing themselves laughing, but I was horrified. She was so earmarked for damnation it wasn't even funny. Later that day The Mouth came over to talk and pray with Trudie about her fondness for guys like Kristofferson and Billy Joel. He told her that in his dictionary *hell* comes after *rock 'n' roll.*

There were so many bizarre categories of things we couldn't do and things we could do and none of it has ever made any sense to me at all. Menno was on a cough-syrup binge when he drew up these lists of dos and don'ts and somehow, inexplicably, they've survived time and are now an integral part of our lives.

When I was ten years old my mom and I had a big discussion about the *Swiss Family Robinson* movie playing at the Rouge Cinema, on Main Street. I wanted to go. My best friend at the time, Agnes, was going but that was because her father smoked and was the town bartender before the purges occurred and The Mouth took over everything and closed the bar and the bus depot and the pool hall and swimming pool and forced all the teachers to follow an oddball curriculum that had nothing to do with the standard provincial guidelines. Our textbook could have been called *Proven Theories We Decry.* The only thing he couldn't take down was the Rouge Cinema but I was never sure why not. Some back-room deal, I guess. A cut of the profits. Who knows. He may have left it there for the American tourists. Something for them to do in the evenings when the village closed. Or maybe he had a dream of someday showing the movie *Hazel's People* non-stop. Or *Menno's Reins.* Those were the films (we were discouraged from calling them *movies*) that we were shown on a regular basis.

If you think that those films were only propaganda, simplistic tales about a group of shy farmers overcoming world pressure to be normal and starting up their own whacked-out communities in harsh climates, you'd be right.

Agnes's family had stopped going to church generations ago. It didn't matter to them. They existed in a vacuum. In the town, but not of the town. They were awe-inspiring. The smell of tobacco that lingered in their house was like some kind of exotic perfume and the clanking of empty bottles was a rare and beautiful music.

Before the purges, when Agnes's dad was working in the bar all night, I'd go over to her place and we always had to play very, very quietly because her dad had to sleep during the day. We usually played a game called hide-the-sponge, but there was no looking involved, just listening. The entire game took place in the downstairs bathroom and the point of it was to put the little green sponge into the cupboard under the sink without making any noise. While one person was putting the sponge into the cupboard, the other person perched on the toilet and listened very closely to see if the cupboard door had made a sound while being closed. If it had, the person listening would whisper *sound* and it would be the other person's turn. Even though I abhor the silence of this town at night, I have to admit I was intrigued with the concept of playing as quietly as we could at the bartender's house.

I had never been to the Rouge Cinema. It wasn't the kind of place families like mine went to. But, damn, how I wanted to see the *Swiss Family Robinson*. My mom said she'd think about it and I said it's this afternoon and she said she'd have liked a little more time. She talked to my dad about it and he of course just didn't know. It was up to her. She walked around the house in her red down-filled slippers doing diversionary things while she figured out what to tell me. I followed her and said well? She asked me what it was about and I said I didn't know. A family, I thought. That lives on an island and is trying to get off. She had a very serious expression on her face. What's sinful about a family trying to survive and fight off things and get off an island, I asked her. She told me it wasn't that, really. It was the problem of certain people seeing me at the cinema. I said I'd wear a disguise and she laughed and said this is utterly unreal. Just go. She said something in the old language that I think meant more or less to hell with it, except, of course, not. We couldn't use the word *hell* casually, although my parents would often say *oba, yo,* which could be loosely interpreted as meaning hell, yeah.

We weren't even allowed to say *heck.* Agnes's family said heck. When we burned her brother's tree house down (another relatively quiet activity), and the tree, she said she would *get* heck. When I asked my mom what that meant she shook her head and asked me not to repeat it. I asked my friend, later, if she had gotten heck. And she said yes, and I remember feeling afraid and envious. Tobacco smoke, clanking bottles, and now getting, *receiving,* heck. What a paradise.

TVs were also on Menno's shitlist, at least they would have been if he'd been around when they were invented. We didn't get one until one of our cousins who was both a first and second cousin to us, and possibly an uncle and future in-law, was on *Reach for the Top,* a show about local high school kids answering questions in very short periods of time and winning prizes for the correct ones.

The whole thing—what was and what wasn't allowed—was so random and absurd it was like playing hide-and-seek with two-year-olds. Billy Joel's okay but the word *heck* isn't. *Reach for the Top,* fine. *Swiss Family Robinson,* no way. The Mouth delivered a sermon once that he had dubbed "Situational Comedies: Harmless Fun?" Trudie couldn't survive without *M*A*S*H.* The melodic "Suicide is Painless," over the sound of helicopters, would tinkle out through the screen window around eight in the evening and into the backyard where I'd be unknotting the garden hose for Ray or burying birds or something and I'd always have this moment, this very brief moment, of thinking ah, now Trudie's happy.

For some reason it was okay to watch *Batman,* even though he fought against man-eating plants and The Joker, which was a nickname that we knew indicated the presence of evil because it was a playing card. We weren't really supposed to

watch *Bewitched* or *I Dream of Jeannie* because of the magic
which meant Satanism, but we did anyway. Trudie said you
couldn't just wriggle your nose to make people trip and dishes
fall and Tash said oh yeah, okay, but you can take a stick and
tap a bush with it so it bursts into flames? Yeah, and check this
out, in my right hand I hold five fish. In my other, a single loaf
of bread. Now watch closely as I . . . My mom said hush and
Tash said you hush. My mom said Tash. And Tash said Mom.
And that was it. Her so-called discipline was so half-hearted.

One time on a comedy show, I can't remember which one, the
comedian wondered out loud if there would be sex in heaven
and Tash, lying on her stomach, chin in her hands, said yes and
it will be divine. I don't know why I remember that exactly. It
was more her deadpan expression that lingers in my mind, and
the reaction of my parents afterwards. There was none. Their
defences must have been down. They were tired. I hadn't
known if it was a joke or not. The very idea of using the words
sex and *heaven* in the same sentence, I thought, would be
grounds for . . . I didn't know . . . a prayer session, maybe. Tears,
verses, hugs, exorcisms.

I spent a large part of my childhood praying for Tash's
soul. I hid her I'M WITH JESUS shirt for almost two years
because I knew she was wearing it insincerely and because I had
inadvertently destroyed it by using my Magic Marker to put an
arrow on it that went up instead of to the side. One time in
church we were doing a call-and-response thing where The
Mouth asks questions and the rest of us answer them in unison
and every answer was supposed to be Jesus Christ but each time
Tash said John Lennon instead. My mom was trying to drown
her out with her Jesus Christs and then Tash started saying her
John Lennons one beat ahead of Trudie's Jesus Christs,

squeezing them in real fast, and I just put my head down on Trudie's lap and prayed for Tash to hear Jesus knocking on the door of her pitch-black heart before she was cast into the burning pits of hell. In the car afterwards my mom said Tash was incorrigible and Tash said my mom was faking it for my dad's sake and my dad said faking what? And Tash said faking being mad. And my dad said mad about what? About John Lennon, said Tash. Mom's mad about John Lennon, asked my dad. Yeah, said Tash, Mom's mad about John Lennon. God. You could *hear* her eyes rolling. And then my dad asked who John Lennon was and Tash requested permission to kill herself—and my mom looked happy, well, not unhappy, and my dad looked confused as usual.

I'm sure that was the day I first heard Tash call me *Swivelhead*. All I did back then it seems was look from Trudie to Ray to Tash back to Trudie to Ray to Tash and on and on trying desperately to understand what it was they were talking about, what the words coming out of their mouths *meant*. The only thing I needed to know was that we were all going to live forever, together, happily, in heaven with God, and without pain and sadness and sin. And in my town that is the *deal*. It's taken for granted. We've been hand-picked. We're on a fast track, singled out, and saved. It was the one thing I counted on and I couldn't understand why my own immediate family would make little feints and jabs in directions other than up, up, up to God.

Why was Tash so intent on derailing our chances and sabotaging our plans to be together for goddamn ever and why the hell couldn't my parents see what was happening and rein that girl in? We were supposed to stay together, it was clear to me. That was the function, the ultimate purpose, the entire premise for the existence of the Nickel Family. That we remained together for all eternity. And it was so doable. It was so close, we could almost touch it, in fact we were touching it. Living in East Village meant we were halfway there already. What more could a pious little Menno kid want?

There were other things you may not necessarily know or remember about my mother. She liked to pat her stomach, especially if she was standing in the middle of the kitchen staring at the cupboards trying to mentally prepare herself for plunging into some tedious domestic task.

Often when she said the word *yes,* in response to a question, she'd spread her arms out like a symphony conductor calling for a big sound from his musicians.

She liked a made bed.

She had an uncanny ability to predict the weather.

She'd snap towels viciously before folding them, often very close to our heads as we sat watching TV.

She didn't believe in waiting for two hours after eating before going for a swim. "Do fish get out of the water after they've eaten?"

She drove too fast and whenever she parked she'd inch closer and closer to the wall or barricade in front of her until the hood of the car bumped against it. She called it Montreal parking. She'd never been to Montreal but she liked to say *Montreal* whenever she could so that everything, parking, hairstyles, sandwiches, were all, according to her, Montreal-style.

She believed in one-hundred-percent cotton. "It wrinkles badly but at least it breathes."

She loved the girliness of my dad's eyelashes and his smile *(oh, Ray's smile!)* and the way his arms got dark brown in the summer. One time she and my dad were talking together in the kitchen and Tash and I heard her say, god DAMN I love your sense of humour.

She occasionally plucked hairs from her chin, which I couldn't watch.

She spoke to strangers whenever she had the opportunity to, mostly tourists here to see the *village,* and would usually get very excited about the various aspects of these strangers' lives.

In the winter she'd warm up my bed for me by lying in it for twenty minutes while I had my Saturday-night bath.

She cried every single time she watched *The Waltons.*

She made a lot of trips to the pencil sharpener in the basement because it said BOSTON on it.

At one point in her life she thought about running for mayor of the town, but didn't want to embarrass Ray.

She sang hymns loudly, which embarrassed me.

She was an expert on drawing horses, especially their rear ends. She'd doodle horses' asses all over the phone book.

She approached life happily, with her arms open. Which could have been a mistake.

She loved white frilly curtains, or yellow ones if they were super bright.

My dad loved the shit out of her and hardly ever knew what to say to her and she loved the shit right back out of him and filled the silent parts of their lives with books and coffee and other things.

I have a recurring mental image of her. When I was about twelve Trudie decided to learn how to ride my first, second *and* third cousin Jerry's motorcycle. He brought it over to our place and he showed her how to sit on it and start it and rev it up and where the brakes were and all that stuff and she said okay, yup, got it, got it, got it. She told me and Tash not to tell Ray because he'd worry. We sat in the grass next to the driveway eating home-made popsicles and watching. Sunlight was flashing off the chrome of the motorcycle and my mom was laughing. She was wearing fake denim pedal pushers and a pink terry-towel T-shirt. She'd wave to us and make faces while Jerry was giving her instructions. So then finally Jerry said okay, time to put this on. He plopped this giant helmet onto her head and she gave us this fake helpless look. Then it was time for her to ride.

She kicked the stand back and then she slowly turned the motorcycle around so that she was facing the highway. She looked at Jerry and he nodded, huge grin on his face, and she took off. She shot off. I mean, she went from zero to sixty in about a second and then she careened off the driveway and onto the grass, hit a flowerpot and went flying over the handlebars. The thing that I keep remembering, though, is how she looked as she flew through the air. She stayed in the exact same sitting position that she'd been in on the motorcycle. Her legs were curved and spread a bit as though she were still straddling the thing and her arms and hands, the entire time that she was flying through the air, looked like they were still holding on to the handlebars. She looked like Evel Knievel jumping twenty cars or whatever but with an invisible motorcycle. It was the funniest thing I'd ever seen. It seemed to last forever.

And then we were all up and running over to her where she lay in the grass, still laughing, and moaning, and Jerry felt awful and Trudie made us promise not to tell Ray which was difficult later on when he came home and wondered how she got that cast on her arm. She told him she'd fallen down the stairs running for the rinse cycle with a cup of softener in her hand and Tash told him the truth but made him promise not to tell her he knew.

It's not really a great or dignified recurring image to have of one's absent mother, I guess, but I get a little thrill from the memory of her flying through the air in that odd phantom position. Later on that summer, when the cast was off, Trudie took me and Tash to the pits for a swim and she told us to go underwater and keep our eyes open. She told us that she was going to do a dive off this piece of board somebody had rigged up and that when we'd see her come under the water she'd be in a perfect frog position. And it was true. She looked exactly like a frog diving underwater.

That's another strong image I have of Trudie but not as strong as the one where she flies. The other day I found her passport in her drawer when I was putting away my dad's laundered handkerchiefs. I wish I hadn't. For the purpose of my story, she should have it with her. I sat on my dad's bed and flipped through page after empty page. No stamps. No exotic locales. No travel-worn smudges or creases. Just the ID information and my mother's black-and-white photo which if it were used in a psychology textbook on the meaning of facial expressions would be labelled: Obscenely, heartbreakingly hopeful.

THREE

~

I met Travis five months ago at a New Year's Eve party at Suicide Hill. Good Mennonites don't technically celebrate the arrival of yet another year of being imprisoned in this world. It's a frustrating night for them. But we weren't good Mennonites.

Somebody had made a big fire and sparks were flying around nicely and people were laughing and coughing. Some were necking in the bushes. A few others were playing flashlight tag in the old Russian cemetery next to the hill. One or two were vomiting in the snow and I could vaguely hear Christine McVie singing "Oh Daddy" from someone's car speaker. I was standing around with some girls from school talking about resolutions when Travis and this other guy, Regan, walked up to us and asked if they could smoke us up.

We all shrugged, non-committal, flipped our hair, bored to death. Enh, said Janine, the verbal one. After sharing the joint me and Travis started a conversation and the other people went over to the fire. You're Tash's sister, right, he asked.

I said yeah.

That's bullshit, man, he said, referring I think to Tash not being around any more.

I shrugged.

You smell like patchouli, he said.

I smiled. We smoked. We looked up at the stars. We shook from cold.

What's your name again, he asked.

Nomi, I said.

He was wearing an army jacket with lots of pockets, and Greb Kodiaks. He'd cut the fingers off his gloves.

You like reggae, right, he asked.

Kinda, I said. Some of it. And he said he did too. And then we just started talking about music because that was sort of the test of potential. Even a Menno sheltered from the world knows not to stick her tongue into the mouth of a boy who owns an Air Supply record. You might stick your tongue into the mouth of a boy who owned some Emerson, Lake and Palmer, but you would not date him on a regular basis, or openly. And then somehow Travis mentioned the name of Lou Reed without acting like a fawning dork about it and I knew then that I wanted to be his girlfriend so I stopped talking for a while and tried to act demure by keeping my lips a certain way.

Be mysterious, I told myself. I'd been going after that laughing-on-the-outside, crying-on-the-inside look for a while. It all had to do with the eyes and the mouth and certain pauses in your speech. It's kind of tragic and romantic. I wasn't very good at it but I liked the bullshit bravado of it, you know, the *effort* of trying to cover something up and show it at the same time.

You said Nomi, right, asked Travis. Yeah, I said, and your name again? Travis, he said. Right. Travis, Travis, I said, making a big exaggerated point of trying to remember. I'd known his name for years. After that we slowly walked towards the bushes and into this little clearing and then we sat down on a fallen tree and his arms were around me and he said talk to me, Nomi, so I started stupidly rambling on and on about the first thing that came to my mind.

I heard something once that I liked and I think about it a lot, I said.

Yeah? said Travis. What did you hear?

Well, I said, these two people, a guy and a girl, were standing on a dark street in some town somewhere and the girl really liked the guy and had thought about him all the time, about being with him, having a relationship, everything, and the guy, I don't know, he might have liked the girl, he was a little older and way cooler, and they just happened to meet each other on the street around ten at night, both of them on their way home from somewhere, and the boy said to the girl, hey, hi, how's it going, you're uh . . . and the girl said uh, yeah, hey, and the guy said so talk to me, and the girl paused and smiled and then she said but you're here. So, I said to Travis, like I had just concluded a lecture on the makings of the A-bomb or something. Do you know what I mean? He said yeah, yeah, he did. He asked me why I liked that and I said I didn't know, it seemed emblematic of something or other, and he said but he was there and I was talking to him and I said yeah, that was true.

And then he asked me if I preferred the people I loved not to be around when I talked to them and I paused because I was confused but he understood my pause to be a dramatically flirtatious pause, maybe, and so when I finally did say no he said okay, good, and we sat there kicking snow and watching our breath evaporate and wondering, at least I was, what came next.

What did come next was a bunch of kids running up to us and saying it's the countdown, it's the countdown, like one minute to midnight, come on, come on, so me and Travis got up and walked over to where a different bunch of kids were pretending to throw this other kid, Kurt, or Little Metal Boy as he was often called, into the fire as a sacrifice to the Devil, and other kids, the feathered girls, loud and drunk as usual, were counting down and everyone was talking with a Scottish accent and Janine passed me a hash pipe and just as I was sucking back on it I got kicked in the face by Kurt's flailing leg and the pipe rammed into the roof of my mouth and tore the skin and my eyes started filling up with tears and Travis put his arm around my shoulders and said happy new year and I whispered happy new year to you too while swallowing mouthfuls of my own blood and when Travis leaned over to kiss me I shook my head slowly but not enough for him to notice and then passed out in the snow.

Afterwards Travis told me I had fallen without a sound. Just like the explosion of chicken blood in my mom's Jackson Pollock painting. That's what snow is good for. That must be why Menno "I love the nightlife" Simons picked this place to wait out the rapture, a place where we could fall quietly and not bother anyone. I woke up a few hours later in the back of Travis's dad's work truck, with a carpet on top of me and Travis sitting cross-legged next to my head. His lips were blue and he could barely speak but what he said was: Oh Christ, thank fucking God you're alive. I thought it was the most original thing I'd ever heard anyone say about me and I began to love him.

Trudie used to work in the crying room at church and we have these pictures of her and Tash and me hanging out in there and there's this one picture of Travis stepping on my face. He was two or so with a giant diapered ass and I was just a baby lying on the floor and obviously in his way.

My mom used to unhook the wire at the back of the speaker in the crying room so she wouldn't be able to hear *the man,* her brother, my Uncle Hans, who was The Mouth. Tash, when she was older, would bring in a transistor radio so we could listen to American stations while we helped my mom take care of the babies.

We had a lot of fun in the crying room. We could see the back of my dad's head, on the men's side, falling over and snapping back repeatedly while he tried to pay attention to the rebukes of Uncle Hands.

It was usually my job to watch out for mothers with screaming infants standing up in their pews because that meant they were headed our way and the radio had to be shut off so my mom wouldn't get busted and disciplined by her brother's notoriously harsh and badly dressed regime. This was the perilous line my father toed and still does, I guess. Torn—at least he was—between the woman he loves and the faith that keeps his motor running. Although with my mom gone, there's not much of a conflict any more. I'd call the aura at our house a perversely peaceful one of hushed resignation. A few weeks ago my uncle came over to borrow my dad's socket set and when he asked my dad how he was my dad said oh, unexceptional. Living quietly with my disappointments. And how are you?

I never know if he's joking when he says things like that or not. He always signs off his Christmas cards to people with: In Sin and Error, Pining . . . Raymond.

Four

〜

Ray has exceptionally large glasses, like an underwater mask, as if he never knows when he'll have to do some welding or shield himself from a solar eclipse. When he blinks at me I'm reminded of the distant city lights, or of the Man from Atlantis or of somebody who has just emerged from a dark underground cell after thirty years of isolation. His glasses are square with thick grey frames and he takes them off frequently to breathe on them. Hah. Hah. Two short punchy breaths, one for each lens. Then he wipes them off with a handkerchief and holds them up to the light, squinting, to see if they're clean. He still uses handkerchiefs. He buys them in packages of three at a store called Schlitzking Clothing. When I empty his pockets to do the laundry I'm always afraid I'll find one.

Doing the laundry can be a really interesting and intriguing process. Emptying people's pockets, noticing odours and stains and items, folding the clothes afterwards, opening drawers, putting everything away. If I were asked by the FBI to infiltrate the Kremlin I'd definitely get a job there doing the laundry. It's where the drama starts. What a gold mine. Anyway. Last night when I got home my dad was sitting in his yellow lawn chair by the front door staring off at the number twelve highway. His eyes shone through his glasses like green Life

Savers. They looked like something you'd want to dive for at the bottom of a swimming pool. Sometimes they're so pretty they're spooky and I have to ask him to shut them. You're still up, I said. He said we need to talk about Nomi and where Nomi's going. I stared at the highway too. I asked him do you mean me and he looked at me, puzzled. I reached out and patted his head slowly. It was a weird thing to do. He lifted his hand and put it on mine and we held our two hands there together on the side of his head, near his ear, as though we were attempting to prevent blood loss while waiting for an ambulance to arrive. Then after a while I said Nomi's going in the house and he didn't let go of my hand right away. Like we were in a crappy play and he'd missed his cue.

Ray once built something. It was a garbage hutch, he told me. A few weeks after Trudie left he'd gone into the garage and started working on it. It took him a few days of straight building to get it finished. I was spending all of my free time listening to one song (Zeppelin's "All My Love"—Trudie had liked it too) over and over in the living room and Ray was in the garage hammering and sawing away on his hutch.

We were little islands of grief. My grandma told me that after my grandpa died she had been very calm. Very, very calm. She bathed, she cleaned the house, she cooked, she graciously thanked people for coming around with their casseroles and condolences. Then, one day, she went to the post office to buy some stamps to send thank-you cards and the guy behind the counter told her she was short two cents and she didn't have any more money on her, and the guy said oh well, too bad, no stamps then, and she said she'd been coming there for seventy-five years, he knew who she was, where she lived, who her children were, who her grandchildren were, whom she sent letters to, everything, couldn't she give him the extra two pennies the next time she came in? No, sorry, he said. If he did it for her he'd have to do it for everyone. But not everyone is short two pennies, said my grandma. Nope, he said. No can do. He didn't want to get into trouble. And my grandma went ballistic on him. She swore. She threw the spongy stamp licker thing at him, she drooled, she snarled, she screamed, she hit him with her purse, and then she left, scattering a stack of Eaton's catalogues on her way out, walked home, felt good, surprisingly good, and sat on her back steps staring at her sugar beet field for the rest of the day. Said her pulse must have been around fifty, some all-time low.

Ray and I never really succumbed to that type of extreme. He built his hutch and I listened to Zeppelin. Inside, probably, our internal organs were chipping off and turning grey. But we never screamed. The big day finally came when Ray unveiled his hutch and dragged it down to the curb on my old Radio Flyer wagon. The next morning we got up really early to watch the garbagemen remove the cans from the hutch. We knew they'd marvel at it. Ray had painted it a kind of mauvey purple and had even laid a piece of Astroturf on the bottom. It had a board across it that kept the cans securely tucked in, and the board was painted a deep red, left over from some school project of his. Right on, Dad, I told him. That's a stellar hutch. He told me that Trudie had always wanted him to make a hutch to keep the dogs and cats from tearing open the bags and spreading crap all over our yard. It would be nice, he'd quoted her as saying, to become the owner of a solid, simple hutch sometime before my throat wattles. We laughed. I'd told him it was a deluxe hutch, state-of-the-art. I knew he was trying really hard not to cry. Turns out the garbagemen thought the hutch was garbage, a colourful mess of boards and nails and outdoor carpeting, and threw the whole thing into the back of their truck. Ray wouldn't let me run outside to tell them they were making a big mistake. He put his hand on my shoulder and said no, no. Don't. He smiled and shook his head. And then he went into his bedroom and quietly shut the door. And I put on "All My Love" and watched the sun rise yet again and thought thank you Robert Plant for all of your love but do you have any more?

I've been experimenting with some vegetarian meals, something called Survival Casserole. A couple of days ago Ray came in and stood in the kitchen and assessed the stuff I had simmering in a pan on the stove. We've been eating an awful lot of vegetables lately, he said. I shrugged. Do you mean horribly many, I asked. Yes, he said, that's what I mean. I found a streak of blood in an egg yesterday, I said. They're very good, though, vegetables, he added. In what way, I asked. Well, he said. Well was his trademark answer to all of life's questions. They'll make you live longer, anyway, I told him. He tilted his head and frowned. Or does it just seem that way, he said. That's quite funny, Dad. He resented vegetables for prolonging his life. I told him we could have pear nectar for supper. It was thick, like a meal. Cooking's not your forte, is it, he asked. I put my wooden spoon on the counter. Do you want meat, I asked. I can't make meat. That's fine, he said. That's A-OK. He likes saying things like A-OK. Things like *legal beagle* and *bean counter* and *shutterbug*. One time I asked him if he had some kind of aversion to saying the real words. What's wrong with *lawyer, accountant, photographer,* I asked him. Nothing's wrong with them, he said. But he looked sad when he said it like he was a kid playing in a puddle and I'd told him to stop fooling around.

Trudie hadn't seemed to mind his word thing but it's always made me crazy. I should try to be more indifferent to it.

I know I would be if I wasn't so wild with the knowledge that he's doing it to seem jivey and laid-back for my sake. He refers to me and my friend Lydia Voth as Tom and Huck. What are Tom and Huck up to? What adventures do Tom and Huck have planned for today? *You mean besides rafting down the Mississippi with a huge man called Injun Joe?*

I think Ray might have wanted a son. One night when I was seven or eight I announced to my family that I wanted to play hockey with the boys on Friday nights and Ray became just a little too eager. Okay! he shouted. All right! We have to get you a stick! We have to get tape! I'll be waiting in the car!

These days Tom and Huck don't have much planned because Tom, or is she Huck, is in the hospital with an illness that has not been diagnosed. Nobody seems to know what's wrong with Lydia. Parts of her body keep breaking down. Yesterday when I popped in to see her she told me she was feeling more and more like less and less and then she laughed her head off for a while until it became too painful. She can't stand the way her socks clutch at her ankles or the way things like lights sometimes hum in her head. She looks like she's lit up from the inside like a jack-o'-lantern. Her cheeks glow red and her eyes are bright, bright electric blue, and her hair is no longer blonde, it's yellow, like penicillin. I lay down beside her in the bed and read to her from one of her old Black Stallion books. She's the same age as me but she likes those books. She doesn't care.

She asked me if it was really hot outside, and I said yeah, killer. It's shimmering. She nodded.

How's the job? she asked. I had a part-time job washing cars at Dyck Dodge but I hadn't been there for a while because I hated the way the tops of my rubber boots chafed at my calves. I showed Lids the raw skin on my legs and she frowned. Basically, I could go in whenever I wanted to and get paid under the table by the guy in the showroom, whose fascination was held by girls who wear short shorts and wield hoses. It's a loose arrangement that surely will not prepare me for a rigid schedule of killing at the plant.

Have you and Travis done it yet, she asked. No, no, no, no, no, God, I said. I waved my arms around like a ref saying no basket. She nodded again.

I will probably, she gasped, never know the pleasure, gasp, of a man. She closed her eyes and smiled.

Lydia was straight-edge but completely, disarmingly, non-judgmental. We had nothing in common. I just liked her weird evanescence and the way she did the most unbelievably nerdy things without knowing it or if she did know it she didn't care at all.

One time she came with me to a Halloween party at the pits and every girl was dressed up like a hooker except for Lydia who was a brown paper package tied up with string, from *The Sound of Music*. In the summer she wore knee socks and orthopedic shoes and a lime-green windbreaker. Sometimes her ears couldn't take loud noises and her eyes couldn't take small print and she'd tell me she couldn't talk but would I talk because if I spoke quietly she would listen to me and she would be *thinking* about what I was saying. And it's true, she did think about what I said. Sometimes I'd say stuff one day and the next time I saw her she'd refer to it and ask me if I was still feeling the same way or if things had changed. Nobody our age did that. We talked about the stuff that was going on, the things we did, not the way we felt. But Lids had no real action in her life, only feelings and thoughts. She lived in her head and that's why it glowed.

She was a decent, kind, sweet person. I guess that's why she had to go to the hospital. I told her stuff, boring everyday stuff about my life, and she liked it. She'd laugh. I liked the way she assumed that the two of us could be friends even though she was a good Christian girl and I was a sad, cynical pothead.

Do you want me to comb your hair for you, I asked her. No, she said, it hurts too much. Can I rub in your moisturizer, I asked her. No, she said, that hurts too. She had a thin layer of white Noxzema skin cream covering her face.

Should I wipe it off with a soft wet cloth, I asked her. No, she said, I'll be okay like this. Are you tired, I asked. She smiled. Should I go, I asked. She shook her head. Can I get you an extra blanket, I asked. Lydia likes extra blankets because she feels cool breezes all the time. Sometimes she asks me to feel the walls for her to find out where the air is coming from. If I'm in a patient mood I feel all the walls all over and then pretend to find the wall with the breeze and then move her bed as far away from it as possible. Sometimes I say Lids, there are no cool breezes in here at all. She likes rooms to be incubator-hot. Sometimes she wears winter scarves around her neck in the summer. I asked her again if she wanted an extra blanket. Her eyes were still closed. She shook her head.

A nurse came in and said: How's the princess and the pea? But not in a nice way. I stared at her. She'd said that because Lydia was lying on a bed that had two mattresses on it instead of one because just one was too hard for her bones. It's a beautiful day, said the nurse, and a young healthy girl like Lydia should be outside in the fresh air. Right, Lydia, she asked. Right, Lydia? Lydia opened her eyes and smiled and nodded and then closed them again. The nurse sighed. I would kill her on my way out of the hospital. My friendship with Lids was often about protection. Or it was a shared desperation. Or it was about recognizing the familiar flickering embers of each other's dying souls. When it was time for me to go, Lids pointed to the table next to her bed. She'd written a poem for me about two girls playing together within some castle's walls. In the left margin she'd experimented with various spellings of the word *requiem*. My mother would have drawn a horse's ass.

FIVE

After supper me and Travis drove around town and ended up at the pits. Saturday nights you'd have a hundred or more kids down there drinking, dropping, smoking, swearing, screwing, fighting, swimming, home-made-tattooing, passing out and throwing up right up until an hour or so before church the next morning when everyone would be back in the pew with Mom and Dad wearing nice (ugly) dresses and buttoned-up shirts flipping through Deuteronomy and harmonizing to "The Old Rugged Cross."

Me and Travis were parked on the windmill side of the pits staring at the water and listening to the radio. We both reached out to turn up the volume at the very same time when the guitars kicked in in a Cars song. That means we're meant for each other, I said. We had a conversation that resulted in a fight. I asked him what he was thinking about and he said nothing. No, what, I said. Well, he said, about floating around in a kind of, you know, vortex of sleeping, drinking and fucking—never quite coming into consciousness. I said oh (we'd never fucked) and he asked me what I was thinking about. Horses, I said. Getting a small horse I can ride but not be scared of. I like to have fun but not fun mixed with fear. I guess it just bugged him that I was thinking about horses while he was thinking about consciousness and fucking and he said he was going to get out and walk over to the diving-board side of the pits to see if The Golden Comb or Eldon was hanging out over there and he'd be back in a bit. Great, I said, because I like sitting alone in a truck staring at gravel. Which was the unsarcastic truth. After he left I got out of the truck and wandered over to the water and saw Sheridan Klippenstein standing there. He wore a Ludwig drum shirt with cut-off sleeves and camouflage pants. He had square brown hands and very thin wrists and a little muscle definition beginning in his upper arms. He cupped his cigarette against the wind and spit a lot.

He and I used to be neighbours before a series of deranged events befell his family. He was also the grandson of this old woman whose leg wounds my mother used to dress. Her name was Mrs. Klippenstein. She lived in a big old farmhouse out on Garson Road. I once wrote a short story about her house and Mr. Quiring corrected me about some detail in the kitchen and I asked him how he knew about old Mrs. Klippenstein's kitchen and he told me that he'd once changed some fuses for her, that he was a friend of the family. Small towns.

In the summer Sheridan and I ran like giant biped mice on spools of hydro wire that were kept in a yard next to his house. In the winter we slid off the roof of his bungalow in shovels. In junior high we kind of lost track of each other.

What are you doing here, I asked him. He told me that his dad had left home to play bass in a cover band from North Dakota. Not a cover band, I said.

I know, said Sheridan. He gathered up a mouthful of saliva and horked it far across the water. It got caught up in a gentle breeze and hung suspended in mid-air. It sparkled in the sun like a tiny chandelier before it dropped softly and disappeared.

He left me an adding machine, he said.

Get out, I said.

No, it's true, he told me. He said he won't know where he'll be for a while.

That's it? I asked.

Okay, he said, I also inherited an umpire ticker. Obviously his dad had enjoyed keeping track of things other than himself. The last time I saw him he was juggling pickled eggs in the rain outside the Kyro, a bar on the other side of the town limits, beyond the reach of Jesus, Menno "Sexy" Simons and Uncle Hands. The not-so-mellow triumvirate. My dad had said don't look, but I'd already seen him. Pickled eggs are the Devil's snack.

Remember when you climbed door frames in your bare feet, I asked him. I looked at his feet. He was wearing Greb Kodiaks. Everybody in town wore Greb Kodiaks, as though we were a people in need of a serious grip, perpetually on the verge of falling to the ground without a sound. Divided we fall politely and modestly.

So what are you doing these days, I asked him. He said on weekends he worked in the Sandilands at Moose Lake.

Yeah? I said. Do you like it?

He said it kind of gave him the creeps because that was where his mom had killed herself years ago. But you know, he said, there are fun things to do there too . . . fishing, hiking, waterskiing. I nodded. She hadn't been aware of her options. I vaguely remembered his mom. She was the first person I'd ever known with highlights in her hair. She owned toe socks. She called Sheridan her little man and made us Nestlé's Quik with extra powder. She taught us skipping rhymes. When she was sweeping and we were in her way she would say get out of my road. She once told me she liked the freckles on my shoulders, they were like stars in the sky. And she let us draw all over the drywall in the basement.

We talked a bit about how we used to say goodbye in all the languages we could remember and some we made up. That was bent, he said. He spit some more and offered me a drag. We'd stand by our front doors yelling stuff like *shalom* and *Faloma* and *nice aroma let's build a snowma* in the dark, we'd just go on and on, in early Menno rap style, until his dad asked him if he wanted a smack. A smack attack jack? Get back on track! He didn't mean it. He was a gentle guy with Brylcreemed hair. We'd hear him laughing his head off somewhere in his house. We'd see Merv Griffin's face reflected in the living-room window. Sometimes we'd hear his dad arguing with his demons in the old language of our people.

What made him go into hogs, I asked. Sheridan shrugged. I thought about how he used to stick his shoulder blades out like little wings.

Hogs, covers, he said. He was right. What difference did it make? I knew his dad had been excommunicated for something but we didn't talk about that. Nobody in town ever talked about that.

When it happened, years ago, Sheridan's mom went nuts. Trudie had told me and Tash that she thought Sheridan's dad should have left town to save his mom the pain of having to pretend he was dead. She'd really loved him. They'd had a lot of fun together when he wasn't too drunk.

But now Sheridan and I were older and staring at the water and sharing a cigarette. I told him I hadn't seen him in school lately and he told me he'd had an entire bottle of Swedish oil poured over his head in woodworking for falling asleep and after that, after being lacquered, he couldn't muster up the energy to come back. I told him that in grade seven science I'd been strapped repeatedly on the hand with a wooden ruler in front of everybody for talking about something other than tuning forks.

We talked about our old expressions like *monkey-doer, wordy* and *I don't give a care.* Remember bubble language, I asked him. He said yeah, but he couldn't remember how to do it any more. We talked about pouring hydrogen peroxide into the blisters we got from playing tag on the monkey bars at Ash Park. And we talked about the stupid things we'd scratched into the metal of the bars like who loves whom forever.

Then I heard the truck start up and some music, some 10cc . . . something about dying . . . playing on the radio and the horn honking and I told Sheridan I had to go. Let's meet here every five years to catch up on our lives, he said. Yeah, okay, I said, and waved goodbye.

Six

~

When we were little, Tash and I would sit in the darkened dining room of my grandmother's farmhouse, listening to the funeral announcements. They came on after supper, on the local radio station we were allowed to listen to because the elders knew that it was better for little children to listen to the names of dead people being read out in a terrifying monotone than the Beatles singing all we need is love. Afterwards my grandma would tell us: They have gone home at last. Praise the Lord. Then we would play this game called *Knipsbrat* with each other until our middle fingers were sore. It was one of the few games we were allowed to play. Golf was another one because it consisted of using a rod to hit something much, much smaller than yourself and a lot of men in this town enjoyed that sort of thing.

When I was a kid I stood in fields pretending I was a scarecrow. It was a sin to pretend we were something other than what we were but I have always enjoyed standing very still in fields. And often, when sin is used in the name of farming, Mennonites look the other way. Farming is very important to us. And I'm talking very important. When I was a kid we played a game in Sunday school, although we didn't call it a game, we called it a pod. Our teacher played the roles of different people in a skit. First, she was Professor Knuf, and she couldn't get on the heaven train. Then she was Rockin' Rhonda, also not allowed on the train. Then the next Sunday she was Slugger Sam and again was denied access to the heaven train. Finally she was Farmer Fred and she was allowed onto the train because she had Jesus in her heart. It was a fun game. We all clapped for Farmer Fred and afterwards drew pictures of the other three people crying at the gates of heaven and Farmer Fred just sailing on by, with spokes of light coming off him. I enjoyed drawing very short shorts on Rockin' Rhonda and a lipstick-stained cigarette dangling from her bottom lip. I drew Slugger Sam next to her, about to slam her over the head with his bat, and a word bubble coming from his mouth that said Jezebel! I didn't quite get why Professor Knuf didn't make the cut, unless it was because he was a professor of science and believed in facts. I considered giving Farmer Fred a word bubble that said Fry, Knuf, fry! but then I realized that that would be gloating and farmer or no farmer, you don't gloat on the heaven train.

One afternoon when I was standing still in my grandma's sugar-beet field I noticed two black dresses, the ugly Fortrel kind that many old women in our town wear on a daily basis, flying around like large crazy birds way up in the sky near the water tower. I hadn't realized, right then, that they were dresses but I figured it out after a while. I stood and watched as they flew all the way over to my grandma's yard. I was amazed that they were flying so close together and I thought it was great because they were dancing all over the place, seriously shaking it in this crazy, free, beautiful way until finally one of them fell onto the roof of my grandma's barn and the other one coasted in for a spectacularly gentle landing right at my feet. It was one of the best things that had ever happened to me, watching those dresses dancing wildly in the wind.

I didn't touch the one lying on the ground beside me, it seemed like some kind of sacred object, but I kicked a little dirt over it and then put a rock on top of the dirt. I said goodbye to it like I was a little kid who didn't know the difference between a dress and a person and I completely ignored the dress that had dropped onto the barn roof. It might still be there. I should check one of these days.

Travis and me just got back from driving around. We drove around and around, not on Main Street, like Bert and his girlfriend do in Bert's Red Phantom, but on country roads with a six of Old Stock between us and some reasonably good shit on the radio. We get dusty when the windows are open but we swelter to death if they're not. I put my bare feet up on the dash and Travis gets bugged when I leave toe prints on the windshield. I can work all the knobs on the radio with my feet and even change the tape and put it back into its case.

Sometimes we race farm dogs, but I don't enjoy that very much because I'm always afraid they'll get caught up under the car wheels. It hasn't happened yet. Sometimes we stick messages of protest onto cows, with wide black electrical tape. HANDS OFF, FARM BOY. Things like that.

Today we climbed a solitary tree in the middle of a field and took turns jumping from higher and higher branches. We saw a gopher that looked exactly like the old guy who bags groceries at Tomboy. Same expression. We thought a flock of crows was plotting to kill us like in the movie *The Birds* which we had never seen but *knew* about and then remembered that a flock of crows was called a *murder*. We threw pieces of dried-up dirt at them and they flew away. We accidentally broke a bottle in the field and spent half an hour picking up all the little pieces so that the cows wouldn't step on them and then another half-hour burying them deep in the dirt. Then I taught Travis how to braid long pieces of grass and we made a little tiara and placed it on the head of a cow that was just lying there and didn't seem to care at all. After that we just sat in the shade under the tree and I asked him if he'd donate one of his kidneys to me if I ever needed it and he said yeah and I said good, thank you, and then he said wait, will having only one kidney affect how much I can drink? And I said probably, and he said then, hmmm, he'd have to think about it.

On the way home I asked him if we could stop at my grandma's old barn to see if the dress was still up there. He asked me what I wanted to do with it and I said nothing, I just wanted to see if it was still there.

My grandma died in the fall while watching a Blue Jays game on TV. Her feet were up and her hair was in curlers and there was a can of tomato soup simmering away on the stove. Now her house was used for missionaries to live in when they were home on furlough.

Travis and I drove up into the driveway and got out and stared at the barn. We went inside it to see if there was a ladder somewhere but there wasn't so we drove his truck around to the back and then he stood on the cab part and I climbed up onto his shoulders and then up onto the roof. The dress wasn't there. I had really been hoping that it would be and when I couldn't find it I felt tired and pissed off and hot and stupid.

Where do you think it went, Travis asked. And I said I didn't know. I don't know where anything goes, I said. Don't be sad about stuff like that, okay, he asked me. He put his arm around my shoulders. I said yeah, okay, I wouldn't be. He picked some dandelions that were poking out of the dirt next to the barn and handed them to me and I said thank you and held them the whole way back to my place. At least if I couldn't have one of his kidneys I could have weeds.

He had to go do some stuff for his dad. Did you have fun today, he asked me. I nodded and smiled and hugged him. He said he'd call me later and then he lifted me up off the ground.

My parents had their first date at church. It consisted of walking side by side for three whole beautiful blocks to the gravel parking lot where my father said to my mother: Well. And my mother said: That's deep. They cracked each other up. Thank God I wasn't there. English wasn't their first language, so jokes were a particular type of achievement. Their mother tongue was an *unwritten language*. How do you write things down, I'd asked Trudie. We don't, obviously, she said, not in that language anyway. The stories are passed around. They come to us.

Should we go inside? That was my dad wondering. He often wondered. Of course, said my mom. We've come all this way. Three blocks only, said my dad. He, like the doomed Professor Knuf, enjoyed specificity. He liked to take note of irrefutable facts. In fact he liked to take *hold* of irrefutable facts as though they were life rafts. Things, unlike wives and daughters, that would not go away. I think he would have walked forever with my mom if she'd suggested it. They'd be walking still. They could be in New York by now.

He had a hard time making decisions. It was tough. The guy arrives at his pre-planned destination with his girl and then wonders if they should go *in*. It seems . . . he said. It seems what, my mom had asked. He didn't know. Take off your jacket, she said. It's so warm. It'll be hotter than stink in the sanctuary. Normally, when my mom made a suggestion, my dad followed through. But not when it came to his suit jacket. It was like Batman's cowl or Samson's hair. No . . . no, he said. I'd better leave it on.

They went inside. They split up to go to their respective sides of the church and listened as the elders, one by one, cast their votes. At the end of the evening, there were three fewer members of the church.

That's all I know about that, my mom told me when I was a little kid. I don't know what they'd done.

Jesus H., Tash said, your first date was a shunning? What did they do, I'd asked my mom. Oh, brother, I don't know, she said. I never really paid any attention. But I pressed her. I was six or seven. What did they do, I asked. Just guess. Well, she said, they may have been fooling around, I don't know. Fooling around how, I'd asked. Oh, she said, misbehaving. Kissing. Just fooling around. And then what happened, I'd asked. They couldn't be a part of the church, she'd say. That's right, Mom. And then? Their families weren't allowed to speak to them, she said. And? I'd ask.

This was a bedtime ritual. I dug the shunning story. I couldn't wait to hear it. What a gem. It completely reinforced my belief system of right and wrong. And everyone had to stand up in church and publicly denounce them. Yeah! I'd say. Denounce them! I'd always loved the sound of that.

And everybody was sad, I'd say. Right? Yes, everybody was sad. It was a very difficult position to be in not only for the person who was shunned but for the people who loved them. God especially, I'd say. Right? Yes, God especially. I loved that hook. Even though he was the ultimate punisher, he got no satisfaction from it. It hurt him, but it had to be done. I thought that was damn heroic.

But Nomi, she'd say, there was always the possibility of forgiveness. Remember that. I didn't like that part. It muddied my crystal-clear waters. But probably not, I'd say. Probably not.

One night my mom said she'd had enough of that story. She didn't like it any more and wanted to tell another one. And they lived like ghosts in their own town, right, I'd ask. No friends, no family. Floating around. Bound for hell, right? Crying all the time? Hey, Mom! For fooling around? Right? She'd make up excuses to leave my room. Oh, Dad needs help choosing his shirts for next week, she'd say. And gently close my door.

My mom had told me about the table trick. How if, say, your wife was shunned, you weren't allowed to sit at the same table as her but if you put two tables together, with an inch between them, and then put a tablecloth over them, it would seem like you were at the same table, which would be nice, but you *wouldn't* be at the same table, so you wouldn't be breaking any rules.

Tash often threw me out of her room with the words *I shun thee!* She didn't take things as seriously as she should have. Like my uncle, The Mouth of Darkness, said, there were eternal issues at stake. And when discipline is properly applied, the one under it needs the humility to come home.

My uncle's name is Hans Rosenfeldt. He is the pastor of our church. He is my mother's brother. Tash once said The Mouth of Darkness has pulled up onto our driveway. Shall I let him in? From then on she and I called him The Mouth, which, if not smart or funny or anything like that, is apt.

There is a woman in this town who was shunned for adultery but didn't leave. She's one of the ghosts. She has health problems and sometimes she just faints on the street, usually in front of Tomboy. People will leave sausages or cheese next to her sometimes but that's as much as they can do. Although I did once see an older woman give her skirt a tug after it had ridden up above her knees.

My mother once told me that her blackouts had to do with stress, which fascinated me. That you could collapse on the spot and wake up a few minutes later feeling ready to go on.

I wanted to be able to do that, although I think my minutes would stretch to days or possibly even years. My mother once told me that there were no adults in our town. But what do you mean by that, I'd asked her. What do I mean by that? she answered. I was never amused when my questions and her answers were the same thing. When she washed the dishes she'd have conversations with invisible people. I'd watch her from the dining room, shaking her head, moving her lips, shrugging, flicking her hand periodically to punctuate some imaginary point. Who are you talking to, I'd ask and she'd look at me and laugh, of course, telling me she didn't know who she was talking to, or what did I mean, or talking? Was I talking? Yeah, I'd say, you were and you seemed ticked off. I did? she'd say, all innocently. That's strange, she'd say. How odd. She'd try to compensate, afterwards, with an abundance of fake enthusiasm that literally felt like an attack. It stung my skin and I'd usually leave the room after enduring a few direct hits of *good cheer*. I wanted to know who the hell she was talking to in the first place.

You know how some people, I'm not sure which people, say that something that happens on one part of the planet can make something else happen on another part of the planet? Usually, I think, they mean some kind of geological event, but I'm sure that my mother's silent raging against the simplistic- ness of this town and her church could produce avalanches, typhoons and earthquakes all over the world. But there is kindness here, a complicated kindness. You can see it sometimes in the eyes of people when they look at you and don't know what to say. When they ask me how my dad is, for instance, and mean how am I managing without my mother. Even Mr. Quiring, the teacher I am disappointing on a regular basis, periodically gives me a break. Says he knows things must be a little *difficult* at home. Offers to give me extensions, says he's praying for us. I don't mind.

SEVEN

~

Main Street is as dead as ever. There's a blinding white light at the water-tower end of it and Jesus standing in the centre of it in a pale blue robe with his arms out, palms up, like he's saying how the hell would I know? I'm just a carpenter. He looks like George Harrison in his Eastern religion period working for Ringling Brothers. Whatever amateur made the sign put a red circle on each of his cheeks to make him look healthy, I guess, but healthily ridiculous. On the other end is another giant billboard that says SATAN IS REAL. CHOOSE NOW.

Main Street is bookended by two fields of dirt that never grow a crop. They lie in *perpetual fallow,* my dad told me. Those words haunt me still.

I can sense that Americans who come here think it's strange. Main Streets should lead somewhere other than to eternal damnation. They should be connected to something earthly, like roads.

Americans come here to observe our simple ways. Here, life is so refreshingly uncomplicated. The tourists are encouraged to buy a bag of unbleached flour at the windmill and to wander the dirt lanes of the museum village that is set up on the edge of town, depicting the ways in which we used to live. It's right next to the real town, this one, which is not really

47

real. It's a town that exists in the world based on the idea of it not existing in the world. It was created as a kind of no-frills bunker in which to live austerely, shun wrongdoers and kill some time, and joy, before the Rapture. The idea is that if we can successfully deny ourselves the pleasures of this world, we'll be first in line to enjoy the pleasures of the next world, forever. But I've never really understood what those pleasures will be. Nobody's ever come right out and told me. I guess we'll be able to float around asking people to punch us in the stomach as hard as they can and not experience any pain, which could be fun for one afternoon.

I once had a conversation with my typing teacher about eternal life. He wanted me to define specifically what it was about the world that I wanted to experience. Smoking, drinking, writhing on a dance floor to the Rolling Stones? Not exactly, I told him, although I did think highly of *Exile on Main Street*. Then what, he kept asking me. Crime, drugs, promiscuity? No, I said, that wasn't it either. I couldn't put my finger on it. I ended up saying stupid stuff like I just want to be myself, I just want to do things without wondering if they're a sin or not. I want to be free. I want to know what it's like to be forgiven by another human being (I was stoned, obviously) and not have to wait around all my life anxiously wondering if I'm an okay person or not and having to die to find out. I wanted to experience goodness and humanity outside of any religious framework. I remember making finger quotations in the air when I said *religious framework*. God, I'm an asshole. I told him that if I heard one more person say it wasn't up to him or her to judge, it was up to God, while, at the same time, they were judging their freakin' heads off every minute of every day (I mean basically they had judged that the *entire world* was evil), I would put a sawed-off .22 in my mouth and pull the trigger. I told him I didn't know what the big deal was about eternal life anyway. It seemed creepy to want to live forever. And that's when he threw me out. I'm not saying he was wrong or anything, I just couldn't ever figure out what was going on. It seemed like we were in some kind of absurd avant-garde theatre, the way our conversations sometimes went.

I once suggested that it was a really risky gamble to bet everything we had in this world on the possibility of another world, and in five seconds he was leading the entire class in prayer.

Please Almighty Father, we just ask you to bring Nomi back within your fold. We just ask you for a miracle this afternoon, dear Jesus. (Was he praying to God, the *Father*, or Jesus Christ, the *Son*? If you're going to terrorize the flock with spontaneous prayer, at least pray to whom it may concern.)

We're kind of a cult with pretend connections to some normal earthly conventions like getting dressed in the morning (thank God, Menno liked to cover up) and going to work or school, but that's where it ends.

There's not a lot of interest in the present tense here. And it's only slightly disconcerting that everyone's related. If a Mennonite couple divorces do they still get to be cousins? Oh yeah, hilarious. Tash once said to my mom: Oh, so it's wrong to move any part of one's body in time to music but it's perfectly okay to penetrate members of one's extended family? My mother told her not to be silly.

Silly was Trudie's ultimate crime. Okay, she'd say, *now* you're being silly, and then we knew it was time to shape up. We'd gone too far.

The Mouth of Darkness loves the word *groovy* and the expression *simply put*. Simply put, we are not a groovy people. He's in love with the notion of shame and he traffics the shit like a schoolground pusher, spreading it around but never personally using. He's not a fire-and-brimstone guy. That's not really our speed. Too animated. Too much like dancing.

He reminds me of one of those statues on Easter Island. I've seen photos of him as a boy and even then he looked like unforgiving granite. Although my grandma once showed me a picture of him sitting in a canoe smiling, looking relaxed and happy, with the sun setting behind him. He's holding his paddle straight up in the air like a spear. I often stare at that picture and wonder what he was thinking about and what happened to the happy little boy before he turned into The Mouth. Well, actually, that sounds really stupid, like the beginning of a lame flashback. Cue the spinning tunnel. I don't really think about him that much. It would be like thinking about time, the nature of time. How it controls you, determines your destiny, and ultimately destroys you.

I do know, because everyone in town knows and doesn't talk about it, that The Mouth had some very bad experiences in his life when he was younger (oh, hmm, tell me . . . and what's *that* like?) and that after those experiences he came back to Shitville to rule with an iron fist. That might have been what that upheld paddle was all about. I think he had tried to rebel against the thing he came back later to stand for and while living in the city doing God knows what he . . . I'm not sure . . . a girl ditched him, I think. Wouldn't have him as her sunbeam. After he'd opened his heart to her and then mistakenly asked her to marry him. (Flash for Uncle Hands . . . it was the period of *free love,* dude.) And he couldn't write poetry like the Beats and was mocked for it. And for his clothing that tried too hard and his eagerness to be hip and his inability to shave properly (don't ask me—Trudie told me this) and countless other crimes of youth and eventually he gave up and came back here full of renunciations and ideas of purging every last bastion of so-called fun in this place and a greatly renewed interest in death and a fresh loathing of the world. In a nutshell. If I'd been his ringside coach I would have said now please get back in there.

Re-enter the world. Just tone it down. Keep your mouth shut a little more often. Try again for the love of God Almighty!

A few months ago I was walking home from Travis's place and The Mouth's house was on the way. It was around three in the morning and the entire town was dead and dark except for the sparkly streets and car tops which were shiny from melting snow. Just as I was walking past his house a light came on in his kitchen, the little stove light, and for some reason I stopped on the sidewalk to look. I saw The Mouth pass by the window, slowly, in a faded green housecoat he'd only half-heartedly closed with what looked like an old tie. I stared at his profile as he stood with his hands on the stove, a little bent over, head down and motionless. He stood like that for a while. The only sound I heard was water dripping out of somebody's drainpipe. Then he raised his head and walked, again, very, very slowly, to his fridge and he opened the top freezer section of it and took out a pail of ice cream. Maybe rainbow ice cream. Maybe Heavenly Hash. Then he took the pail and disappeared from view for a few seconds and then returned with a spoon and put the pail down on the stove, under the little light, and opened it up and started to eat. He ate and ate and ate, not like a pig or anything, just steadily and continuously for at least twenty minutes, maybe half an hour.

I stood on the sidewalk and watched him and thought every once in a while that now he'd quit and put the pail back and switch off the light and go to bed, but he didn't. He kept eating the ice cream.

When he was finally finished he disappeared again for a few seconds and then came back and leaned his head against the top part of the stove, near the fan, the way he had earlier, like a guy completely defeated by life, with holes he could never fill with ice cream no matter how much he ate, and I almost started to cry thinking about poor The Mouth being dumped by the city girl and just wanting to be able to write a poem that someone in the world would dig. I thought: He's my uncle. I should love him. And then I walked the rest of the way home.

A while later, maybe a month or so, I noticed my mom leaning her head against the window over the kitchen sink in the very same way The Mouth had leaned his head against the fan part of his stove. She was watching the neighbour's dog. She said: I envy that dog its freedom and obliviousness.

When I said obliviousness to what, she said: Hey, Nomi, how'd your friends like your new haircut? She was a master in the art of off-kilter conversations. I never knew where any of my questions would go, or if her answers were answers or clues or jokes or what. Some questions resulted in songs. Some in hugs and kisses. I needed a map.

When I was ten years old I had to memorize Bible verses in order to attend Blue Mountain Bible Camp. I'd stand in The Mouth's office and say: In the beginning was the world and the world was with God and the world was God. And he'd correct me. No, Nomi, not world, *word. Word, word.* I'd try again. In the beginning was the world and the world—no, Nomi, *word,* not world. None of it made any sense to me.

I hadn't even wanted to go to Bible camp. The only thing that appealed to me about the whole experience was the bus trip there and back because the route they took went through part of the city and I wanted to stare at the human beings who lived there. I've tried staring at people here but they just stare back, like babies. It's not an aggressive stare or anything, just a completely unsocialized one. Most people around here are quiet and polite and a little stunned. Somehow all the problems of the world manage to get into our town but not the strategies to deal with them. We pray. And pray and pray and pray. If I could live anywhere else in the world, anywhere, I would. Although my preference would be NYC.

My dad has never missed a Sunday. He's received many awards for perfect attendance. But he never talks about it. At first I was embarrassed by it. Later, I realized the mortification would kill me if I didn't change my attitude and so I began to imagine my dad as the noble captain of a sinking ship. Or, sometimes, as a faithful lover, waiting for a passionately planned rendezvous that would never happen.

I conjured up all sorts of reasons for him to be there every Sunday other than the real one, which seemed to be that it fulfilled a need to be reminded of his powerlessness, over and over and over again.

Americans who come into our real town are either surprised or disappointed or both. They see some of us sitting on the curb smoking Sweet Caps, wearing tube tops, and they don't like it. They pay good money to see bonnets and aprons and horse-drawn wagons.

A tourist once came up to me and took a picture and said to her husband, now here's a priceless juxtaposition of old and new. They debated the idea of giving me some money, then concluded: no.

I speak English, I said. The artificial village and the chicken evisceration plant a few miles down the road are our main industries. On hot nights when the wind is right, the smell of blood and feathers tucks us in like an evil parent. There are no bars or visible exits.

But I suppose there are ways to leave if you know the terrain. My mom and my sister easily made tracks when it was time to split. (Mr. Quiring has advised me to "lay off the jive talk." It just happens sometimes. I can't control it. I'm Sybil. I used to do it to entertain my mom and my sister, calling them child and talking about the pusher man and all that stuff, you know, funkifying—to make them laugh. I was just a kid imitating Tash's records. So now, when I talk about them, I sometimes become Curtis Mayfield. I don't really know why it happens. I'll try to curb it.)

My mother, Trudie Dora Nickel née Rosenfeldt, has gone away. Irrefutable fact, although where she is is up to me, right? I mean I don't *know* but who cares—that's not how stories work around here. Every day at Happy Family Farms a few birds somehow manage to escape and fly away. Some of them end up dead in the ditches.

Like I said, I don't know where she is, but I imagine different scenarios. The scenarios that I imagine most often involve my mother, with passport in hand, travelling around the world. That's why I was so profoundly disappointed to find her passport in her top drawer. That discovery posed the hateful question of where she might be if not somewhere in the world.

I use drugs and my imagination to block that question.

She left seven weeks after my sister, Natasha Dawn Nickel, left with Ian, Mr. Quirings's nephew. Different people have different theories but they don't talk about them as a rule. I believe that they're all alive and that one day we will be together except possibly without Ian. Tash and Ian may be rearing their own love child somewhere in northern California right now. I could be the aunt of somebody named Tolerance. My mother might be an activity director on a cruise ship. She likes water and she likes activities. She's a Cancer. Did she pack warm clothes for herself when she left? No, she did not. Did she pack *any* clothes for herself when she left? No, she did not.

A detail that falls into the same disturbing category as the one about her passport still being in her dresser drawer.

I'm only mentioning these things because they *weigh* on me. Not because I let them control my life. Or this story. Who cares about facts, right? We're talking about miracles. Jesus died on a cross to save our sins and three days later he rose up from the grave and pushed a giant boulder away from the opening of the cave they'd put him in. Good enough.

Eight

~

I like to ride my bike to the border and stare at America. I like to ride my bike to train crossings in empty fields and watch graffiti fly past me at a hundred miles an hour. It really is the perfect way to view art. I silently thank the disenfranchised kids from Detroit or St. Louis for providing some colour in my life. I've often wanted to send a message back to them.

Nomi from Nowhere says hello.

But the train doesn't stop here and I don't have any spray paint. At night, I like to go to Purple City. It's when you stare at the giant caged light in front of the post office for exactly sixty seconds and then you stare at all the lights in people's houses and every single one is purple. The moon and the stars, if there are any, are also purple. Nobody but me and Lids knows about it. We are the only two residents of Purple City.

I like to ride my bike to the old fairground and smoke in the rodeo announcers' booth and look at the things written on the walls. THE WAGES OF SIN IS DEATH. DON'T WAIT TIL PAYDAY. WHO ARE THE PEOPLE WHO TIE KNOTS IN BARBED WIRE FENCES? MY FAMILY DOES NOT HAVE A DISEASE RIDDLED HISTORY AND I AM ESSENTIALLY NORMAL. IS THERE A CRIMEA RIVER? I USED TO LIVE HERE.

That last one is my favourite. I often wonder if my sister wrote it, and if so did she write it before she left, or did she come back. But it could have been someone else.

I like to ride my bike on the highway and hang on to the back of RVs with American plates going seventy-five miles an hour. I once caught a ride all the way to Falcon Lake on the back of an Airstream trailer from California. A little girl stared at me through the back window and held up stuff to show me. A pinwheel, a stuffed bear, a drawing she'd made, a tiara. I'd nod and smile, my hair whipping all over my face in the wind, and she'd go off to get something else. Her parents must have wondered why she was so quiet back there. When they stopped at a gas station I rode away and the California girl waved goodbye to me and made her bear wave goodbye too.

When Tash was twelve one of her molars came out and she put it in a glass on the bathroom counter so she wouldn't lose it and a while later I came in from playing kick the can and filled the glass up with water and drank it and accidentally swallowed her tooth. It's still in my stomach, my doctor, an irritable man, is sure of it. And it'll probably stay there forever, like the image of the little California girl waving goodbye in her tiara, which makes me happy.

I've decided to walk around today and say goodbye to people despite the fact that I'm not going anywhere.

Bye Gloria, I said to Gloria.

She said hey, we used to play soccer together when we were, what, five, right? She reminded me of the only two rules that the coach had given us: No hugging and no picking flowers. All I remembered was him lining us up against the snow fence and kicking frozen balls at us while we scrambled, screaming, to get out of the way.

I laughed for way too long and then she told me I could have my Coke for free because her manager was gone.

Right arm, I said. (I wished I hadn't.) Gloria had given herself an anarchy tattoo, near her wrist.

Is that a promise ring, I asked her.

Oh this, she said, holding out her hand.

Yeah, I guess, technically, she said.

To who, I asked.

Marvin Fast, she said.

Seriously? I asked.

I guess, she said, and laughed hard.

Marvin Fast used to chase me home from school and whip me with branches and then the next day he'd give me five bucks, I said.

Really, she asked. That must have been after he was run over with a combine and had his neck broken.

Well, congratulations, I said.

Ew, she said, it's not official.

Where are you going, she asked.

Well, I said, starters the city. It wasn't true, just a thing I liked to hear myself say. She nodded and said the big schmake eh? Good luck.

The city was the dark side, the whale's stomach. It flickered off and on in the distance like pain. It was the worst thing that could happen to you. If you go for any length of time you don't come back, and if you don't come back you forfeit your place in heaven's lineup.

Hey, she said, is that a picture of you in the new building? I should have said no but I waited one beat too long for a convincing lie. She was referring to a photograph taken of me as a young volunteer at the museum village. I'd been a butter churner. I stood in the hot sun in front of the hot outdoor bread oven robotically pushing a broom handle up and down in a ceramic jug of cream while Americans took pictures of me for the folks back home.

One day I lit up a smoke and my bonnet, which protruded from my face stiffly like a pipe, caught on fire. The entrance of the tunnel leading to my face was in flames. I tried to untie it but couldn't. I screamed and ran in circles around my ceramic urn until a quick-thinking tourist grabbed me from behind and plunged my head into a barrel of rainwater in front of the old general store. It was so vaudeville. I imagine everyone moving really fast and jerky in black and white.

Yes, yeah, that's me, I said. Gloria scanned my face. No scars though, she said. I wanted to scream: THAT'S WHERE YOU ARE SO UNBELIEVABLY WRONG!

Yeah, well, I said. What's a little inferno in your bonnet. The photo had been taken while I'd been on fire, before the dunking. It had been framed and mounted in the archival area of the new building, where you paid to go in. I don't know why. The caption is: Young Pioneer, Naomi Nickel, learns valuable lesson.

Hey, said Gloria, do you hang out at the pits now?

Yeah, sometimes, I said. I shrugged.

No offence, she said, but I always thought you were straight-edge.

Mmm, yeah, well I was for a long time, I answered.

She said oh and smiled.

I could smell the wind coming through the open window behind her and it was like a present or a compliment or something. The sweetest winds blow over us Mennos sometimes, when the poultry massacre stops long enough for us to smell them, and they can literally stop you dead in your tracks and break your heart. It's the certain smell of that wind and the sudden whoosh of heat that just undoes me. It's a June wind, mostly. An embrace. (Did I just say *embrace*? Asshole.) I could smell it now.

You know what would have been nice, asked Gloria.

What, I said.

It would have been nice, she said wistfully, if our stoner periods had coincided.

I nodded again and smiled and said yeah, it would have been. I thought about taking her hand but other things happened instead. I wanted to stay in Gloria's store and talk to her about soccer and anarchy and Marvin Fast and our childhood but I'd already walked over to the door and put my hand on it and said goodbye and it would have seemed pathetic of me to change my course. Walking along Main Street felt ominous. It was way too bright. This is what an autopsy must feel like, I thought. I could feel the sun burning holes in my retinas.

I walked past Tomboy and there was a new sign up in the window that said COME ON IN AND BURST A BALLOON. I wasn't sure what it meant. A man in a cowboy hat carrying a baby walked past me and I said goodbye. The baby waved.

The wind was my best friend but I couldn't smell it any more and I was glad because it was killing me. I said goodbye to everyone I passed and trudged towards the outstretched arms of George Harrison.

When I got to the lights I turned left on Second Avenue, past the post office. I dropped in on Mrs. Peters. She gave me home-made popcorn balls and I gave her the opportunity to talk about her dead son who, if he were alive, would be my age. I was her barometer. Although I was a girl, she used me to imagine what her son would be like if he hadn't drowned when he was four years old. This had been going on for a while. It started in church when I was five or six and she leaned over one day and whispered: You fidget like my Clayton.

I saw his body in the coffin at Wohlgemuth Funeral Chapel. He wore light blue seersucker overall shorts and a white shirt with a Peter Pan collar and flat buttons with tiny yellow ducks on them. His hair was blond and slicked over to one side, and he had a bored expression on his face. There was a tiny scar near his left eye. I asked Mrs. Peters if I could touch his arm and she said yes. I asked her if she was sad, and she said yes again. I stared at him for a long time. I moved my small grubby hand slowly up and down his cool forearm. I think I felt him move, I told her. She said no. Other people came to look at him. She hugged them but they didn't talk. She asked me if I was needed at home. I didn't understand the question, and said nothing. Finally she suggested that I go home for supper because it would be dark soon.

She had chocolate puffed wheat balls this time. Clayton had loved them. She was older than most parents of kids my age. Even her husband had died, or been called home, and her other children lived in Bolivia and Akron, Pennsylvania. I changed a light bulb for her and cut her bangs after she wet them in the kitchen sink. She had all-white appliances in her kitchen because she said that coloured stoves and fridges were *pre-sins,* like pre-cancerous cells. Same with touch-tone telephones and soft-top cars.

I can't believe he'd be graduating from high school already, she said. What will you do afterwards, she asked me.

I moved her wet hair to one side like Clayton's. I don't know, I said. (I did know. Hello, abattoir!)

No, I don't imagine he'd have known either, she said.

Was he like that, I asked.

In some ways, she said. But not in others. I nodded. She told me she liked her hair to be asymmetrical.

That's a good choice, I said. That's my signature cut.

Clayton would have liked this too, she said. She was pointing at a thin piece of leather I'd tied around my wrist.

Yeah? I said.

She said yes, he would have. Very much.

When I was done cutting she got up and looked at herself in the toaster. Perfect, she said. Thank you.

She got a broom out of the pantry and started sweeping up the bits of feathery white hair.

What do you do these days, she asked me.

I didn't want to tell her the truth. I didn't want her to imagine Clayton doing what I did. Well, I said. I walk around a lot.

Do you enjoy it, she asked me.

Sometimes, I said.

Clayton liked to run, she said. She told me how he'd been running down the sidewalk one day and had tripped on his new shoes which she'd bought a couple of sizes too big, for the savings. He had a hole in his head the size of an Aspirin, she said. At the hospital he'd been so brave. When they asked him his name he'd said: My name is Clayton. Clayton Peters. The real Batman.

What did they say when he said that, I asked.

They said next time he was in such a hurry he should take the . . . what did they call it?

The Batmobile, I said.

That's right, she said. The Batmobile.

Did he get stitches, I asked.

Yes, she said, right here. She touched her temple.

How many, I asked. She loved to answer questions about Clayton.

Was it three or four, she wondered. Three, I think, she said. I lifted my shoulders and held them for a few seconds near my ears before letting them drop.

She said something in the odd unwritten language of our people, a language that is said to sound vaguely Yiddish.

Can you translate that, I asked.

She thought. Then she said: I don't know. I just don't know. To the point of knowing I will never not know as much about something as what I don't know about him.

She smiled. I can't wait to see him in heaven, she said.

I said yeah and looked at my feet. Will he recognize you, I asked.

Of course he will, Nomi, he's my son.

But I mean you'll have aged, right, I asked.

Oh no, she said, I'll be young again.

But I mean, how young, I asked. Young like when you had Clayton? Or young like . . .

Don't worry, she said, we'll recognize each other. God will make sure of that.

Who would you say hi to first, your husband or your son, I asked.

Oh, now that's a good question, she said.

What if you had remarried, I asked her. And that husband had died too, and then when you got to heaven there would be your son, your first husband *and* your second husband. That could be awkward, eh? Like, who would you live with?

Hmmmm, she said. My son, I think.

But I mean which husband, I asked. First or second? Or both?

Not both, she said. I'm not sure. God will know. He'll have a plan.

But, I said, what if . . .

How's your dad, she asked. People asked me that a lot.

Great, I said, smiling back at her. He wasn't great, he was on life support, but she didn't want to hear that. She wanted to listen to the funeral announcements on the radio, so I left.

Goodbye, I wanted to say to her, I may not be back for a while. But that sounded ridiculous. I was pathetic. I couldn't even follow through with my plan to say goodbye to people in the manner of a person going away for a long time. Maybe my heart wasn't in it or maybe I was just a bad actor.

I decided to visit Lids in the hospital. I wouldn't say goodbye to her.

When I got there she was lying on her tall bed with her eyes closed and a surgical mask tied around her face. She must have smelled fumes or something. Maybe from a car in the parking lot or somebody doing some painting two hundred miles away. There was a pile of papers on her stomach.

Hi there, I whispered. She opened her eyes and smiled and said come in.

What is this, I asked her, pointing at the papers.

Mr. Quiring brought them so I wouldn't fall behind, she whispered. She pointed at her throat.

Can't talk? I asked. She nodded.

Do you want these on your stomach? She shook her head and whispered that she couldn't lift them.

The nurse just plunked them on your stomach? I asked. I picked them up and put them in the drawer of her bedside table.

Thank you for your poem the other day, I said. I wish you *could* come out and play.

Soon, she whispered.

Yeah, I said.

She pointed to a small piece of paper on the bedside table. I wrote another poem for you, she said. I picked it up and read the title: "C'mon, Get Normal." I said thanks and told her I'd read it later when I was feeling odd.

She opened her eyes wide and looked at me. That meant I was supposed to talk about my life. I told her about some things, seeing Gloria, finding out that she was engaged to Marvin Fast. When I said Marvin Fast, Lids put her hand over her mouth and I said I know and started to laugh. The nurse came in and said she'd heard laughing. Maybe Lydia wasn't as sick as she thought?

No, I said, that was me laughing.

Well, she said, I guess there's something really funny going on in here. I told the nurse I had found a place for Lydia's papers besides her stomach.

Oh, said the nurse. I thought she'd have been able to do that herself.

Well, I guess it's not a good idea to make assumptions, I said.

Well, said the nurse, if you had twelve patients to take care of maybe you wouldn't be quite as sure of yourself.

I'm not sure of myself, I said.

You sound very sure of yourself, said the nurse. She was fiddling around with things near Lids's bed. It was the biggest sin in our town to be sure of yourself.

Lydia, said the nurse in a loud snippy voice, you didn't eat your lunch. Lydia didn't move a muscle or open her eyes. Lydia! said the nurse.

She needs it to be softer, I said, or it hurts to chew. She needs everything cooked an extra couple of minutes.

Oh really, said the nurse. Lydia needs a lot of things, doesn't she?

Yes, I said, she does. The second biggest sin in town was to need a lot of things.

Isn't that what a hosp— . . . I started but the nurse announced that both Lydia and I needed to have our wings clipped.

What? I get so mad. I go fucking insane sometimes with people like her. You know what? I said to the nurse. I don't . . .

She put her hand up and told me she didn't have the time or the patience to listen to my self-indulgent prattle. Lids had started making a low, moaning sound.

All I'm saying, I said, is that . . .

Whatever you're saying is a lie, Ms. Nickel, your entire family is . . . cuckoo. She moved her index finger in small circles around her ear.

I picked up Lids's apple-juice container and winged it at the nurse's head and missed which was a good thing in some ways. Lids opened her eyes and stared at me. Apple juice trickled down the wall by the door. Sorry, I said. Sorry, I said again really loudly to the nurse. I'm sorry. Please . . . But she'd left the room.

First she told me I was as crazy as my mother and *then* she left the room. I put my hand over my mouth and looked at Lids who stared back at me with big eyes peering out from over her green surgical mask.

Oops, I said. Lids was shaking in her bed trying not to laugh. Next time, aim, she whispered. The nurse came back with another nurse and an orderly that me and Lids vaguely knew. He used to be in our school but then decided he'd rather be an orderly. He was the boy who had eaten his entire gym bag over the course of one year, in protest.

Hi, I said. He said hi back. He pointed at the wall. You? he asked.

Sorry, I said.

He shrugged. I'll get her another one, he said.

Thanks man, I said.

Lids, he's getting you another one, I told her. She smiled with her eyes closed. No big deal, said the orderly.

The other nurse asked me nicely to leave. The short-tempered nurse glared at me the whole time and I told her, lamely, to take a picture, it lasts longer, and Lids opened her eyes for a second to roll them at me. I shrugged. On my way out I stopped at the nurses' desk and asked the nice one, the one who'd asked me to leave but to come back soon *when the dust has settled,* if they could please take good care of my friend and cook her food a little longer and keep the room warm and things off her stomach and the nurse nodded and smiled and assured me that she would try. She told me the short-tempered nurse was under a lot of stress and that next time I was upset about something I should see her, not the short-tempered nurse, personally, and we could try to fix it up. I wanted not to be overwhelmed by her kindness because it made me sad to be so happy about something like that but on the way out, walking into the sunshine, I felt like my chest was going to explode and I looked straight into the sun to give me something painful to concentrate on.

NINE

Travis is teaching me how to drive. He likes to teach me things. Consider this: Our people's contribution to civilization is the housebarn—a dwelling in which people are encouraged to sleep with livestock. Or this: The word written on the cap of the guy on the Players cigarette pack is HERO. We go out to fields and take shots at each other's heads with dried-up turds.

Travis wavers between hippie and punk. When we play soccer he often wears a Pistols T-shirt and his Patrick "football" shoes. Last night we drove to La Broquerie in his dad's work truck and bought a bottle of Black Tower at Chez Felix. There are lots of small French villages scattered around here. During the war all the French men had to go off to fight, but the Mennonites didn't because Mennonites are conscientious objectors (*man*, can they object), and so while the French guys were off fighting in Europe, the Mennonites went and bought up a lot of their farmland really cheap from the women left behind who were desperate for money to feed their kids and just survive until their husbands and sons came home.

I found out all this stuff by riding my bike into the neighbouring villages several years ago when I was a curious, hopeful child and asking them what they thought of Mennonites. I compiled all the information and then tried to hand it in for a social studies assignment and was rudely rebuffed by Mr. Petkau, who said it wasn't relevant.

Not relevant to what, I'd asked him and he asked me if I wanted to spend the rest of the semester sitting in the hallway. When I said yes he goose-stepped me out the door and called me wicked.

I had once tried to hand in an essay titled "How Menno Lost His Faith in the Real World (Possible Reasons)," which was similarly rejected.

Anyway, it was bad form on the part of the Mennos, but me and Travis are trying to make up for it now by buying really large amounts of booze off the French since we can't buy it here. Wealthier Mennonites, even though they're not technically supposed to be wealthy, do their drinking in North Dakota or Hawaii. They are sort of like rock bands on tour in that the rules of this town don't apply to them when they're on the road. An embarrassing situation for wealthy Mennonites is to meet other wealthy Mennonites at the swim-up bar at the Honolulu Holiday Inn.

After the driving lesson we went into Travis's basement bedroom to drink the wine and listen to Cheap Trick again. He showed me his *Joy of Sex* book including charcoal sketches of elated, naked hippies with armpit hair. We read that armpits can be extremely erotic. He had a bargain tub of Vick's Vaseline on the top shelf of his closet. And a gerbil named Soul who was on antibiotics for a tail infection. He asked me if I was cold and I said no, I just shiver sometimes.

We talked about some things. That he'd had an operation to pin his ears back when he was eleven. I looked closely at his ears.

They looked quite good. He thought they were slowly growing out again and would one day need to be re-pinned. I told him they looked perfect to me. Everything about him looked perfect to me. Everything. Most of the time I couldn't even believe that somebody like me, the person immortalized in celluloid as a pioneer with her head on fire, was sitting in the bedroom of a guy like Travis. He told me he loves to wear sweaters together with shorts. And hockey socks with Greb Kodiaks. These are some of his favourite combinations. He asked me what some of my favourite combinations were.

What do you mean, I asked. Like, opposites? His questions always made me nervous because I knew he appreciated creative answers.

He played songs for me on his guitar. Bob Dylan and Neil Young and James Taylor. I didn't like the pauses in between the songs because I didn't know what to say other than that was nice, play another one. Sometimes I said wow, crazy. I lay on his bed and stared at the ceiling thinking about Tash, and also the feasibility of blowing up a laundry bag and floating away on it from a place like Alcatraz. Travis was singing Dylan's "You're a Big Girl Now," in a soft voice that kept getting softer and softer until it finally stopped. His fingers were long with square tips. He also wore a thin piece of leather around his wrist.

Tash phoned a couple of times after she left and then stopped calling altogether. A lot of teenagers hit the road in the seventies looking for peace and free love and ended up on communes and being brainwashed and having a whole bunch of babies with bearded men who enjoyed thinking of themselves as new messiahs. But I don't believe that happened to her because that would be way too similar to how this place, this town, came to be, and she never had anything good to say about it. We're a national joke, she'd say. Seriously, she'd say, we're the joke town in the joke province in the joke country. Everybody mocks us and the more they do the more The Mouth goes: We won't give in! We'll fight the good fight! We'll keep the faith! We'll ban more books! We'll burn more records! Have you ever noticed how the media make us out to be religious freaks with no fashion sense and shit? Oh my god, it's humiliating beyond belief! My mom and dad and I would sit at the kitchen table and listen to her rant and when she was done my mom would put her arm around Tash and say stuff like: Have a warm bath.

I have some things of hers. Piano books I can't play. Her metronome. Her collection of Lee jean labels, her old *Seventeens*, her *Lives of Girls and Women,* and her Lady Schick. My dad and I used to have heart attacks when the phone rang but not quite as much any more. We've become a little sluggish. The phone hardly ever rings. I mentioned that fact once to Ray and he said that didn't mean people weren't calling us.

I think that is exactly what it means, Dad, I told him. I worried that he was hearing voices. Then I worried that I wasn't hearing voices.

One weekend, we were both sick with the flu, we lay around the house the entire time hardly moving, hardly talking, and the phone didn't ring except for once on Sunday evening and it sounded like an alarm and Ray said: Whoah, sensory overload. He said I laughed too hard at that one, that my reaction discouraged him from future attempts at humour because I'd either (a) built him up to a standard where he'd be too paralyzed to perform for fear of failure, or (b) been insincere. He told me that he thought my laughter was tinged with desperation. That I so lacked stimulation that any little thing would set me off inappropriately.

Hey, I said, you're a lot of fun. I love the way you don't analyze simple moments to death and he said what simple moments. And then, the way he does after confirming that life really is all about pain and suffering, he cheered up. He spun a disc. He played table football with me. He polished his shoes. He turned up the volume on *Hymn Sing*.

After Tash and Trudie left, The Mouth of Darkness came over to pray with us and told us we couldn't live in crisis forever. Right Nomi? he said.

I wanted to say no, I thought I could with very little effort. He stuck his arm out and said shake? It was like putting my hand into a bowl of warm mashed potatoes or a freshly pissed diaper. I wasn't sure what I was agreeing to.

He slapped my dad on the back and my dad's face froze into a grimace he'd been trying to pass off as a jocular grin, the manly type.

Well, he said, I need to check the level of softener salt in my tank but I do appreciate your visit that's for sure.

The funny thing is that it wasn't even a lie. My dad did need to check things like water softener the way other people needed blood transfusions. He checked and double-checked things all the time. He was the kind of person who secretly took his pulse at various points throughout the day. Two fingers held flat on the inside of his wrist. *Yes, hmm, still here, well.* I had mixed feelings about it. Oh, it was disconcerting, yes. Often instead of hello he'd say to me: Oh good, you're here. The gap between our feelings, his and mine, on that particular point was immeasurable. But again, I was never entirely sure what he meant by *here*.

I like to sit on my driveway and push the melting asphalt around with my fingers. Sometimes I buy bags of little fake seashells and stick them in there. I like the cracking sound when a car drives over them. I can imagine I'm in some Latin American capital where they celebrate good things with random gunfire.

My dad came riding up on his Red Glider and said what are the youth of today up to, and I said how could I possibly know the answer to that question.

Well, he said. He reached into his pocket and then held his hand out to me and said here, have some chalk. It resembled a cigarette. When I was a kid I ate chalk and clay and sand, if it were a fine grain. I was one of those people. I only ate white chalk. There was so much of it around the house. I tried the coloured stuff but it had an oily taste. I also tried paper, but didn't enjoy it.

My dad gazed into the neighbour's yard. Looks like the little girl's got herself a new two-wheeler, he said.

We say *bicycle* now, Dad, I said. Or, sometimes, bike. He put the front tire of his Red Glider into a concrete stand by the garage, took the pant clip off his leg and saluted me before going into the house. I had never seen him salute before. Were we saluting now? Was this some new *playful* thing we were doing now? God, Ray deserves a better daughter than me. He deserves Laura Ingalls Wilder saluting him back exuberantly, clicking her heels even, and saying oh, Father, and gazing at him the way a daughter should. I took the chalk and wrote in tiny, tiny letters on the driveway: Dad, don't think I'm not saluting you when I'm not saluting you. And then I scuffed it out with my foot before anybody would see it.

I used almost the entire length of the driveway to write my favourite quote in chalk. LIFE BEING WHAT IT IS, ONE DREAMS OF REVENGE. It's by Gauguin.

My neighbour came out to look at it. She's an unhappy housewife with the flattest ass I've ever seen. Swaths of fabric allocated for a person's butt billow emptily around hers like a sail. She walked slowly up the driveway, reading out loud in a voice like a little kid just learning how to. Then she said Go Gwin, eh? I said *Gauguin*. She asked me how I would feel living in a house with all primary colours. I said I didn't know. She said seriously, how would you feel, so I said not great I guess. Then she folded her arms and looked at me and said: It. Sucks. Bag. Really, I asked. That bad? Hey, she said, where're you from? Crazyville? I smiled and nodded. What do you call those colours, she asked me. She was pointing at our house. My mother called them salmon and sky, I said. Tash called them flesh and vein. She hated them. Well, said my neighbour, what do you call them? I looked at my house and shrugged. I don't know, I said. I've never thought about it. She left and I surveyed my chalk work. I realized I enjoyed the sound of my favourite quote more than anything.

I never dreamed of revenge.

I sat on the driveway pushing tar into the cracks until I was in a shadow I couldn't move out of. I walked to Abe's Hill, the big pile of dirt on the edge of town named after the mayor, and smoked a Sweet Cap and watched the dusk move in and the lights come on in the faraway city. The magical kingdom.

The lights of the city came on, slowly at first, and then faster, like they were giving in, like the people in charge of turning on the lights were thinking all right already, it's dark, let's just get this night over with.

When I got home I found a book on my crate next to my bed. It was *The Screwtape Letters*. My dad had written something inside it. For Nomi, that it may inspire, love Dad. I thought: Letters from Satan?

My dad's favourite writers were C.S. Lewis and W.B.

Yeats. He said they were deft wordsmiths. He once told me he enjoyed the sensation of being pulled along by the mysterious fullness of initials. I whispered thanks Dad and then stared at my *Christina's World* poster.

I lay on my bed thinking about Travis, about his large-pored green hands and his favourite combinations and the way he always reminded me to signal when I turned. Nomi, he said, you just need to wake up to the fact that other people need to know where you're going. But there's nobody behind me, I told him. And he said, reassuringly, that someday there may be.

I put on Tash's Keith Jarrett record and watched the needle wobble around and around, six inches from my head. I liked the way he moaned when he played the piano. I decided to like anybody who would allow their moans to be taped and distributed to the world. I wanted the world to hear my moans, I thought. And then realized that I would have to also learn how to play an instrument brilliantly. Wake up to the fact, I said out loud. I don't know why. I wondered if it was possible to donate my body to science before I was actually dead. I wondered if a disease were to be named after me what the symptoms would be.

Ten

You are a pathological liar, Travis told me. Like that guy in that movie, remember?

I am not, I said.

But your mom, he said. With your dad? I mean, quote me if I'm wrong, but . . . you think there was chemistry there?

I think I would know, I said.

Or you just tell yourself, said Travis.

Like, are you a shrink or something, I asked him.

No, but I mean I'm just saying. He blew smoke rings.

Well, I said, you're full of shit. He shrugged.

You'd know, he said.

Oh slay me, I answered.

We were sitting in the truck outside The Golden Comb's trailer. Travis took my hand and put it in his lap. Feel that? he asked. Obviously, I said, my hand is on it. It's not a wooden hand.

You're a pathological liar, he said, but you're also very literal. Spooky, he said.

I just don't like it when you're suddenly telling me about my own life, I told him.

I'm not, he said, it's just that your dad always reminds me of that boy, you know? The one with his finger in the dike. Like standing there forever saving the town, like a hero, but kind of not, sort of goofy.

So, I said, you're telling me that I'm a liar and my dad's a moron and you're coming on to me at the same time?

No, I'm not saying that you're a liar and your dad's a moron. I'm talking about the human condition.

Oh, I said, well, the human condition. That's nice. Little Menno boy in a bubble suddenly becomes freaking Balzac or someone. Look at this, Travis, we're in a fucking field in the middle of nowhere. There is no human condition here.

Okay, said Travis, okay. He told me I needed to relax.

The Golden Comb came out of his trailer and walked over to my side of the truck. What's up, he asked.

Waiting for my man, I said. He leaned in through my window and smiled. I looked at his hands. He had once had a job at the killing plant and had learned how to catch four chickens in each hand by sticking their legs into the spaces between his fingers. He could dislodge their brains from their brain stems with one quick violent shake of his hand and throw them on the conveyor belt so they landed neatly in a row, all eight of them. He'd always had a crush on Tash.

Looks like the weather's shaping up, said The Comb. I nodded. Looks like Mr. Green's back in town, he said.

Excellent, I said, and handed him the money. He took his pick out of his back pocket and jabbed at his blond Afro. Travis rested his head against the steering wheel.

Looks like Mr. Brown may be joining Mr. Gre—

Fuck, man, said Travis. Give her the shit.

You simmer, douche bag, said The Comb. He looked to the left and to the right and then craned his neck for a look over his shoulder.

We're in a field, I said. How many more people would I have to tell that to, I wondered. Who do you think you're looking for, I asked him. The FBI? Normally I didn't sass The Comb, he was our only hope, our Mayo Clinic, but the whole scene was ticking me off.

The Comb spit and tossed a Baggie through the open window and into my lap. Seen your sister yet, he asked.

I'll let you know, I said.

I'm waiting, he said, and grabbed his crotch.

I'll let you know, I said again, hoping to sound more agreeable. This sounds so Hollywood, but the truth is this: You don't annoy The Golden Comb. He was a rare example of a person who lived freely in our town completely outside the structure of the church and who didn't care and who didn't leave. He was so far removed from any responsibility or guilt or any of that stuff that he and Eldon, another complete reject, could pretty much do whatever they wanted in their scuzzy little trailer out in the bush. I guess it didn't hurt that The Comb had managed first to identify an overwhelming need in this community and then, secondly, to single-handedly go about filling it. Menno Simons himself would have had to congratulate the guy for self-preservation. They even shared the same obsession with escaping from the world, only The Comb made a huge amount of money from his.

Being seasick at sea is not the same as being homesick at home. I sat in the vacant lot across from Darnell's Bakery writing profound things on the sidewalk with my piece of chalk and watching Bert drive his Red Phantom up and down Main Street. He had a jean jacket with the sleeves cut off and he'd taken a Jiffy Marker and written LED ZEPPEL on the back of it and then under that the remaining two letters.

I wished so badly that he had taken the time to measure the letters out and sketch them on with pencil first. I thought to myself that there really were so many simple ways we could make ourselves look less like idiots. I counted the number of times Bert drove past me. Twenty-three times. I suppose that if Bert were looking for me he would have found me by now. The only real conversation Bert and I ever had was an argument and I forget what it was. All I remember about it is Bert saying end of story. End of Story. And how it left me speechless and depressed. But that's because endings are my weakness and I hate them and mistrust anybody who knows when they occur.

When I was twelve Bert picked me up outside the Sunset and let me drive around some country roads. When I told him I had to go home he asked me why and I said my parents would be worried. He told me he didn't have any parents. He did have parents but they'd been shot out of town in a cannon. He lived with his grandma. His grandpa lived in a little garden shed in the backyard and had his food brought to him in a margarine container. He'd been thrown out of the church a long time ago for being sick. Although the elders don't think alcoholism is a disease so it wasn't presented that way to the congregation.

That's sad, I said. No parents. And he laughed and said I've got something else and then he held up his cigarette in one hand and his bottle of Old Stock in the other hand and said: Mom. And Dad. When he dropped me off my own parents were playing badminton in the front yard. My mom was wearing white canvas Keds that she'd got in the States, and pedal pushers. And my dad was in his suit, of course. They waved to Bert and I told him to hide his mom and dad or I'd never get to go driving with him again. It turns out I never did go driving with him again anyway because he started dating a wild French girl from Marchand. They're still together. Usually she drives up and down Main Street with him in his Red Phantom. She sits right beside him, practically on top of him, and smokes du Mauriers, one after another, lap after lap, night after night. She's really hard-looking. She doesn't smile much. Bert acts goofy a lot and she'll shove him away by pushing one hand against his chest. She has Fancy Ass jeans with bolts along the sides. Sometimes Bert will park the Phantom in the Tomboy parking lot, under the light, and play music loudly and the two of them will sit on the hood of the car like the kids in *Thunder Road*.

I once had a dream that Bert and Brass Knuckle Girl (I don't know where that name came from but her real name was too hard for repressed Teutonic types like us to pronounce and we of course enjoyed distilling individuals down to what we thought was their core essence) were sitting there in the Tomboy spotlight and they started to dance old-style, like Fred and Ginger. Bert said sweetly: Brass Knuckle Girl, will you dance with me? And she said Bert, you know I'd love to. And then Bert took one deep drag off her du Maurier and flicked it, swirling, onto the dark asphalt outside of the spotlight, and they slid off the hood of the car, hand in hand, and waltzed around all over the parking lot and one by one people were coming to watch them and everyone started to cry because they were so beautiful and doomed. After twenty minutes or so of dancing they bowed to the audience, which applauded politely, and then drove off in the Red Phantom, which halfway down Main Street lifted right up off the ground and soared off into the blackness. Since I had that dream I heard through the grapevine that Bert and Brass Knuckle Girl like to have candlelit dinners together on top of silos and that they've signed a suicide pact so that one won't have to live without the other. I wondered if it was signed in blood and where they keep it and how long they've agreed to live before dying. If they have a prerequisite number of laps they need to make around Main Street before jetting.

——

I also wondered how Travis's version of "Fire and Rain" was going and what I would say the next time he played it for me. He'd picked me up on Main Street and told me I looked kind of like Federico Fellini's wife and I said who's that and he said I wouldn't know her and I asked him oh, from *Raiders of the Lost Ark*? And he said that was funny and I asked him if he wanted to sign a suicide pact and he said that was insane and I said nothing but I did notice that he had some ketchup or something on his cheek which I thought I would try to ignore while focusing some more on things to say between songs.

I spent way too much time thinking about what I'd say in between songs. I could say trippy or choice or deadly or wordy or *hey, nervy*. I could say naked. But no more wow, crazy. I'd heard about a girl taking a boy's hand and putting it on her heart so he could feel it racing. That's not bad, I thought. But what would I say if Travis didn't get it. That's my heart? Beating? Fast?

It didn't really matter because mostly he was interested in running around naked in fields. I could do that. All it required afterwards was lying on the ground and staring silently at the sky and I appreciated activities that in the end required silence. The one time I attempted to speak, out of politeness, Travis put his hand on my stomach and said don't talk, let's synchronize our breathing. In. Out. Easy, Nomi, there, yeah. I felt like I was being tested for pneumonia. I wondered if a boulder were to be dropped on us from a height of one hundred feet how many seconds we'd have to roll out of the way.

I must have fallen asleep thinking about it because when I woke up Travis was sitting in the truck and I was wet. I walked over to his window and tapped on it. He rolled it down a crack.

You left me lying naked out in the rain? I asked.

I couldn't move you, he said.

Or wake me up? I asked. He said there was lightning and the truck was the safest place. I put my clothes on and climbed in next to him.

Oooh, you're wet, he said, so I moved back over to stare out the window. I told him his version of "Fire and Rain" was destroying my soul. Except not out loud.

Do you know, I told him, that when it rains, or threatens to rain, even cows and horses bunch together to protect one another from the elements.

Really, he said.

Yes, I said. Look over there. We stared at a thick clump of horses in the field across the road.

When I got home my dad was on the roof. Feel safe up there, I asked. He shook his head. He was crouching and looking at something.

I put my fist around my mouth like a bullhorn and said please come down from the roof. I repeat, come down from the roof now. My dad stood up. Little lightning bolts seemed to radiate from his head. He looked like the less angry, less commanding brother of Moses coming down from Mount whatever. I asked him what he was doing and he pointed to the eavestrough and said cleaning this stuff out. I said okay, don't fall. I went to my room and looked out the window. I wondered if my dad had intentionally waited for an electrical storm to strike before going up on the roof to do some cleaning. Giant chunks of crud were dropping to the ground. I could have stuck my hand out the window and caught them.

My sister's leftover Valium from her wisdom teeth being removed were still in the cupboard above the stove. I took two and my Sweet Caps and left for Abe's Hill to stare at the lights of the city.

The neighbour kid was playing in her yard as I walked by and I did what I always do. I spun her for a long time until we both fell over. I told her she should go inside because it was dark and she asked why, which I thought stood out nicely from all the questions I'd ever been asked. She had a green shiny purse hanging from her shoulder.

What's in there, I asked. She opened it up and showed me the contents: a lipstick and a gun, a plastic one. You're all set, I said. Then she asked me if I knew Jesus drank wine. I said no and she said see, nobody knows the bad side of Jesus. I walked across the yard with her hanging on my leg. The only way I could get her to let go was by agreeing to make my *famous face*. And then pretend my face wouldn't go back to normal and get all panicky about it. It was a routine, I guess. An uninspired one but it cracked her up.

She had a carton of chocolate milk with her and she told me to watch as she drank the whole thing in one gulp. When she was finished she said listen to this and started jumping up and down and sure enough I could hear the chocolate milk sloshing around inside her stomach.

My life is an embarrassment of riches. On the way to Abe's Hill I passed The Mouth and his wife going for a bike ride. Hello Nomi, said The Mouth. *Vo est deet,* he said in the non-romance language of our people. He had so many large grey teeth. Some were jagged, some pointy, like a mountain range. His wife mimed some kind of weak acknowledgment. I exhaled a little louder than usual. It was about all I could muster in terms of a greeting. That's your mother tongue, he said, referring to the bit of unwritten language he'd just laid on me. He wanted people to speak it all the time. English pained him.

They had a daughter who was living in the Black Forest. She also enjoyed physical exercise. She used to be my Sunday-school teacher and she sometimes cried over us because she loved us and couldn't bear to think of us in charred pieces. Our classroom window led onto the fire exit at the back of the church and we'd often escape when she left the room for felt-board supplies. She could really get a buzz on from arts and crafts, particularly the ancient art of gluing macaroni onto jars and spray-painting them gold. Isn't it exciting, she told us, how many ways there are to serve Jesus? She once asked me and the other girls in our class if we were gymnasts, but really fat ones, would we think we could just go out and win an Olympic medal one day? No? Well, that's what Christianity is all about, she said.

The Mouth's wife never spoke. She was in charge of Brides of Christ so maybe she spoke then but what do you say to the Brides of Christ? I once liked one of their sons for a while and he and I would sit in the empty school buses when they were parked in a field for the summer and talk and sometimes hold hands or even kiss. We didn't let the fact that we were cousins stop us from fooling around. We played Bus Driver and Lost Girl. He was the bus driver and I was the lost girl. I would have to let him kiss me if I wanted him to take me home.

After spring break he started liking another girl who stole STP motor-oil stickers for him to put on his banana seat, and he doubled her all over town until I gradually realized we were through.

The Mouth spoke. How's your dad, Nomi, he asked. Why don't you ask him, I said, and rode away.

———

I tried to ride my bike uphill but it didn't work very well. I'd get about twenty feet up the hill and then roll backwards. Then I'd try again. It would have been a fun thing to do with someone else. It was very hard work. It made me think I should stop smoking. Instead, I left my bike at the bottom and trudged up the hill on foot.

It's sad but I don't know what I'd do without my cigarettes. I've tried to quit. I've tried to switch to cigarettes that have less tar, but I don't think I'll ever quite forget the feeling I get from a Sweet Cap. They're my brand. It's hard to explain but it feels good to own something, like a brand. When I go to the store to buy cigarettes I'll think to myself oh there, I see my brand on the shelf, and it's comforting. This your brand? the cashier will ask, and I'll say yeah, those are mine. It's like some people with their TV shows, the way they say I gotta get home for my show. Like it's theirs. Like the way my dad owns *Hymn Sing.* I was always envious of people who had a show, something to do at the same time every day. Like my friend who got heck. Having a show, getting heck. What punctuation things like TV and punishment could bring to a disorderly life. That's what my Sweet Caps do for me. They're my commas and my periods, and they'll probably be the end of me as well. I'll try to quit when I'm forty. Who wants to smoke after that. Really, who wants to live after that? At forty, I'll have worked for approximately twenty-three years chopping heads off chickens. It'll be time.

~

ELEVEN

It's easy to revere you in absentia. To think of you as having a master plan. Did I just say that?

I stayed on top of the hill for a long time. I told myself when it cooled down I would go home but it took a long time to cool down. I spelled Travis's name in the dirt. I practised my new signature, which Travis had helped to design. It was basically a capital *N* and then a straight line similar to the one on a dead person's heart machine. That part of it bugged me but Travis said it was enigmatic. I tried out a few fancier signatures. They didn't work. Tash had warned me about trying too hard. There had been an *a* in my name a long time ago. *Naomi*. But when I was born Tash couldn't say it. We were Natasha and Naomi.

We were going to live together in Prague because Tash said it was the place to be. We were sitting in my grandma's tree and she told me that there were tiny colonies of Mennonites in a place called Kazakhstan. Stalin put them there during the war, to help with the hard labour. They have twenty kids to a family. Say it, she said. Say Kazakhstan. I said it and she said no, really say it. Like a knife, slicing. It's my favourite word now. It's so conducive, she said. *Conducive* was another one of her favourite words, although she never said something was conducive to something else, just that it was conducive. I practised saying Kazakhstan until I got it just right.

Someday we'll go there, Nomi, she said. We'll liberate those kids and take them with us to Prague so they can sit at outdoor cafés with their cute Czech lovers and laugh and drink. I had wanted to laugh and drink, only not with hordes of liberated Mennonite children, but I nodded anyway and said okay.

It did finally cool down—with a northerly breeze that can be so refreshing if it's not also carrying with it the odour of deceased poultry—so I went home.

I saw Mr. Quiring on the boulevard, with his little son, but he was busy tying his shoe and didn't notice me. I thought it was a little late for the son to be up but I guess Mr. Quiring knew what he was doing. Maybe he was on a night walk. Trudie used to take me on night walks when I was really little and we'd talk about the moon and the stars and what we'd have for our "night lunch" before going to bed.

I had an imaginary friend then who hated me and was trying to kill me. The night walks with Trudie helped me to forget my problems.

When I got home I found my dad in his yellow lawn chair. Practising your sitting? I asked. He shrugged like a Mafia don with his eyes closed like he had to do what he had to do. I hated to admit it, but Travis was right. I could imagine my dad standing forever with his finger in a dike saving a town that only mocked him in return. And not knowing it. Or knowing it but not caring. Or knowing it but not knowing what else to do.

I went to my room and put on Keith Jarrett quietly and lay on my bed. I got up and walked to the kitchen for a drink of water and saw that my dad had come inside to have a staring contest with the kitchen table. I got my water and said good night to him and he said good night to me but in a way that made me think he wouldn't actually make it through the night. I thought: He's going to go to Minnesota for a coffee. I can tell. He'll be driving around in another country listening to religious radio while what's left of his family sleeps.

I went back to my room and lay down on my bed. I stared at the old bloodstain that was near my pillow halfway up the wall and considered, like always, getting a cloth and wiping it off. It, the blood, had originally come from my face after I fell off my bike and landed in gravel.

I'd been careening home on my little bike with a giant box of Kotex pads for Tash who had, ten minutes earlier, hissed at me from inside the bathroom instructions to take the money from off Dad's dresser and get the shit she needed before she filled *the entire fuckin' bowl.* Those boxes were huge, the size of a small refrigerator, and I had this one balanced on my handlebars completely obliterating my view and I hit the curb with my front tire and skidded out of control and landed face-first in somebody's pebbly driveway while Tash's pads sailed off into the middle of the road and once again blood poured from my face.

When I got home, finally, after making separate trips each with the bike and the box, Tash said geez, I thought I'd spend the rest of my life stranded on the fuckin' can and I went into my bedroom and lay on my bed picking out bits of gravel and congealed blood from my face and smearing them onto the wall above my pillow in a way that resembled the Mandarin language. If you look closely at my right cheek you can see a whole bunch of very tiny holes that look like an Aero bar. It bothered me in a kind of Charles Manson way to have a brown smear of blood on my wall but I also liked it because every time

I looked at it I was reminded that I was, at that very moment, *not* bleeding from my face. And those are powerful words of hope, really.

Trudie had her kids and her husband and her books. She had a car and nightgowns and white lace curtains. She had friends. She had equanimity. Everything was good. She lived in a town where every single person knew who she was and where she came from and sometimes that made her crazy but most of the time she liked that because it made her feel like she was a part of something. She believed in God and heaven.

She talked about her dead father a lot, my grandpa. His name was Nicodemus. They'd been very close even though at times he couldn't remember her name. Even when he was young and healthy he sometimes had problems remembering the names of his fourteen children. Half of them died when they were babies. We have his old, crumbling bible on a shelf in the den and inside it is a place to write about important events like births and deaths. Nicodemus did all the writing but you can see that there were times when my grandma would correct things for him. He'd thought that his son Peter's first name was Walter but in fact it was Albert. Walter had been the name of an older child of theirs who had died. My grandma twice crossed out Walter and wrote in Albert, next to Peter, in the birth section and then again in the death section. In one place she had crossed out his Mina and written in Minty. She also corrected his Gorge and Hellen.

I think that my grandpa, Nicodemus, was my mother's hero. She missed him. She missed sliding down the stairs in a cookie sheet and having him time her with his pocket watch. She missed watching him run around the yard on stilts and then knock on her second-storey window. He had taught her how to drive at the age of thirteen by sending her off alone in the car on a short business trip to Ontario. She loved to drive. Trudie and Ray were always going for drives, little piles of Wrigley's Spearmint Gum wrappers sitting on the seat between them. Going to little towns near the border and having lunch or dessert, or just coffee.

In church, she was one of the loudest singers. She knew all the words to all the hymns and when she sang she reminded me of a bird or a political prisoner who had just been released from her cage. When I was really small I put my head in her lap. I could see individual hairs poking through her nylons. She rubbed my back. During Communion the women washed each other's feet without removing their nylons. Oh, she said, they dry in a jiffy. She'd snap her fingers. The men however did remove their socks and I saw my fair share of podiatric horror.

After church she'd say let's go in a crisp, very unambiguous way. You were supposed to walk down the aisle to the back and shake hands with The Mouth and various laymen but she'd usually grab me and my sister's hands and take us out the front door, next to the organ. She'd say whew, it's so hot in there. I needed air.

We'd sit in the car and wait for my dad because he always went down the aisle to shake hands, the way you were supposed to, and it took a very long time. Often, our car would be the last one to leave the parking lot.

While we waited for my dad to finish inside, my mom would stare straight ahead with a funny little smile on her face. Sometimes my dad would come out and say I think I'll walk home and she would say oh, now you tell me. The girls and I have been sitting here waiting for you. All right then, my dad would say, we'll drive. No, my mom would say, it makes no difference now. You may as well walk if you want to. Should I, my dad would ask. Oh my god, my sister would say. Do you want to, my mom would ask. I had planned to, my dad would say. Then do, she'd say. And so he would. He loved her ass off. That's what I believe.

I may be a disappointment to Menno Simons but I would like him to know that I have carved, out of the raw material that he has provided, a new faith. I still believe that one day we'll all be together, the four of us, in New York City. Lou Reed could live with us too. We would all sleep until noon, then play Frisbee in Central Park, then watch him play in clubs. We'd be his roadies. People would say hey, is that Lou Reed and his Mennonite family of roadies?

Trudie liked to talk about her childhood. Oh, I had the run of this place, she'd say, about the town. My mom's family was one of the original ones to come here. My sister would laugh and say what place? This town is like a movie set. Nothing real is allowed to happen. It's a ghost town. It's Brigadoon.

My mom told her that we could have stayed in Russia and had our barns set on fire and our stomachs torn out. In war, she said, the oddballs are first on the chopping block.

Oh, is that an original thought? Tash would ask her.

I mean they left with next to nothing, my mom would say. Maybe a dozen buns. Or a few blankets. Most of them fled in the middle of the night. Okay, that's a cliché—the middle of the night, Tash would say. People flee throughout the day as well.

A lot of the families were separated along the way, said my mom, or simply died and were left by the side of the road. There was no time to bury them. We're lucky they let us come here.

My sister would say oh yeah, I feel so lucky. From Stalag 14 to Studio 54. My mom laughed at her when she said things like that and Tash would suck in her cheeks.

My grandma tried to get my mother to keep a cleaner house. Do you need motivation, she asked her. My mom said no, she didn't need motivation because she didn't care so fervently about a clean house. A clean house, my grandma said, is rather like a calling card. If the Rapture occurs while you're out and the Lord God descends upon us and enters your home, he will know, by its cleanliness, that you are one of his sheep. And then what, asked my mom. And he will wait for you to return, said my grandma. And if my house is a mess, asked my mom. He'll leave quietly, said my grandma. Oh, said my mom, I see. I never knew if she really did or if she only said she did, or if she was maintaining one of those infuriating airs of bemusement.

Our house stayed the same, in its level of disorder. My father would sigh, and escape into his world of isotopes and carbons. I learned that radioactive elements are by nature unstable and that they lose mass over time because of emissions from their nuclei.

But who cares? I'd ask my dad.

Well, he'd answer, holding his chin between his thumb and index finger. These radioactive elements decay in order to become more stable. I rather like that, he'd say. This is where the Second Law of Thermodynamics comes into play. *My dad and his Second Law.*

Don't talk, I'd say. I'd put my hand over his mouth.

My mom loved to play Dutch Blitz, which is a card game invented by the Amish people of Pennsylvania. We are offshoots of each other, although they are even more perturbed by the real world.

The game has to do with speed. Trudie often kept me up past midnight so she'd have someone to play Dutch Blitz with her. She was crazy for Dutch Blitz. One more game, she'd say even though in between rounds, during the shuffling, I'd have put my head down on the table and closed my eyes. Sometimes Tash would come home while we were playing and say oh my god, you're playing Dutch Blitz, and Trudie would say okay that's it for me, thanks Nomi, that was fun. I think she used Dutch Blitz to keep herself awake until we were all safely in the house. But I didn't know it at the time. She didn't worry outwardly, ever. She hated public displays of agony, although there would come a day when she would have one.

One day The Mouth came over to our place and asked to speak to her alone outside on the driveway. She said oh for Pete's sake, Hans, what's the problem? Tash and I watched them from inside the house, through the living-room window. She sat on the trunk of the car with her back to us and The Mouth stood with his arms crossed, talking to her, and listening to her occasionally. Although we couldn't see her talking. Sometimes her hands would swing upwards in that universal gesture of helplessness. Then she hunched over and rested her face in her hand. I could make out the keel of her spine pushing against her summer blouse. (I just employed the words *keel* and *blouse*. I'm seventy years old.) I asked Tash what they were talking about and she said how the frig would she know.

Once, while The Mouth was doing the talking, she turned around and looked at us and waved. She waved, I told Tash, and Tash said she wasn't blind.

She's happy, right? I asked Tash. Otherwise, why is she waving?

It's involuntary, said Tash. Mothers wave. We're supposed to smile. I smiled at my waving mother. Tash didn't.

Is she crying? I said. Hey Tash, is she cry— . . . you should wave back.

He wants her to do something, said Tash. She blew a bubble with her own spit.

What? I asked. What do you mean? Tash pointed at them.

Look at that asshole, said Tash. Look at his goddamn . . .

Shhhh, I said. I put my hand over her mouth and she grabbed it away and told me to get lost. She stood up and said, okay, this is the tail end of a five-hundred-year experiment that has failed.

What? I asked.

What? she said, and got up to put on a record.

The Mouth seemed to want to talk some more but my mom had got off the trunk of the car and was slowly backing away from him, towards the house. She was nodding and looking over her shoulder at us as if to say that's fine, okay, but now I have to get back to my kids. Eventually he left and she came inside. What did he want, I asked her and she said oh, pfff, nothing. Nothing? I asked. She smiled and went into the kitchen to fill a pot with water. I followed her. Nothing? I asked. He wants me to work in the library at the church, she said. Like, a job, I asked. Yes, she said. Will you, I asked. And she laughed in a way that bothered me. Well Nomi, she said, of course I will. And then smiled that big, fake spooky smile that I admired and hated at the same time.

Twelve

~

One summer when I was eleven and Tash was fourteen, she and my mom went away for two weeks to work at a Christian camp on an island in the Lake of the Woods. You'll be able to take care of Dad, won't you, she asked me. How hard can it be, I said. Yeah, said Ray, throw a piece of meat in the cage every once in a while.

Tash was really excited because it was a boys' camp. My mom was going to work in the infirmary and Tash was just going to fool around and look hot and drive guys crazy.

That's when my dad and I developed the alphabet routine that has served us so well since. I started with Alphaghetti and then moved on to Bread and Cake. After that, my dad took us out to the Sunset Diner for a break and because I couldn't think of a *D*.

Tash came home from the camp and told me she had had the most amazing romance with a junior counsellor named Mason McClury. God, even that name, she said. He was nuts about her and kept leaving his group of nine-year-olds asleep in their cabin so they could go skinny-dipping together. But, okay, I said. Weren't you like the only girl on the island that whole summer? She hissed at me and held up her hand like a claw. It reminded me of when we used to play White Fang in the backyard.

She told me that when she and my mom had left the island on the camp boat, Mason had stood on the dock blowing her kisses and then, oh my god it was so sweet, he dove into the water in his clothes and pretended to swim out to the boat because he couldn't let her go. Did he make it to the boat, I asked. No, obviously not, she said. It had a motor on it. It was a gesture, Nomi. Like, of love. She told me that Mason had promised to write her and that they'd somehow hook up together in the future, when he got off the island at the end of summer.

When fall came around he still hadn't written and Tash said that he'd probably lost her address, that was so like him, but that he had told her he played basketball for his school team and that he was from a small town and sometimes his team played our boys' team and so she started going to all the games even though she hated sports and one time his town's team was there and she asked all these people if they knew Mason McClury and they said no, who's he? And she sat there for the whole game pretending to cheer for our team and smiling a lot and trying not to cry hot tears of shame. And when she walked home along the highway she thought about what it would feel like to throw herself in front of a livestock truck. She wondered who would miss her, really, and concluded no one. She didn't tell me any of that, actually. I read it in her diary. I was impressed with *hot tears of shame*.

After that I tried to be really nice to her and when she went places I'd say why do you have to go or I sure hope you're coming back, but she wondered what my problem was. And then she burned her diary in this ceremony that indicated the end of her little-girl period and threw the ashes into the Rat River, a properly embittered woman.

Recently, in the top drawer of her dresser, I found a little card and envelope with her name on it. Natasha, my love, "And the

Lord will guide you continually and satisfy your desire with good things and make your bones strong; and you shall be like a watered garden, like a spring of water, whose waters fail not." I wish you joy, peace and contentment. My thoughts will be continually with you, and they will be thoughts of love and goodwill. I will picture you in safety and beauty. Mom.

Puzzling. Had Trudie known all along that Tash would one day leave? Or had Trudie been fooling around with the idea of leaving herself and then stashed this card into Tash's dresser. If so, where was *my* card? But also, Tash left months before my mom did which would mean . . . I don't know. Either my mom was saying goodbye to Tash, knowing she was on her way out of town, and Tash either didn't find the card before she left or found it and forgot it OR my mom was saying goodbye to Tash long before she herself actually left. A dress rehearsal. Before she had the guts to really leave? Before she felt she had to leave for Ray's sake? It's raining questions around here. A person could drown in them.

Travis is putting blinds up today for his dad. We sat in his dad's work truck on my driveway and he told me that I should go on the Pill. I thought yeah, probably. Good idea. Travis had quit school to work for his dad and learn things on his own. He had just turned eighteen. I liked to tell him things that reinforced his idea that school was ridiculous.

I told him that my English teacher didn't know what a codpiece was. He called them grossly enlarged sex organs. Codpieces were the height of fashion in Shakespeare's time, said Travis. He says *height of fashion* in a way that bugs me. I told him that my biology teacher, while teaching us about the reproductive system, pointed at the penis on the overhead and mumbled er, no function. Simians, said Travis. I made a mental note to look up *codpiece* and *simian* in the dictionary when I got home. Then off he went to hang blinds. I had to go to a farmer's field with my history class and pick rocks. It was supposed to help us appreciate how excellent our current lives were.

In the field a few of us spelled out SOS with the rocks although nothing but a crop-duster flew over us and we almost died choking on the poison. It was so hot our eyes dried out to the horrific extent that we couldn't blink and Mr. Quiring had to open up the first aid kit for drops.

I found a note blowing around the field that had been torn in half, right down the middle. It said: I'm sittin in I want to get drunk but I have no flo'? kid here at S.H. that name's Andrew. I ugly but the point are bitching that guys. So one day you with some sexy off, ha ha. Well shit face, me and Sherise ways I guess I'm just my sister for a while if you forgot my pants hope you won't ght you should ditch you could do so much She always a bitch, you don't do what erv, walking around She's gonna trap your thing!! I'm just biz, I'm your gurl here or not. I'll always playboy. Your gurl!

A couple of us looked around for the other half but the wind must have blown it to another town. I knew exactly what your gurl was talking about because I also only ever said half of what I meant and only half of that made any sense, which is, I admit, a generous appraisal of my communication skills.

I had a thought, on the way home from the rock field, that the things we don't know about a person are the things that make them human, and it made me feel sad to think that, but sad in that reassuring way that some sadness has, a sadness that says welcome home in twelve different languages.

When we got back to school our principal told us he had cancelled the Queen City Kids from playing in our cafeteria on the last day of school because a number of large parents had complained about the negative ramifications. Instead, we were given tablets that turned our mouths pink to indicate cavities. Hard to keep up with the changes around here.

After school I went home and had a nap. When I woke up I discovered bite marks on my arm. I bit my arm, experimentally, and the patterns matched. I wondered if this was the beginning of insanity. My *Christina's World* poster fell on my head again because Ray disapproved of tacks in the wall. I got pink shit from my mouth all over my Noah's Ark pillowcase. I thought to myself: The world can be divided into two types of people. That's where I stopped. Travis had suggested I broaden my horizons and attempt to finish my thoughts. He said I should make a list of ways to improve. Oh that'll help, I thought.

1. Topics chosen for conversations: To be filled in later.
2. Plan of action: Read books by philosophers (*The Outsider* by Albert Camus).
3. Form opinions about news stories, possibly read world news section.
4. Become really funny.
5. Pin down current definition of existentialism.
6. Career options: School superintendent, city planner, stone breaker, freelance detective, underwater explorer.
7. Personality development: Read Jung, Adler, Freud. Listen to The Jam.

I went into the living room and stared at the piles of newspapers. I read: Summer, 1982, is the season of the nautical stripe.

I went back into my bedroom and knelt at my bed the way I did when I was a kid. I folded my hands and pressed the top knuckle joints of my thumbs hard into my forehead. Dear God. I don't know what I want or who I am. Apparently you do. Um . . . that's great. Never mind. You have a terrible reputation here. You should know that. Oh, but I guess you do know that. Save me now. Or when it's convenient. We could run away together. This is stupid. What am I doing? I guess this is a prayer. I feel like an idiot, but I guess you knew that already, too. My sister said that god is music. Goodbye. Amen. I lay in my bed and waited for that thick, sweet feeling to wash over me, for that unreal semi-conscious state where the story begins and takes on a life of its own and all you have to do is close your eyes and give in and let go and give in and let go and go and go and go.

Thirteen

~

Trudie lost her job in the crying room when the wife of Uncle Hands, my Aunt Gonad, snuck up on us one morning and caught us grooving to The Knack instead of to her husband.

For a while Uncle Hands made my mom take a bunch of girls, including me and Tash, to the foul-smelling Rest Haven, to sing hymns for The Oldest Mennonites in the World. They sat hunched over in wheelchairs with trays and gas tanks and as we filed past some of them would moan and reach out and try to grab us with spotted papery hands from another century. One man in particular would smack his wet lips together about forty times and wave his one good hand around until the nurse made us go over there and sing "What a Friend We Have in Jesus" and he'd sing along but not with words or melody. The grip some of them had was amazing and terrifying. I wasn't sure if they were trying to drag me along home to heaven with them or if they were desperate for me to pull them back to safety, to a life of running and playing and independent breathing. A nicely dressed woman who seemed functional and completely out of place there sometimes came out of her room to listen to us sing and one time when we were just about to leave I went up to her and said hello, my name is Nomi, and she told me to go to hell.

Tash and I begged Trudie not to take us there ever again and she knew what we were talking about. I guess that'll be my life eventually. First about fifty years of killing chickens and then the Rest Haven. What a relief that will be. I'll probably also be the type of old woman to tell friendly little girls to go to hell.

After the Rest Haven, Trudie got that job as the church librarian. She liked people a lot, anthropologically speaking, so it wasn't too bad at first. She enjoyed helping them find just the book they were looking for. Would you like three weeks for that? she'd ask them. Two weeks was the standard time, but my mom wanted them to be able to finish the books without getting anxious about the due date.

Sometimes she'd let me and Tash skip out of church upstairs and hang out with her, putting books on shelves, sticking numbers on their spines, reading. We read every single Sugar Creek Gang book, stories about a group of mischievous Christian children. Bad things happen. They get into trouble. But always, always, they learn something about sin and forgiveness at the end. We read books by Billy Graham, and books about staying quiet and clean when your husband comes home from work, and books about punishing your children.

It was okay. I liked the way the library smelled and the way the rads would hiss and clank and scare the shit out of us. For some reason, when we were in the library, Tash and I often pretended that we were German spies and we called ourselves Platzy and Strassy. We'd hide bits of information in books and then give each other clues about how to find them. There are probably still little notes stuck in Billy Graham books that say things like: I was brutally tortured for several hours this afternoon but I am fine. Let's meet for drinks at the Über-Swank at eight. Platzy.

Sometimes parents would bring their kids into the library to chew them out about misbehaving during the sermon. One time I heard a little three-year-old kid screaming: I didn't bite him! I didn't kick him! I didn't pinch him! I'm a good Christian!

After church my dad would come downstairs to get us and we'd all go home. My mom worked at the library a lot, it seemed. My dad sometimes built new shelves for the books and she'd sit on her desk, legs swinging, and tell him where to put them. The Mouth told her it was nice to see her taking ownership of her job and being an obedient soldier of Christ. My dad was happy to help out whenever he could. He just wanted to be with her. It didn't matter where.

Speaking of obedient soldiers, Tash wasn't one. She secretly got her ears pierced with a needle and a potato. She kept her eyes half closed all the time when she talked to us which was hardly ever. She'd mumble stuff sometimes and if you asked her what she said she'd say nothing, forget it. She started bringing her radio and candles into the bathroom with her when she had a bath. My dad would gaffer-tape her radio to the counter so it wouldn't fall in the tub and kill her. She wrote Patti Smith lyrics on her bedroom wall, and also the words: DON'T IMPOSE YOUR NOSTALGIA ON ME.

She started going out with Ian, who instead of Greb Kodiaks wore motorcycle boots with chains on them and put his hand on her ass when they walked around town which they didn't do very often because obviously they wouldn't *walk*. And they never ran either. Tash had warned me about running. It's for idiots and children. Ian had a faded red Econoline van with no windows in the back, just a mattress and a cooler. They had matching home-made tattoos of small blue stars. Ian sometimes wore eyeliner. Tash had shown him how to put it on really thick so that it highlighted his pupils and made him look dead. He liked napes, which he compared to vaginas. He told me what *mitosis* was. I loved the way his voice sounded when he said: Two daughter cells. I loved the way he took my sister's hand like he was sure she'd let him. He had wet brown eyes, really long arms, and a slight underbite like Keith Richards'. He once gave me five bucks to go away.

Tash just shot up one night. My mom said, Tash, you must have shot up in your sleep. Tash said she didn't think it was possible to shoot up in your sleep and Trudie told her that of course it was possible and Tash was saying yeah? Really? Okay, how? She liked to pretend she was this wasted junkie girl but I think Trudie just played along to hear her laugh at something because Tash hardly ever laughed around us any more and derisive laughter was better than nothing, I guess.

In the morning when she came to breakfast we all stared at her. She really was about a foot taller than the day before. Are you standing on something, my mom asked. Do your joints ache? Oh my god, said Tash. Trudie put her arm around her and asked her how a girl who was still growing in her sleep could be so tough. Tash told her that made a lot of sense, meaning that it didn't, but at least they were having a conversation. Tash had string bikini underwear and a light blue bra. I loved to watch her get dressed for school in the morning. She liked to use Nazareth's "Love Hurts" as a soundtrack to getting dressed. Every morning was the same. We'd all get ready for school and work, my dad shaving, my mom making lunches, while a litany of bad things love can do blasted out of Tash's stereo speakers. I loved the professional way she put on her bra, fastening it in the front and then whipping it around to the back and sticking both arms through the straps in one smooth motion. She could remove her bra while walking home from school by doing different things under her shirt and pulling it out of her sleeve. She wore orange men's shirts, or sometimes white ones, low-riding Lee jeans with a leather belt that had a Wesson gun buckle on it, and a choker woven out of white leather, with a blue bead in the middle. Her hair was black and straight and parted in the middle. She had very pale skin and dark green eyes like Ray's. She took excellent care of her teeth. She introduced the concept of flossing into our home. Her perfume was Love's Baby Soft. She taught me how to spray it away from me and then walk through the misty cloud for a subtler scent. She understood the meaning of *fascism.* She had three small drops of white paint on one of her jean legs and tiny, minuscule, pink embroidered letters that spelled EAT SHIT AND DIE. She was in possession of real textbooks. Math, science . . . She was more than I could ever hope to be.

It may have been the light at 5:36 on a June evening or it may have been the smell of dust combined with sprinkler water or the sound of the neighbour kid screaming I'll kill you but suddenly it was like I was dying, the way I missed her. Like I was swooning, like I was going to fall over and pass out. It was like being shot in the back. It was such a surprise, but not a very good one. And then it went away. The way it does. But it exhausted me, like a seizure.

I wrote Travis's name in the margins of my notebook today. There are still smudges where I erased all the Travises. I left a print of my right elbow too. It could be useful for identifying my body at some point in time if my teeth can't be found.

He wouldn't let me call him Trav. *Trav-iss,* he said.

Do you know, he asked me, that Günter Grass refers to our people as coarse? What a cunt, I said. I had meant it to be a joke but Travis said no, he was a great writer and I didn't have the energy to explain anything so I just said oh, yeah, I know.

Travis showed me the Vistula River on a map on his bedroom wall. And Danzig, which was also called Gdansk. I watched his finger snake around the Vistula and felt my stomach flip. I imagined the coarseness of our people. What did they do, I asked Travis. He shrugged. They burned down feed mills, he said. Feed mills that didn't belong to them. Oh, I said, that's pretty coarse, right?

Travis put his hand under my shirt and began to suck on my neck. I wish my last name was Grass, I said to him.

Change it then, he said.

I was joking, I said. Travis said oh and then I told him that I almost never meant what I said and he asked me why I was so hedgy and I said it wasn't that, it was because I never knew what to say and yet felt the pressure to say things so I would try to but when I did they lacked all conviction and nothing made much sense.

He ran his finger down the section between my breasts and told me I was sweating a little. I know, I said, I'm always nervous except for when I'm stoned and even then I am.

Nomi Grass, he said. It's kind of nice.

I laughed. I couldn't change my name, ever, because then how would I be found by my mother or my sister, but I didn't tell Travis that because he would have said oh God no, Nomi, not your little scenario again. Or something along those lines.

Why don't you play your song for me, I asked him. What song, he asked. I have all sorts of songs.

Oh, you know, I said.

"Fire and Rain"? he asked.

Yeah, I said, it might relax me.

I'll draw you while you play.

As in sketch? he asked. Can you draw?

I said no, but that wouldn't matter because it would be an abstract representation of a boy playing his guitar for a girl. It'll be my feelings in charcoal. I thought that sounded amazingly cool and Travis seemed to think so also. When he had finished singing I showed him the picture I had drawn.

Who are these people, he asked.

The Grass family, I said.

You drew a picture of your family to represent me playing my song for you? he asked. He looked disappointed.

I'm sorry, I said. It was when you were singing that part about endless . . . about days not . . .

What? he said. How is that . . . I kissed him slowly on the mouth and closed my eyes and held his head so he couldn't move it very well and I did it for a long time even when he tried to move me back a bit with his hands on my shoulders and remove my shirt and put on a record with one hand and switch off the light and move all the shit off his bed and get his guitar out of the way I kept kissing him and kissing him until I had stopped crying long enough for him not to notice.

He went upstairs and got me a glass of water and a pepperoni stick and told me I was bony and hot.

You're beautiful, I told him, and . . . kind of mean. No, I didn't say that last part. And he said he liked it when I took the initiative once in a while and I said well, baby, you really *schteck me ohn,* which in our town means, baby you light my fire (if Jesus really was watching over me he would have prevented me from saying such retarded things to people I was hoping to impress), and then I flicked the lights off and on while he did a Donna Summer routine for me that made me laugh hysterically and also worry about whether or not I was a manic depressive.

———

I have a feeling, a sneaking suspicion, that Mr. Quiring thinks I'm nuts.

I mean, just because he knows my family history and all that. The problems it caused. The messy endings. The whole town knows, right? How could they not? He's probably thinking hey, this girl does have a legitimate claim. And I wouldn't blame him or anything. How can you argue with the crazy genes? But don't worry, I'm hanging in there, remembering to keep my pants on, etc., etc. My school assignments have helped me to focus and organize some of my thoughts. And soon I'll be able to spend my pre–Rest Haven days murdering chickens which should help me to release some of my pent-up psychosis.

But still, it bugs me slightly to think that Mr. Quiring thinks I'm insane. Not that I can be bothered trying to convince him otherwise. Today in school he sat on my desk and told me it was against the law to mow your lawn on Sunday morning in East Village. Tell your dad, he said. You know he was out there at 7 a.m. the other Sunday mowing his lawn?

Fourteen

~

My mom was loving her library job, it seemed. And my dad was loving her. And Tash was loving Ian. And I was loving Tash. But there was a vibe happening in the house. I didn't know exactly what it was. I was too young to understand philosophical shifts. There was a look in everybody's eyes that I couldn't explain. Like they could see something that I couldn't see. Like I was four years old again and lying in the back seat of the car pretending to be asleep while the rest of my family sat together in the front and said things that I couldn't quite make out. One night I heard my dad say to my mom: I can't help but think of the good times we're having now as being painful memories later on. And my mom saying, c'mon now honey. Oh super duper, I thought, now my dad has started mourning the future too.

Tash started staying out really late with Ian and when she did come home she went straight to her bedroom and slammed the door. The Mouth came by often to talk with my parents. He'd bring Aunt Gonad with him sometimes and my mom would get out the TV trays and make tea and The Mouth would sit down on the couch with his legs crossed so that one of his pant legs rode way, way up his leg and exposed a shiny, hairless shin. Pure bone. I would occasionally stroll through the living room and glance surreptitiously at his leg just to freak myself out but that was long ago. I remember wanting to tell Tash about it one evening, it was the type of grotesque detail that could almost make her smile, but when I knocked on her bedroom door she said piss off, Swivelhead. And that was long ago too.

When I was a kid I was afraid of the dark and one night I thought I saw Jesus standing at the foot of my bed with a baseball bat poised to smash my head in for a lie I'd told Rhonda Henzel that day and forgotten to ask forgiveness for. I ran to my parents' room and hid under the bed and eventually fell asleep.

When they came to bed I woke up and heard my mom asking my dad where everything had gone and I remember wondering if we'd been robbed. I think I'm losing Tash, she said, and began to cry. And I heard my dad, in his wordless way, shift around in the bed to offer what comfort he could in the form of his arm. I waited for them to fall asleep and then I went back to my bedroom and slept with the light on all night. The next day my dad and I went to church and my mom told him she couldn't go with him because she wasn't feeling well. My dad stood staring at the closed bedroom door. I could see his outline in the dark, from the living room. Then he knocked on Tash's door and said Tash: It's time to get up. And she told him to go to hell.

If I had a clue as to what constituted an ending I'd say that that day marked the beginning of the end. My dad and I walked to church together holding hands. Afterwards, we walked back home. And I listened while he talked to me about the half-lives of isotopes. Take radon, he told me. For it to break down into its daughter nucleus, polonium 218, requires 3.82 days. Others take only seconds.

I didn't know what he was talking about, but I felt happy knowing he was happy about something even if it was about something breaking down.

And potassium, on the other hand? he said. To break down into argon?

I'd hum.

Nomi, he'd ask. Are you with me? It takes fifty billion years! Fifty billion years to find a little stability. A molecule's worth.

I laughed, and then I realized that I had just laughed the type of laugh my mother often laughed. It was the kind of laugh a person laughs before consuming two or three bottles of Aspirin. And I had another thought: that Tash had stopped laughing for a good reason. And that she was the sanest person in our family. But that didn't make any sense at all.

When someone complimented Tash she'd suck in her cheeks to keep herself from smiling because she enjoyed looking pissed off and dangerous. I liked the way the shadows fell on her face when she did that. She looked like Sophia Loren. When I did it I looked like Alexander Solzhenitsyn after all those years in solitary confinement. Ray had his book.

I went to the garage and sat on the cold cement floor and opened and closed the garage door with a little black box that said STANLEY on it. When we first got the automatic door opener I loved to roll under the door and clear it at the last second. It was fun to think I could be sliced in half if I made even one tiny tactical error, until my sister told me the door was designed to stop as soon as it made the slightest contact with any surface, even flesh. Thanks for ruining my fun. I remember the way her knees looked while she stood on the driveway saying to me as I rolled under the door, don't let's be the kind of family that fights about who gets to kill themselves next.

When Tash was four and I was a fat baby, she threw herself out of a tree and broke her elbow in two places. She thought that God had let it happen. My mom told her that God had saved her life. She could just as easily have broken her neck and died. Then she had wanted to throw me out of a tree to test God's love and my mom said no, there are such things as accidents.

These were simple, barely considered statements that Trudie threw out like confetti and forgot in a second that she'd said but they stuck to me like the kind of wood tick that crawls through your ear into your brain and lays eggs. What did she mean, *accidents?* What about God knowing how many grains of sand there were on every single beach? What about him knowing what we'll do before we do it? Obviously if my sister were to throw me out of a tree there would be an ending ordained by God. He'd have known that she was going to do it and he'd also have known what the outcome would be. If Tash felt like throwing me out of a tree, wasn't that because God was making her feel like throwing me out of a tree, and for her not to follow through on that feeling, wasn't that a sin? Wasn't Satan speaking through my mother when she was preventing Tash from throwing me out of a tree and following God's will? Technically, I should have been thrown from that tree.

I remained in the garage but moved from the floor to the top of the freezer to get away from the ants. I realized while lying down on it that my body could easily fit inside. I imagined Tash walking up to me, in frayed cut-offs with cotton balls between her toes, saying: No, it wouldn't. It's designed to hold casseroles and pork chops and things. Don't let's be the kind of family discovered in freezers.

———

My sister once gave me a Valentine's card that said Jim Jones loves you. It had a rainbow decal inside that I stuck into the exact centre of our large picture window.

When my dad saw it he asked me what it was. A rainbow, I said. He said no . . . no and shook his head. He gave me a razor blade and a wet cloth. My dad wasn't big on overt symbols of hope. His famous line was: Let's not call it a celebration. He said that when his school was planning a twenty-year anniversary thing and the kids were making up the invitations for the general public to come and eat a sandwich and look and marvel at how things hadn't changed, he suggested they use the words Twenty Years: A Retrospective.

Trudie had said but honey, I think celebration sounds nice and Ray had said yes, it does sound nice. Tash had suggested Twenty Years: A Long, Arduous Journey, which my dad had liked and didn't realize until later that she'd been joking.

On long drives Tash would be forced to share her thoughts with me in the back seat of the car. Her big thing was noticing things nobody else had, like: Ever noticed how nobody names their kid Cain any more? Ever noticed how Mom and Dad can say *open house* and *come and go* and *do* but never *party?* We had parents who couldn't say *party.* We were in the car on a long, boring trip somewhere. We thought of ways to make them say *party.*

Okay, said Tash, we'll do word association. I say *birthday,* Mom, what do you say? *Cake?* said my mom. *Suit?* Then I tried: Okay, Dad, this is more like a fill-in-the-blanks game. I go to a restaurant, the hostess person comes up to me and says how many people in your . . . ? My dad said *family? Car?* Tash said god and rolled down the window just far enough for her to put her head through it. When my dad said Tash, please don't do that, please get your head back inside the car, she closed the window even tighter around her neck so it looked like she would eventually pinch it right off and her head would go sailing off into the sky like a lost balloon. Her hair was whipping around wildly and her lips were stretched back and turning blue in the wind and she slowly dug her thumbnail into her arm until she'd engraved in herself a little bleeding crescent moon. That was how badly she needed to hear my parents say *party*. Finally my dad stopped the car somewhere around the exit to Falcon Lake and we waited for Tash to sit properly in the back seat. That took about five or ten minutes. My mom said: Honey, we were playing along. We were only teasing you. I had to get out of the car and go around to give Tash a sip of my Coke, so she wouldn't dehydrate in the sun. I don't know why it meant so much to her. Everything always did. I sometimes wonder if they'd said *party* that day if things could have been different. Things shouldn't hinge on so very little. Sneeze and you're highway carnage. Remove one tiny stone and bang, you're an avalanche statistic. But I guess if you can die without ever understanding how it happened then you can also live without a complete understanding of how. And in a way that's kind of relaxing.

FIFTEEN

It was an idea, more than anything, that started the whole thing. It was the seventies then, and although our town was a secret town (The Mouth suggested that when we look in the mirror there should be no reflection because who we are is something that we cannot see), some of the less oppressed teenagers were able to pick up signals from the outside on their invisible radars. Tash especially.

The Mouth came to our house one evening to tell my sister that her physical self was irrelevant. She said okay, thanks for that. Thank you for coming over here to tell me that. And when he left, she shouted oh my god and got on the phone immediately to tell her friends about the latest Buddhist-tinged interpretation of the gospel according to The Mouth.

That was around the time our Aunt Gonad asked Tash to burn her *Jesus Christ Superstar* soundtrack. Tash could do a hilariously sexy version of "I Don't Know How to Love Him" where she basically worked herself into a complete fake orgasm during that big crescendo. Ian could play it on the piano because every good or previously good Menno kid knew how to play the piano and she'd drape herself all over him and sing and moan while he banged out the tune and laughed his head off.

Please don't *schput,* Ray would say. He never made a big scene. He'd go into the basement and practise his typing or work on his watercolours.

Tash was gone a lot of the time. In the summer she'd sleep till one or two in the afternoon and then get up and put on loud music and cool clothes and grab an apple or something from the fridge and leave. She had this thin silver chain that she wore low around her waist and sometimes when she walked out into the yard it would catch a ray of sunlight and the reflection was so bright and flashy it made me have to look away and I liked to think it was a message of some kind. Like, zap, I love you. Or something like that.

My parents and I would stand in the living room staring at her through the picture window. There she goes, my dad would say. Jingling the money in his pocket the way he did for an entire day and night when my mom left. And my mom would say well, it's normal, honey, let's not make too big a deal out of it or it will just get worse. But although my mom was philosophically cool about a lot of stuff, her eyes lingered on things, like Tash when she walked down the driveway and got into Ian's van. I used to count the seconds that passed between the time Trudie would first fix her gaze on Tash as she left and the time she would turn to look at me all bright-eyed and smiling saying well, what's next? Nine or ten seconds, usually. There's very little turnaround time for a mother to go from careworn to (fake) enthusiastic but Trudie was a pro and I loved her for it and it didn't occur to me then that that sort of bravura could have a shelf life. For all I knew Trudie was also taking heart from the quick laser reflection of sunlight off Tash's silver waist chain.

It was around then, during the days of Tash's silver-waist-chain period, that Mr. Quiring came to our house for a meeting with

Ray and Trudie about Tash skipping out of classes and not
getting her assignments in and, quote, leading the class, when
she was there, in mini-revolts that she thinks are humorous, etc.
etc. He told Ray and Trudie that he considered himself to be a
patient and long-suffering man but that it had to end
somewhere. It does? Trudie had asked.

Ray was outside watering the flowers and Trudie was
cooking something in the kitchen and I was . . . I don't know
what I was doing. I answered the door. Tash wasn't at home. And
my mom was flustered at first because she didn't know what Mr.
Quiring wanted or why he was there and he seemed a little
nervous too, standing there in the front entrance. And then Ray
came in, his hands all dirty, and Mr. Quiring asked if it was a
good time to talk about Tash, and Ray and Trudie thought it was
and I made tea and sat on the couch and listened.

But he was really nice about it and he told Trudie that he
thought Tash had a lot of talent and a sharp intellect. And he
said she had dramatic flair and that it was a shame there was no
place in town where she could develop that. He was wearing
sandals and jeans. And just those three things combined—saying
that Tash had dramatic flair, expressing regret that it would
probably never be realized in East Village, and wearing jeans and
sandals—made him seem like the original hipster man,
especially next to Ray who hadn't even taken off his tie to do the
gardening and had probably never used the word *flair* in his life
except maybe to describe somebody with a flair for modesty. Ray
seemed so much older than him but he isn't really at all.

I would ask Mr. Quiring if he remembers all that but
I don't really want to have conversations about the past with
anybody but myself. It prevents discrepancies from creeping in.

After Mr. Quiring left, Trudie slammed her cup down on
the kitchen counter and told Ray that even Almon Quiring
could see that Tash didn't belong in this town. And Ray asked

her what he should do about that, take an Almon Quiring course on Natasha Nickel?

Even I knew the answer to that question. Uh, Dad, we all move to NYC? But I kept my mouth shut. Sometimes I think that Trudie blamed Ray for Tash leaving town with Ian because if Ray had agreed to leave first, had taken us all off to some other place, Tash wouldn't have had anything to rebel against and would have stuck around.

But, on the other hand, sometimes I think that Trudie appreciated the fact that Tash had an awful lot of things to rebel against because if she didn't she might not have developed her dramatic flair and pursued all sorts of adventures off in the city and in the world that Trudie herself more than anything also wanted to experience.

Anyway, from that day on, Trudie would periodically invoke Mr. Quiring's name, telling Ray that at least there was one person in this town who could see that Tash wasn't like everyone else. And Ray always agreed with her and said Mr. Quiring was absolutely right which didn't leave Trudie any more or less frustrated.

Basically, I think that Trudie and Tash were kind of the same person. And maybe me and Ray are too. What was it Mr. Quiring told the guidance counsellor? Nomi's problem is a general lack of self-esteem that feeds into an eroding sense of purpose. Yeah, okay, sounds right, I guess. I'm sure once I begin to spend nine hours a day separating chickens' heads from their bodies I'll feel a lot better and more useful.

My parents weren't crazy about the fact that Tash was drinking and hanging out with Ian so much, sometimes until five or six in the morning, at the pits or in the bushes around Suicide Hill or in any of the other rustic settings we young pioneers relied on to get us through the night, but it wasn't that, really, that my mom was concerned about. Not really.

I do remember The Mouth coming to our house and my mom saying Hans, for crying out loud, what is it this time, and him saying Trudie, you know as well as I do that Tash's been hitching rides to the city, and my mom saying something sassy like well, can you blame her and The Mouth telling her she was treading on thin ice. I didn't know if he meant my mom or Tash or both of them and I didn't know what *thin ice* meant exactly and when I asked my mom she said oh, it's just the heat. Everybody's cranky these days.

Later that evening we had supper at my grandma's place and The Mouth was there also with his wife and kids, my first and third cousins, and my grandma said but where's our Tash, and The Mouth cut my mom off and said Mother, this is a spectacular pot roast. I had never heard The Mouth use the word *spectacular* in any context whatsoever. I'd vaguely thought it was a sin to say *spectacular*. So while I was busy chewing over his use of that particular word, I hadn't noticed that my mom was getting more and more pissed off with her brother and his habit of controlling every single aspect of her life. Which in fact was still not quite the thing that bothered her. She was used to that by then, obviously, and she could ride that out.

I did know that Tash and Ian had applied for library cards in the city, and were bringing home books not by Billy Graham or about the Sugar Creek Gang. And pamphlets about communism and Albania being a great place and if there's one thing other than John Lennon that gets The Mouth's back up, it's communism because it was the reason why the Russians took everything away from the Mennos and sent us all packing when life had been so coarse and sweet back there on the banks of the Vistula.

Tash had learned the meaning of the word *metaphor*, and had started applying it to almost every aspect of her life, and ours. I heard my dad say to her: Tash, some things are real. Some things are nothing but what they are. And Tash asked him how he knew that and he said he didn't know that, but he believed it. And some things are more than they appear to be. What things, she had asked. And my dad said he didn't know exactly. I remember being frightened by that conversation and making a mental list of the things I knew, and then wondering if they were real or not.

That may have marked the beginning of my self-biting period. I wondered if Tash was possessed by the Devil. Suddenly, in comparison to loving metaphors and communism, it seemed tame and typical and status quo to be drinking at the pits, to be staying out all night with a boy, and to be storming around the house in a bra and panties swearing along with Marianne Faithfull and saying oh my god to everything anybody ever said to you. Why did my sister require more than that? What the heck was she doing with that library card of hers? She'd gone too far, I knew that much.

Sixteen

~

This evening I tried to explain to Travis how it was that he found me lying on the shoulder of Highway 23. It's my chain, I said. It's faulty. It happened to me frequently. One second you're flying down the highway to America, the next you've got your Wrangler flare pant leg caught in the chain and you're down, stuck pinned to the road staring up at the clouds and picking gravel out of your skin, waiting for someone to come along and rescue you.

Usually it was a farmer passing by. He'd get my pant leg out of the chain and throw my bike in the back and give me a ride to the border. Once I got to shift gears for a carny named Snake. Now! he'd say. It was fun. He made me wear one of his hats with the carnival logo on it so if someone saw me riding with him they'd think I was a co-worker and not report him. He told me he was on antibiotics because he'd gotten the clap from the cotton-candy girl. He told me that a kid like me could make twenty-five cents per rat at any fairgrounds if I knew how to swing a bat. I didn't have a clue what he was talking about. He told me he could not afford one more felony. I said man, tell me about it, although I was only ten and had never heard the word *felony* before. It sounded like a pretty girl's name to me.

Travis put my bike into his dad's truck and asked me why I didn't tuck my pant leg into my sock. Somebody might see me, I said. I'd rather fall.

I made Travis promise me that he would never become the type of person who tucked his pant leg into his sock while riding a bike and he said I was superficial but he knew what I meant. He said he'd take off his pants and ride around in his underwear first.

Where would you put your pants, I asked. You're not gonna have a carrier!

What's wrong with a carrier, he asked and I said no, no carriers. Carriers are for little kids.

Well, then he said he'd get a clip for his pant leg and I said no, no clips, and he said my bike etiquette was extreme. I felt like an idiot for feeling good about knowing how to look on a bike. I had to get my driver's licence soon.

He asked me if I felt weird lying beside the road under my bike. Now that you mention it, I said. He drove us to a field and we smoked a joint and climbed into the back of the truck where we could stretch out and stare at the sky. Just another hard surface to lie on while contemplating infinity.

Let's talk more about bikes, I said. We talked about when we were kids and dressed up our bikes for the July 1 parade, which included a contest.

You don't want to win though, I said. He agreed. (In this town, if you win something you're dead.) Hey, we actually agreed on one thing, I said.

He asked me if I was warm.

Yes and no, I said. And I'm not on the Pill yet, I told him, which he said was cool but when would I be. Maybe two weeks, I said.

Should we take off our clothes anyway, he asked. I guess we could, I said. We lay in the open box of the truck like two dying fish on the bottom of a small boat. He told me I was cute in the moonlight. I wished he'd said beautiful. *Cute* made me feel like a garden gnome.

He said we should go to Europe together and I could learn how to bake bread and he'd sell his writing and we'd have this little place up hundreds of stairs in a building in Paris with a courtyard and we'd ride bikes everywhere and play in fountains and make love continuously. I said: I do ride my bike everywhere. No, he said, but in Paris, with a big carrier that could hold baguettes and wine and fresh flowers. I said: Baguettes? Then why would I have to learn how to bake bread? And hey, I said, what did I just say about carriers?

Nomi, it's romantic, he said.

Well, but how would we get to Paris? I asked.

We'd save money from our jobs, he said.

What jobs? I asked.

Nomi, you have . . .

No, too many variables, I said. What's that bright light headed straight for us? I asked. It could have been a seeder. It was some kind of giant farming implement bearing rapidly down upon us like the Apocalypse.

What the fuck is that, asked Travis.

It's like we're in *Jaws,* I said. He told me to roll myself up in the shag carpet in the back and then he jumped out and ran around to the cab and started it and took off. The field was really bumpy and I felt my bike fall on top of me again, although this time I was rolled up in a carpet so it didn't hurt as much.

He drove to The Golden Comb's trailer out on Kokomo Road and parked behind the purple gas tank and that's where I emerged from the carpet like a cute but not beautiful butterfly and put my clothes back on. I had orange wormy pieces of rug in my hair. He pulled them out one by one. He was so gentle and sweet and he sang an Eric Clapton song in this weirdly satirical operatic voice but underneath he seemed to mean it so I put my hands on his waist and up under his shirt and we waltzed around, badly, and then we fell.

We sat in the grass and sang stupid nursery songs that had perverted hand movements. We tried to whistle "Crying" by Roy Orbison straight through without laughing. We loved Roy Orbison. Let's name our baby Roy Orbison, said Travis.

Do we have a baby? I asked.

We will someday, he said.

Hmmm, Roy Orbison, I said. What if it's a girl?

Nova, he said.

Nova? That's a car.

No, it's a star, he told me.

I don't want to have kids named Nova and Roy Orbison, I told him. I liked the name Miep. Miep was the woman who had saved the letters of Anne Frank and had also done kind and dangerously heroic things for her. A real star.

Anyway, said Travis. We did this thing where I lie on my back in the grass and he stands at my feet really rigidly with his arms straight out like he's on a cross and then he falls forward and I scream quietly and he puts his hands down at the last second, mere inches away from crushing my body. After that we just sat around sniffing purple gas for a while, lighting matches and flicking them off into the dark, and I asked him if he wanted to go halfers with me on *Wish You Were Here.* He said what if we break up which made me kind of sulk a bit and made him act tough like he'd have four thousand girlfriends in his life and I stopped talking except to answer his questions.

I hated the way I always wrecked beautiful moments. We saw The Golden Comb open his trailer door and spit and then slam the door shut again. Spitting is how people in this town both mourn and celebrate. It's the standard response to everything that occurs. The screen on the door was covered with moths. Travis and I stared at it longingly. Do you have any money, he asked me. I didn't.

What about the carpet, I asked. We could trade it for dope and tell your dad it fell out the back of the truck somewhere and we hadn't noticed and that when we retraced our route we couldn't find it.

Travis told me that when I was dying to get high was when I was the most together and brilliant.

Well, I said, it's the dying part that makes me feel alive.

I asked him if we were waiting for something and then he got up and hauled the rolled-up carpet out of the back of the truck and we each took an end and walked over to The Comb's trailer and banged on the door.

Oh my God, said Travis, they're listening to Yes.

The Comb opened the door and looked at us. He wasn't wearing a shirt and he looked pissed off. No, he said, I don't want an orange carpet, but thanks anyway. He was just about to slam the door but Travis put his foot in the way, movie-style, and said it was a shag carpet with triple-thick inlay. The Comb came outside and rolled the carpet out in the dirt and lay down on it for a minute. We stood there staring down at him. He ran his fingers through the shag.

Well? I asked. Yes or no?

He got up and told Travis to roll it back up and bring it into the house. I stayed outside and leaned against the ripply aluminum outside of his trailer and said thanks, man, you're a lifesaver. The Comb smiled and put his hand on my arm and then leaned over and kissed me on my fuckin' lips and said he'd seen me getting dressed by the purple gas tank.

Hmm, bionic eyes, I said. I shrugged. He tried to kiss me again and I asked him if we were doing the thing or not and he said I didn't really have much of a choice, did I, referring to the fact that there was nowhere else that we could go, and I said no, not much of one, but that Travis would be out very soon and shit, we had given him a carpet, so . . . then Eldon yelled something from inside about not being able to find the scales and The Comb said he'd be right there and Travis came back out and The Comb went in and I lit up a smoke and tried to act intensely nonchalant while we waited for The Comb to come back out again.

I hate that motherfucker, Travis whispered.

What does that have to do with anything, though, I asked him. On the way home Travis told me that when he was a boy he'd asked his mom whom she loved more, God or Dad. God or Dad! he said. God or Dad! She wouldn't answer, just hummed. Then she finally said God already! and Travis was weirded out by that but he'd said: Thaaaat's right. For some reason I laughed hysterically while he was telling me about it and afterwards I felt like an idiot.

We drove past my high school and the junior high and the track and the Sunset Diner and the cemetery and past a few houses and up onto my driveway which made a nice cracking sound that bothered Travis because he thought his tires were being punctured.

I was relieved to see my dad not sitting in his yellow lawn chair. We sat in the truck for a while listening to an American radio station.

Music really is the glue of our relationship, isn't it? I said. Travis said yeah, shhhh, I'm listening to this song.

I mean really, I said. It's brought us together, right? Yeah, it has, said Travis. He turned up the radio a bit.

Music's probably altered our DNA so you and I are like twins now. You know? I said. I *know,* said Travis. We'll feel the same thing at the same time even if we are miles apart, I said.

Can you be quiet for a minute, please? said Travis.

I shut up after that, thinking about the words *salve* and *salvation.* I got out of the truck without kissing Travis and said ciao for the first and last time in my life.

That night it rained softly. I could hear it through my screen. And then I felt it on my face, and it was warm, but it wasn't rain.

In the morning I watched dust enter my room through a crack in my blind. No, I heard my sister saying, that dust has always been there. It's the sunlight that illuminates it. I checked myself for bite marks. I wondered what it meant to bite yourself in your sleep. Would I soon begin to tear out clumps of hair? Would I be able to kill myself eventually without realizing it?

My dad and I used to dust with Lemon Pledge but when it ran out we stopped, although we talked about it a couple of times. Some pledge, my dad had said and I gave him credit for being funny intentionally.

Ray had already left for school. He had put his coffee cup on the counter, on top of the plate he'd used for his toast. I put them into the dishwasher and then I looked into the fridge to see if there was anything to make for supper. There was a knock on the door and I went over and opened it and the neighbour girl was standing there wearing her bathing suit and rubber boots.

Hello, I said, I have to go to school.

Can you play charades with me? she asked.

I said no, I didn't have time, but she looked so sad and forlorn and kept saying please over and over so I said fine, quickly. I stepped outside and sat on the front step and she sat down in the grass.

Start, I said, hurry up. I'll guess.

She didn't move.

Are you doing it? I asked. She nodded.

Are you a . . . weird little kid? She shook her head.

Hmmmm, I said. Hang on. I went into the house and got my smokes and sat back down on the step and lit one up and said are you a rock? She shook her head. She was just sitting there in a vaguely square shape. God, I said. I blew smoke rings at her. Can't you do some kind of action? She shook her head and started to giggle. Are you a book? I asked. She shook her head again. A fridge? She shook her head. Okay, forget it, I don't know and I have to go to school now, I said. I threw my butt into the grass and went into the house and slammed the door.

Three seconds later she knocked again and I opened it and she told me she had been a Shreddie. Okay, I said, I'll pour some milk over you and eat you, and she screamed and ran away. I thought probably I would not be a very good mother to Roy Orbison and Nova.

On the way to school I stopped to watch a group of twelve- or thirteen-year-old boys throw rocks into a new abattoir being built next to the junior high school on the other side of the highway. There was a twenty-foot wall of concrete cinder blocks around it and every day it got higher and higher, but the men were working from the inside so you couldn't actually see them. I heard a loud clank like a rock had hit somebody's hard hat and then an angry scream and five seconds later a bunch of the workers came flying out of an opening in the side and were throwing rocks back at us. Most of the kids had taken off but one of them got hit in the back and fell shrieking to the ground.

I went over to him and put my hand on his back and asked him if he was okay but he didn't say anything because he was gasping for air.

Three or four of the construction workers came running up to us and they pulled him into a sitting position and said c'mon buddy, breathe. There were many occasions in this town where people encouraged others to breathe, it seemed. C'mon, c'mon, said one guy with no shirt. He was moving his hands around the boy's chest, trying to get the air circulating inside him. There we go, he said. There we go.

The boy began to cough and cry. I picked his ball cap off the ground and put it on his head.

Do you know this guy, asked the construction worker. I shrugged. I know of him, I said. We all knew of each other.

I'll take him to school, I said.

Hey kid, said the man, see what happens when you throw rocks? The kid nodded. Gonna do it again? asked the man. The kid nodded.

He means no, I said. He better mean no, said the worker. C'mon, I said, let's go. The boy got up and we headed off in the direction of the junior high.

What's your name? I asked.

Doft, he said.

Do you speak English? I asked. He shrugged. Are you from Paraguay? I asked. A lot of people who had left town for Paraguay for even more hardship and isolation than this place could provide, although we did our best, were moving back. The Paraguayan girls wore dresses over pants, and the boys wore suspenders and men's shirts. He nodded.

Hey, I said, don't cry. You're gonna be okay. You had the wind knocked out of you, that's all.

He wiped his nose with the side of his hand and pulled his cap down really low over his eyes. Do you smoke? I asked. It was all I had. He nodded. I handed him a Sweet Cap and lit it for him and we sat on the curb smoking with our backs to the front doors of the junior high. When I was finished I flicked my butt onto the road and Doft put his on the ground and jumped on it with both feet.

You should go in now, I said. I pointed to the door. Doft took his ball cap off and handed it to me. Please, he said.

His English wasn't very good but then again none of ours really was. Then he did six or seven cartwheels in a row down the sidewalk and back again. I handed him his hat and said fuckin' A, Doft. *Bueno.*

We waved at each other before he disappeared inside the school. I have made two children happy in the course of five minutes, I thought to myself.

I was moved in typing today for flippancy. Flippancy was the big sin. I should have realized the inherent gravity of fjfjfjfjfjfjfjfjfjfjfjfjfjfjf the fox jumps over the log. And *how* will this help me to kill chickens faster?

On our report cards every letter of the alphabet signifies a different behaviour problem and I always without fail get a big red circle around the *F* for Flippant Attitude. But I don't really give a fuck. (Oh, funny, eh?)

Travis had phoned me in the morning, before the Shreddie incident with my neighbour, and said he was mad at me for saying he looked like Ian Tyson when he holds his guitar so high up, which had put me in a bad mood. I just like them better held low, I said. He told me I was shallow. First about pant legs being tucked into socks and then about how a person holds his guitar. Well, what the hell am I supposed to think about, I asked him. I told him he was fishing around for stupid things to be mad at me for because he knew *he'd* said a stupid thing last night and couldn't just apologize and tell me we'd never break up because he loved me more than life itself. And then I hung up.

Five seconds later I phoned him back and said I was sorry and he said he was too and asked me what I was wearing and I lied and said his Blumenort Jets sweatshirt.

At lunch it was raining so I didn't go home. I went to the gym and sat way up in the bleachers and watched Rhinehart Bachenmeir shoot hoops. Man, he was good. He was *conducive*. That fast break and all that spinning around to the left, to the right, and his arc, stellar, beautiful like one of those marine-show dolphins. Dribbling between his legs making all those three-pointers and left-handed layups and slam dunks. What a pretty shooter. The only thing missing was the ball. I clapped anyway and he gave me the finger because I guess he thought he was alone with Kareem Abdul Jabar.

At 2:30 the guidance counsellor came to my class to tell me I should talk to her. We walked together in silence to her office next to the principal's office and she pointed at a chair and said have a seat.

She asked me if I had any specific goals or aspirations for after high school and I smiled.

Hmmmm, I said. Lemme think. I told her I'd thought about becoming a city planner someday. She asked me if I wanted to spend the rest of my life spacing fire hydrants. No, I said, but I like looking at cities and thinking about them. She told me I needed exceptional math skills for that.

Like, for instance, I said, that our main street has two dirt fields on either end of it is weird to me. Shouldn't it lead somewhere?

That requires engineering, she said. I nodded. Any other goals? she asked.

I told her I'd like to be able to do one chin-up. One chin-up, she said. She looked at me. I mean that would be something, right, I said. Holding my entire self up by myself. Like, my self by myself. No? She was writing something down.

Nomi, she said. Talk to me about English.

English? I asked.

Your written assignments, she said. Forgetting about
"Flight of Our People" for now. You're having some problems
getting them in?

I'm not having problems getting them in, I said. They're
not . . .

Mr. Quiring says the . . .

It's just . . . I don't know. She nodded. I blew my bangs
out of my eyes. She looked at her watch. I shrugged. She wrote
some more stuff down and then she stood up and said she had
to see someone else.

Okay, I said. Well, thanks a lot. I stood up and she came
around from behind her desk with her arms out like an extra in
Night of the Living Dead.

Can I give you a hug? she asked.

I . . . it's just . . . I mean philosophically a hug is a great
thing, I said. But . . . I smiled and left quietly. It's so good to
talk to someone who cares. I had a doctor's appointment after
school.

On my way to my appointment I stopped in at Barkman's and
stared for ten minutes at a floor model of a plastic bird whose
head goes up and down into a cup of water. I wondered if it
would hurt Travis to know that I was more interested in plastic
birds than in procuring the female hormone that would allow
our love to "progress to the next level."

How much is that, I asked Mr. Barkman. I thought
maybe my dad would like it. It seemed like such a
straightforward thing for that bird to be doing. Head in. Head
out. It made sense. Mr. Barkman said it was six bucks so I
bought it for my dad and Mr. Barkman gave me ten or fifteen
Icy Cups and a parachute jumper on the house for taking it off
his hands.

I left the store and bumped into two girls singing "Let My Love Open the Door" into microphones made from screwdrivers and tensor bandages.

There was a little kid, maybe three or four, walking down Main Street by herself with a doll's stroller strapped to her butt. Every few steps she'd stop and sit down in it for a rest and then get back up and keep walking.

From the back all I could see was the stroller and two little legs. I wondered what she was thinking. I wonder what three-year-olds think. I wonder if somebody had told her she was too big for that stroller. I wonder if she felt the way I did about people who told you something that you knew was just not fuckin' true and if she felt like screaming at them and hurting them and plunging herself into a chemically induced oblivion.

I admired this kid for keeping her cool. She just strapped herself into that doll stroller and took off walking, probably without a word. All the way down Main Street. She'll show the whole town that no, in fact, she still fits into the damn doll stroller.

I took a shortcut to the clinic and bashed my head on the air conditioner coming out of the wall while reading the directions on the bird. Although you would expect the directions to a bird whose head went in and out of a glass of water to be fairly minimal, they weren't.

When I got to the clinic all the chairs were taken by Hutterites, also not especially a groovy people except for the fact that they are allowed to wear only polka-dot clothing, and the women must wear kerchiefs and the men, beards. My dad buys eggs from them. They are another sub-sect of our larger clan, except they live in colonies. Kibbutz-style. We are all, though, knock, knock, knocking on heaven's door. The same door.

I sat on the floor and kept my face hidden in a big thick

book of Bible stories for children. I thought to myself: Dear
Jesus, please let me one day hang out with Neil Young and Joni
Mitchell and turn all my grief into hits.

The doctor asked me if my dad knew about me going on the
Pill and I said of course, you can phone him if you like. He
should be at home right now—I can give you the number.
I pointed at the phone on his desk and said go ahead. Then
I stared at a dot on the wall and astrally projected myself into a
Greenwich Village coffeehouse until the doctor said uh, that
shouldn't be necessary and my heart began to beat again.

I thought I had seen a book on his shelf that was titled
How to Incorporate Mental Illness into Your Daily Routine. So,
he really did understand us. Dr. Hunter was English. That's
what people in my town called anybody who wasn't
Mennonite. He might have been Estonian or Moravian for all
I knew. In church The Mouth called him Brother Doctor
Hunter and made snide comments about his fancy education.
He had a reputation in town as a shit disturber because he
believed in supplying birth control for the women here who by
going forth to bed and multiplying often had ten or twelve or
fifteen kids. He also liked to prescribe antidepressants. He'd
written an article for the city paper that said our town has
colossally huge numbers of depressed people. He talked about
the emphasis here on sin, shame, death, fear, punishment and
silence and somehow, *God knows how,* chalked that all up to
feelings of sadness and galloping worthlessness.

The Mouth said the piece was fiction. He said we, the
followers of Menno Simons, were used to being misunderstood
by outsiders. He'd tried to shut his practice down a few times
but that only strengthened Brother Doctor Hunter's resolve.
Either way, he wasn't particularly cheerful about doling out

birth control but then again he was a man on a mission, and missions aren't supposed to be fun.

Any history of clotting?
 Pardon me?
 Blood clots.
 No.
 Do you smoke?
 When I'm on fire.
 Do you smoke?
 Yeah.
 Asinine.
 Thanks.
 I said that's asinine.
 Got it.

I have realized that my personal yearning to be in New York City, wandering around with Lou Reed in Greenwich Village, or whatever, is for me a painful, serious, all-consuming kind of thing and is for the rest of the world a joke. When you're a Mennonite you can't even yearn properly for the world because the world turns that yearning into comedy. It's a funny premise for a movie, that's all. Mennonite girl in New York City. Amish family goes to Soho. It's terribly depressing to realize that your innermost desires are being tested in Hollywood for laughs per minute.

Seventeen

~

I walked home down the number twelve sensing the beginnings of my nightly face ache, despite the fact it was the middle of the afternoon. Giant semis filled with pigs and chickens whipped past me at four thousand miles an hour three inches from my left arm. My right eye twitched from lack of stage-four sleep. I decided to cut across town and go to the hospital to tell Lids about my prescription.

When I got there I was dripping in sweat and the cut on my head from bashing it on the air conditioner had started to bleed a tiny bit. My eye also had not stopped twitching. The mean nurse saw me coming down the hall and made a Herculean effort to cut me off.

These are not visiting hours, she said.

Okay, I said, we won't visit. I kept walking.

Lydia is rather agitated today, she said. She wants to be alone.

No, she doesn't, I said. By then the nurse had clickety-clacked off to some other dire emergency.

Lids was wearing her so-called normal clothes instead of a hospital gown but she was fast asleep. Her hair was really greasy and she was wearing gloves. They were white and puckered on the sides and had pearl buttons at the wrists.

I sat down in the chair next to her bed and started flipping through *The Black Stallion*. I wondered if there was a way I could wash her hair for her while she was sleeping so she wouldn't feel the pain but then with the heat of the room and my own personal fatigue and everything else I fell asleep in the chair and when I woke up Lids was quietly singing "Shine a Light," the Stones song from *Exile on Main Street* (an album named for the Mennonite people if there ever was one), and staring at me. It was one of the songs she liked because it talked about the good Lord.

I smiled and said hey, hi, you're up. Her eyes were even brighter than the last time I'd seen her. Remember when we were Georgina and Alberta: Granny Sleuths? she asked.

Yeah, I said. That was fun. We'd had healing powers. When our gym teacher hurt girls in our class, emotionally, by saying cruel things to them, we could heal them with our powers. For one whole year girls would come running up to us in the hall to tell us what Ms. Weins had said to them in gym and then we would heal them with our powers.

We talked about stuff, about how she was feeling, how I was doing, ordinary things, and then I told her I'd just got the prescription for the Pill. Lids didn't agree with premarital sex but she told me congratulations and said she meant it. I hope it all works out, she said. It probably won't, I answered. She nodded.

She asked to see the prescription and I showed it to her and she held it in her gloved hands and stared at it for a long time and then said wow. I know, I said. It was kind of embarrassing and sad. I don't know why.

You know you have a little blood on the side of your face? she said. I told her about the air conditioner. I showed her the bird I'd bought for Ray.

That is so sweet, she said. She said she missed Ray asking her what she knew for sure. Whaddya know for sure, Miss

Voth? Lids's parents were nice, quiet people. They didn't really believe in medicine or banks or social insurance numbers, just miracles. They were trying to cure Lids with tomato juice, gallons and gallons of it. Dr. Hunter didn't get along with them. Lids had once heard him talking to a nurse about her parents and he had called them *those holy roller shitsqueaks.* Lids told me they were fighting over her soul.

How's school going, she asked me.

Meh, I said. I shrugged. I told her I had learned that it was illegal to mow your lawn on Sunday morning. Then I asked her if I could wash her hair if I did it really, really gently so that she'd feel hardly anything at all, just warm soft water and a light tender touch of my hand.

At first she didn't want me to. She touched her head like it was a premature newborn and said she knew it was awful but it hurt so much and I told her again how ultra, ultra gentle I'd be and that I'd stop as soon as it began to hurt and she finally agreed.

The logistics of the thing got pretty complicated. We had to strategize for about half an hour as to how to actually do it. She'd already used up her "air" by walking twice to the bathroom that day so we had to somehow do it with her in bed. Eventually we decided that she would lie diagonally across the bed with her head resting on my legs. I'd have a bowl of warm water right under her head, on the floor, between my feet, and I'd just kind of cup the water in my hands to rinse out the shampoo and it would all run back into the bowl.

It all worked out more or less. I could tell Lids was in pain but the whole time we hummed "Shine a Light" together over and over like a calming mantra and eventually it was done. Although there was quite a lot of water on the floor. After cleaning that up I patted her head a bit, gently, so that her hair would dry faster and we also debated the idea of putting a scarf or something over her head so she wouldn't catch a cold. But then I told her that her hair would never dry with a scarf on and that colds come from viruses not wet hair. That sounded kind of bossy to me, though, and I told her I was sorry, and she said no, no, don't be.

Mmmm, I said, sticking my nose close to her head, smells like apples. Then I thought hey, how about blow-drying it dry, and Lids said she didn't have a blow-dryer. I had wanted to comb it but she said no way. At least it was clean and soft and smelled good.

Does that make you feel any better? I asked her. She smiled and nodded and closed her eyes. It made me feel better.

I asked her if she wanted me to read some more from *The Black Stallion* and she said no, that was okay, she just wanted to sleep. Then her voice was gone for good, or for the time being. She touched her throat and grimaced apologetically. I said okay.

I didn't want to go but I didn't know what to do next. I stood next to her holding on to my prescription and stupid dipping bird. The apple scent wafted up from her hair. She opened her eyes and whispered one word: Travis. And then she pointed at the prescription.

Oh, I said, I have to wait a couple of weeks before the thing kicks in. She nodded and smiled again and then I kissed her on her bright red cheek and said I'd see her soon and that I loved her.

When Lids was in her feeling-good periods we'd walk each other exactly halfway home. Halfway was this spot in an empty lot on Main Street, next to the feed mill that looks like a ship, and on that spot we'd kiss each other goodbye like two French girls, once on each cheek and then a third time.

I left the hospital and trudged towards Main Street and when I got to the halfway spot in the empty lot I stopped and lit a Sweet Cap.

———

I walked up my driveway and waved to my dad who was warming up his yellow lawn chair for a little highway staring adventure. He lifted his hand like he was pushing against water. Like, rapids.

I was officially on the Pill.

Hey, I said.

Oh good, he said. You're here. He told me he was planning to take down the badminton net. Since my mom left he'd walked into it about thirty or forty times. He'd just head on out the door to work, eyes down, brain stuck in reverse, and boing . . . into the net.

Probably a good idea, I said. And I'm thinking of selling some of my tools, what do you think?

Well . . . I began.

Say, said my dad, could you stomach a walk downtown? Would you be at all interested in helping me buy a suit? *Was he on speed?*

We had a nice walk to Schlitzking Clothing. We didn't take the long way. We could hear families in their houses, talking and clanking and playing the piano. We heard an entire family harmonizing to "How Great Thou Art." I felt like holding his hand but that would've been pathetic.

At the red light on Main Street and First my dad looked at me from behind his wall of glass like he was surprised I was still there. Waiting for a different shade of green? I asked him. When we got to Schlitzking Clothing an extremely thin man in a three-piece suit took out a measuring tape and told my dad to stand in front of the mirror. I sat on the floor in the back and looked at the different styles of Stanfields underwear for a while. Then I took out my Pill directions for perusal.

My geography teacher walked out of a changing room wearing a lemon-yellow ensemble that included not one natural fibre.

Oh, he said when he saw me. I stared at him. A couple of weeks ago he'd slammed me into the lockers for not standing at attention properly during the anthem. I'd told him I wasn't into individual nations, man, and he'd said I was a lunatic.

I looked at his tiny feet sticking out from under all that piss-yellow Fortrel and then I moved my eyes up slowly to his face.

It's you, I said.

What do you think of this fabric? he asked.

I squinted at him. Why would he ask a lunatic for her opinion?

It's worsted in such a way that it breathes, I said. You'll enjoy its versatility.

I went back to my medical information. I learned that my body would think it was pregnant.

There would now be yet another part of myself that would not know what was really going on.

I overheard my dad and Mr. Schlitzking talking. Mr. Schlitzking was stroking my dad's shoulders from behind and saying eh? Who's calling the shots now? My dad blinked at himself in the mirror. Let's take a walk over to the sock table, said Mr. Schlitzking, and my dad followed him to the back of the store where I was sitting. He looked at me like this was all my fault.

Well, he said, I have socks at home.

He does, I said.

No, said Mr. Schlitzking, I mean socks for this particular suit.

Well, said my dad . . . and then Mr. Schlitzking said: You think they're not looking at your socks? He rested his chin on his collarbone for dramatic effect and then said: They're looking at your socks.

My geography teacher came out of the change room wearing a mint-green leisure suit with chocolate-brown outer stitching.

Oh hello, he said to my dad. My dad said hello. Looking forward to the summer holidays? asked my geography teacher.

No, said my dad.

Any vacation plans? asked my geography teacher.

None, said my dad.

The beach? asked my geography teacher.

Never, said my dad.

I tried to imagine my dad at the beach. I saw a man in a yellow lawn chair wearing a black suit and tie and reading *Notes from the Underground.* He smiled and looked at me. Shall we? he asked.

We went home with a suit and socks he'd never take out of the package. On the way we stopped for an ice-cream cone at the Sunset and sat down at a picnic table next to the takeout window. We were quiet, just licking our cones and staring off at the sky, listening to the crickets.

Nomi, said my dad.

Yeah? I said. He had a grim expression on his face. His brow was furrowed. Yeah? I said again.

You think they're not looking at your socks? he asked. I nodded gravely. They're looking at your socks, we said in unison.

On the way home my dad asked me if I minded the way he was. He was mournful like he'd been drinking too much wine which he never did because what would Jesus do without his blood? Sobriety was enough to make my dad's world spin. I punched him in the shoulder. I sang the whole theme song to *The Partridge Family* and poked him in the stomach. C'mon get happy. Oh, cut it out, he said. Then we walked in silence.

Finally my dad said: Really, I'm not much of a father. No, you are, I said. No, he said. He shook his head. You are too, I said. I dabble in parenthood, he said. No you don't, I said. *Deusant,* he whispered. It was his favourite curse. His only curse, actually, but it covered a lot of territory because it meant thousand.

When we got home I gave him the dipping bird and he cleared the spare change off his dresser and put it there, next to a picture of my mother. Well, he said. This is quite a surprise. Thank you very much. Thank you very, very much.

We sat on the end of his bed watching the bird dip its head in and out of the glass of water.

How do you like that? he said. He patted me on the knee. Then he went downstairs to watch *Hymn Sing,* his favourite show, where a group of men and women in black suits and long dresses stand in even lines on risers singing hymns for half an hour. You can watch it with me if you like, he'd said from halfway down the hall. Hmm, I thought. And leave the bird? In *Hymn Sing* the words bounce along on the bottom of the screen in case you want to sing along, but my dad never does. He just watches. But why would you want to sing along to "He Was Nailed to the Cross for Me"?

I went into my room. I threw a T-shirt over my lamp, lit some of Tash's incense and put on a Bob Marley album. I played "Redemption Song" about twenty times.

EIGHTEEN

~

I turned thirteen three days before Tash left town with Ian. The drama focused on her and Trudie, really. My dad and I hovered in the wings like stagehands, not entirely sure of what was going on but looking forward to it being over. They spent a lot of time speaking in code, it seemed.

I was sure my sister was a pusher. We'd seen a film in church called *Hey Preach, You're Comin' Through!* and it was all about a girl like Tash who'd gone bad and veered off the road less travelled onto a thoroughfare of sin.

Once, during this perceived pusher period, my dad and I went for a walk and I suggested to him that he hold my hand. He told me he hoped I could thrive from benign neglect, like an African violet.

Well, then I will, I said. And he told me I'd need more than his faint hopes to thrive like a plant. But he did take my hand, and that made me think things might work out, although I still didn't know exactly what was wrong.

One night Ian dropped Tash off in the middle of the night. I heard his low voice and her soft laughter and the door open and close really, really quietly. I heard my mom open her bedroom door and head down the hall towards the kitchen. After that I couldn't hear anything and I went back to sleep.

When I woke up a few hours later I went into the kitchen and read a note that was lying on the table: My mom had gone to do some shelving at the library, in the middle of the night, and my dad had gone for what he liked to call a toot, which to him meant a drive. Which made Tash almost wet her pants one day because in her circle *toot* meant toke. Tash, herself, was asleep on the couch.

I thought she must be in very big trouble this time and I wondered what would happen to her. Nothing bad had ever happened to us before so I didn't even know what the consequences *could* be. I went into her room and pulled out her high school yearbook and stared at the black-and-white photographs of her classmates. I lay in her bed and imagined that Ian was lying on top of me, wiping the hair out of my eyes, cupping my face in his strong hands, and telling me how he shouldn't be doing this but he just couldn't help himself and we must never tell Tash. Never.

I went into the living room and played an Irish Rovers record loudly until she woke up screaming what the fuck is that? Oh my god! I was sitting in the big green chair, trying to be both sinister and casual. I slowly lowered the newspaper that I'd been pretending to read, and looked at her. So, I said, you're awake. Perhaps now you'd be willing to answer a few questions? Oh my god, she said, and stumbled out of the room cursing. I had thought a little sketch comedy would soften her. You'll burn in hell! I screamed. Forever! I thought I heard her laughing in her room, but I couldn't be sure. I ran to my room and fell into my bed sobbing.

That morning Trudie came home to find both of her daughters crying in their bedrooms, only for entirely different reasons. I was convinced that Tash would fry like butter for her sins and she was . . . well.

I didn't know why *she* was crying, until I heard my mom say honey, what is it? What's wrong? And Tash said: I think I'll go crazy. I can't stand it. It's all a fucking lie. It's not right and it's killing me. It's killing me! Mom, it really is! And then something happened that took me completely by surprise. I heard my mom say, I know honey, I know it is. And then she began to cry also, not with the same intensity but with a pacing that made it seem like she knew what she was doing and I remember thinking to myself: Are they equally as sad? Why is my mom not angry? What is killing Tash? Drugs? Sinning? Books like *The Prophet* and *Siddhartha* and *Tropic of Cancer*? And when my mom said *I know it is,* did she mean she knew it, whatever it was, was killing Tash, or did she mean she knew it was all a lie. And I'm pretty sure that's when my nightly face aches began. Like my head had suddenly been filled with ideas and suggestions that it couldn't contain. Or maybe I was just choking. I was wrong about everything. I thought that what Tash meant when she said it wasn't right and it was killing her was the pusher's lifestyle that I'd imagined she'd been living. Selling drugs in the city, whoring around with a bad boy, cleaving to ideas of communism, telling Dad to go to hell. It was obvious to me. And after a while I started feeling good again because I realized that Tash was about to get back on track, that she had figured out she needed saving, and that God and Mom and Dad and The Mouth and everyone else who mattered would forgive her. And we could go back to being a normal family again, even with small amounts of desperate laughter.

I heard my dad come home and knock quietly on Tash's bedroom door and my mom saying it's okay, honey, we're in here, make yourself a sandwich, there's fresh ham in the fridge.

I could hear Tash and my mom talking but I couldn't make out the actual words. Then I heard my mom leave her room and go into the kitchen to talk to my dad. I got up and went into the hall and knocked on Tash's door. She told me to come in. Her hospitality made me nervous. She was sitting cross-legged and barefoot on her bed in her orange men's shirt and white choker with the blue bead. It looked so pretty. She'd put a red T-shirt over her lamp so the room had a pink glow. Want to burn some incense? she asked me. Would you like to listen to a record? I sat down beside her and smiled. She looked at me. What's wrong, she asked. I started laughing which is what I did back then when I was sad or freaked out. It was the kind of laugh that alarmed people. Nomi, she said, don't. And she put her arms around me and said everything would work out. Everything's gonna work out, man. I promise. I wouldn't let her go. Nomi, she said, I know you're crying. Please don't cry. I whispered to her that I didn't want her to go to hell, and she started laughing and said hell was a metaphor. I didn't know what she meant of course, and it wouldn't have mattered to me even if I had known. I was a believer and I was convinced that my sister was going down. God is love, Nomi, she said to me. That's all you need to know, man. God is love. She was so doomed.

When Ian came to pick her up, I went into the living room to read the paper. I put the Irish Rovers on again, loud. Tash came into the living room and said oh my god, Nomi. But this time she was smiling. A really tender genuine smile that killed me. There was no sarcasm, no faking. I knew that something horrible was going to happen. She'd freed herself. That's what a real smile meant. I knew it. She told me I could have her records.

My mom put some blankets and pillows into a garbage bag and carried it out to Ian's truck. She put bread and fruit and the fresh ham she'd bought that day into a box and Ian carried that out.

I remembered my mom telling us about the Mennonites in Russia fleeing in the middle of the night, scrambling madly to find a place, any place, where they'd be free. All they needed, she said, was for people to tolerate their unique *apartness*. Nomi, find my purse, she told me. She could never leave it in the same place. I found it on the floor in the dining room and gave it to her and she took out two fifties and handed them to Tash.

Then it was time for them to leave. Ian shook my hand. He said: Stay cool, kiddo. He also shook my mom's hand, but my mom said oh phooey and put her arms around him. He said hey thanks man. Then he went and sat in the truck while my mom and I took turns hugging Tash in the front entrance.

Again, Nomi? she'd say. Oh my god. We all laughed. My dad stayed in his bedroom. For a very long time, in the dark. He didn't come out even for *Hymn Sing*.

I went into the washroom and took my first Pill out of its Monday slot. My body was now in the early stages of believing it was pregnant. I thought about the name Credence for a baby girl. It was way better than Nova. By the time she was in school CCR would have bitten the dust and it would be okay. Credence.

I lay on my bed remembering conversations and agonizing over things I'd said or hadn't said until I heard my dad coming back upstairs and going into his room to his own large bed. We took turns lying on our beds, sneaking out at night, driving around in the dark, and pretending certain things existed just beyond our reach. I lay there imagining what it would be like to have another human being growing inside me. Would it panic? I heard my dad begin his special brand of snoring that sounded like he was being choked but refusing to die, all night long. It reached a frightening crescendo and then he stopped breathing—I counted to seventeen before he exploded back to life—and then started from the beginning again. I got up and went into his room and rolled him over and told him: Seventeen seconds this time Dad, you need to have that adenoid operation. You're making me mental. Sorry, sorry, he said. But he was sound asleep. He lay there on his side curled up like a Cheesie with his hands stuck between his knees in prayer position. I pulled his blanket up around his shoulders. I noticed that he had some hairs growing on his shoulders. I imagined him living at the Rest Haven. I put my face next to his and whispered: Seven. Teen. Seconds. I sat on the bed and watched him for a while. I looked at the bird on his dresser. It had stopped dipping for the night. I looked out the window. I told myself those lacy white curtains would need washing someday. They were the same sad grey as the floors in my school. And as the artillery of teeth in The Mouth's mouth.

It was two in the morning, maybe, or three or four, and Travis and I were bobbing around in the moonlight on an inner tube at the pits talking about how it feels to go crazy.

I think it's a gradual loss of peripheral vision, he said. Oh no, I thought. I knew he wanted me to say something almost as brilliant, but not quite. What do you think? he asked. I know you're not sleeping.

I opened my eyes. Is there something wrong with just bobbing? I asked him.

What do you think? he asked me again.

How it feels to go crazy? I asked.

Yeah.

I don't know, I said. Sad and easy, I guess, like losing a friend? You say a few wrong things, you ignore the obvious, you act stupid in an unfunny way. Travis told me that Kafka or someone like that had said insanity could be defined as the attempt to reconcile one's overwhelming urge to write things down with one's overwhelming conviction that silence is the most appropriate response. Oh, I said. Okay.

Travis told me how one spring his Aunt Abilene went nuts and after her funeral The Mouth said that like children and retarded people who were not capable of making an informed decision to ask Jesus into their hearts, Abilene, although she'd not attended church since she was sixteen, would automatically make it to heaven. Wild eh? asked Travis. They stayed up all night seriously discussing, like they *knew*, where Abilene would park her ass for all eternity. So wild, *wild*'s not the word, I said. Poor Abilene.

We drifted around in the darkness and quietly tried to harmonize on "Delta Dawn" which got stuck in our heads from talking about Abilene's own mansion in the sky. Travis told me I had a loose commitment to the melody. I was preoccupied with the meaning of the lyrics, I told him. The line about walking to the station. I didn't tell him I'd just had an awful feeling that the song was really about me. And then Travis said: Hey, it's like you, Nomi. And even though tears in my throat were starting to suffocate me, in the nick of time I remembered Travis telling me once that I was boring when I was offended, and to be boring was the ultimate crime, and I put my head back and made a laughing sound. And I splashed him. And he splashed me back, conveniently, so that all the water on my face looked the same.

After that we tried thirty-nine times to stand together on the tube until we finally did. It was fun. I liked the falling part, and holding hands. Relationships were so easy when all you had to work on was standing up together.

Nineteen

~

It was still early, my dad was asleep, and I didn't so much want the night not to end as I wanted the next day not to begin so I walked over to Second Avenue to The Trampoline House, which was next door to the boarded-up bus depot, a disastrous experiment that had resulted only in people leaving. If you threw a dime into this coffee can they kept between the doors and took your shoes off you could jump for a while, at least until the next person with a dime showed up or until the family woke up.

It felt good to be alone, jumping, while the rest of the town remained unconscious, and I tried with every bounce to go higher and higher without knocking my head against the hydro wire. I tried to sort out my problems by putting them into categories. Travis. School. Environment. I wasn't pretty enough to be the complex, silent girl and yet I never knew what to say. I didn't want to be the ugly, quiet girl. There was no such thing as the ugly, mysterious girl. I could be the tortured, self-destructive girl. But where does that lead? I remembered a conversation I'd had with Tash on the same trampoline a hundred years ago when it only cost a nickel.

Tash: What do you say to a boy you like when he passes you in the hall?

Me: Hello?
Tash: Nope.
Me: Hi, how are you?
Tash: Nooooo.
Me: Okay. *Bonjour?*
Tash: (says nothing, gives me a look)
Me: What then?
Tash: Nothing.

I jumped up and down, hands at my side like a punk until I heard the Trampoline House people open their door and take their can with my dime inside which meant they were closed. I had to go to school in two hours and write a fifteen-hundred-word story that included a triggering point, a climax and a resolution. On my way home I came up with my first sentence: The administration passed her around for beatings like a hookah pipe at a Turkish wedding.

Which got panned by Mr. Quiring. No . . . no, he said. He tapped me hard on my forehead. He didn't even bother reading the rest of it. So far in English I was not allowed to write about Kahlil Gibran, Marianne Faithfull lyrics, marigold seeds, Holden Caulfield, Nietzsche, Django, Nabokov, preternatural gifts for self-analysis, urges, blowtorches, and now Turkish weddings.

So what should I write about? I asked him. He sat on my desk and crossed his legs and clung to one knee with both hands like it was hurting him. I stared at his belt buckle. Hmmm . . . he said. Let's use our imaginations. What do you see when you close your eyes? Nothing, I said. He frowned. Are you not upset when you get your paper back and everything is underlined in red, he asked. No, I said, not really, in the Bible the words of Je—

Get out, he said. I got up and walked away and he threw my pencil case at me. It hit me in the small of my back, near my kidneys. I thanked him, picked it up, and left. I went into the doorless girls' can and threw up, said hello to the stoners sitting on the sinks throwing wet toilet paper at the ceiling and walked out into the killer sunshine. It was 9:08 a.m.

Suddenly I wished I owned a dog. He and I would spend the day exploring some place off in the bush, maybe make a fire, roast a gopher he'd have caught. Fall gently asleep together in a pile of leaves. Maybe save a life. I decided to walk downtown and check out the latest old-man boots at the Style-Rite.

I saw my simple cousin Norm sitting at his lottery booth outside Economy Foods. When me and Tash were younger we weren't allowed to sit on his lap. I waved from a distance and he said what he always says: Awwww, c'maawwwnn. I sat for a while with my other simple cousin, Jakie, at the post office and smoked a Sweet Cap. We watched sixteen Hutterites emerge from a parked Land Rover.

I shook hands with Jakie. That's a big hand, I said, and he looked at it. Then I got him to tell me the day I was born. Thursday. I told him he was automatically saved. He nodded his head slowly for a really long time, like he was listening to music.

Jakie used to have a full-time position sitting on the bench with the high school boys' basketball team. I never knew what that was all about. They just let him sit there during the games and at half-time he'd get up and shoot hoops with them. He'd always get up and do the three cheers thing with them too and then shake hands with the other team. He loved shaking hands. I never knew why he stopped doing the bench thing, unless it made some people nervous to have a forty-year-old guy in a ball cap sitting next to their kid. But the team didn't mind at all. They sometimes let him go with them to away games.

I never made it to the Style-Rite. Jakie and I shared a bag of chips and a Coke and I got him to tell me the birthdays of everyone I knew. That's cool, I told him, reaching out to take his hand. I'm a character, he said. I asked him how many hours a day he sat at the post office and he stared off at something and said dogs love better, which made me wonder if he was psychic because I'd just been thinking about dogs. We shook hands again. And then again. When I said goodbye he looked away.

I passed the church and read the sign outside: AND THEY SHALL GO FORTH, AND LOOK UPON THE CARCASSES OF THE MEN THAT HAVE TRANSGRESSED AGAINST ME: FOR THEIR WORM SHALL NOT DIE, NEITHER SHALL THEIR FIRE BE QUENCHED; AND THEY SHALL BE AN ABHORRING UNTO ALL FLESH.

How sweet. The Mouth must have been in a good mood when he dug up that ol' chestnut. I walked down the shady side of Main Street thinking about triggering points.

There was a new sign in the Tomboy window. COME ON IN AND CHECK OUT OUR NEW MEAT DEPARTMENT! I stared at it for a while. And then I crossed the little parking lot and went in and walked to the back of the store and looked at the pieces of meat behind the glass. The butcher, who was also the man who opened the windows in church with a long stick that had a hook on the end of it, said hello and wondered if there was something he could do for me. I told him I was just checking out the meat.

Is this the new meat department? I asked.

That's right, he said. We've expanded our selection. He spread his arms.

I nodded. It's nice, I said. It's very um . . . you have a lot of interesting meat products here.

Yes, he said, we're very happy with it.

Yeah, I said. Well, me too. I smiled. He smiled.

Is there anything I can help you with, he asked me. He seemed much friendlier now than in church when he sombrely walked down the aisles unhooking windows with the broom handle.

Do you sell Klik? I asked him.

Klik? he said. You mean the luncheon meat? I nodded. Well, this here is fresh meat. This is the fresh meat area. Canned meats are in aisle four near the pet food.

Oh, right, I said. Yeah. I nodded. Sorry.

That's okay, he said. He looked a little sad and I didn't want to disappoint him so I asked for a pound of meat.

What kind of meat would you like? he asked.

Well, I said, um, just . . . meat that I could make for my dad. He likes meat. He enjoys meat.

Hmmm, said the butcher, how about a roast?

Yeah, that would be perfect, I said. I left the store with a giant roast gift-wrapped in brown paper and string. He'd written the price on it with a Magic Marker.

I stood at the new crosswalk for a long time with my arm out. I pushed the button to get the lights to flash. The crosswalk was a new concept in town. It was feared and loathed as an extravagant expense.

Nobody stopped, although a couple of guys in a truck slowed down long enough for me to hear them shout Nomi you doob. *Doobs* are what we call condoms around here. I don't know why. Voices inside my head told me not to throw the roast at the truck.

I met Marina Dyck and Patty Pauls on Autumnwood Drive pulling the Funk kids in a wagon and they told me they were babysitting and I could come back with them to the Funk house for some Bundt cake and vodka from the hidden stash. We were there for a while watching TV and eating cake, but I was waiting for the vodka.

Then Marina said, oh the parents are coming home soon, you guys better go. So Patty and I took off in separate directions. About ten minutes later I was standing in the kitchen drinking water looking out the window and I saw Pat going back over to the Funks'. Oh, I thought, I get it. I understand. I am a doob.

Ray came in from watering his flowers and sat down at the kitchen table. Hey Nomi, he said. I didn't look at him. I fooled around with the taps. And then he asked me how my day had been and I asked him what he saw when he closed his eyes. Obviously nothing, he said.

I think he figured out that I was crying because I didn't say anything and I still wasn't looking at him and he'd said to me in his tragically cheerful voice: How about accompanying me to the nuisance grounds.

We say *dump* now, Raymond, I told him. For Ray the dump is consolation. He appreciates specific areas of waste as opposed to the type of wide-range, free-floating mess that has taken up too much of his life.

Tash once told me that Ray had proposed to my mom at the sewage lagoon behind the parka factory outside of town.

Help me unload some of those old two-by-fours from your playhouse and that rusty bed frame taking up room in the garage, he said. Ray has a way of offering comfort in a well-meaning but ridiculous way. He tends to go overboard in the same spirit as people who overwater thirsty plants.

I remember my mother tearfully telling him that she had to go to the morgue to identify her sister after her horse-and-buggy accident and Ray walked over to her and put his arms around her and said don't let it be an entirely negative experience, honey. He couldn't understand why my mom had peeled out of the driveway. Tash and I watched him walk outside and stare in befuddlement at the blackies her tires had left behind, like there'd be clues.

It was nice seeing Ray's tanned hairy arms draped over the wheel, like he was in control of something. I put the visor down for him so he wouldn't have to squint and he said how do you like that. Simple things that make life easier, like visors, don't figure into his world.

What was my first word? I asked him, and he said: *Don't.* I asked him what my second word was but he couldn't remember. I think I'd have made something up if I was him. Like *go.*

Hey, I said, I bought a roast today but I lost it on the way home. I'd forgotten it at the Funks' when we left in that big hurry.

Oh, really? said Ray. That's okay. Roasts are an awful lot of work.

Actually they're not, I said. The butcher said they were easy. You put them in before you go to church and when you come home they're done.

Well, said my dad. They're easy to lose.

Well, no, I said. Only complete idiots lose roasts. He told me I wouldn't believe the amount of meat he'd lost in his life. Yeah, yeah, I said, and stared out the window.

We can always get another roast, Nome, he said. I didn't say anything. I closed my eyes.

Right? asked my dad. He turned to look at me briefly and I opened my eyes and noticed him smiling so I smiled back at him and said yes, he was right.

We were supposed to pay a dollar to get into the dump but the guy there knew Ray and waved him right in. VIP? I asked him. Well, he said, he hadn't wanted to brag but he never has to pay when he goes into the dump. Then he told me that he sometimes cleans up at the dump late at night after the guy at the gate goes home and the dump people liked that.

You clean up the dump? I asked him. At night?

No, no, he said.

Yeah you do, I said.

Well, yes, he said, I do.

That's cool though, I said thinking Jesus, let's not be the kind of family that tidies up the dump at night. The dump is the dump though Dad, I said. The central idea at work in a dump is that it's not a clean place.

Ray said: Well, yes, but I organize the garbage in a way I feel makes sense. I patted him on the arm. Not so much to encourage him, but because I needed to feel something solid right then.

Being there was kind of nice though, like the beach but less oppressive. Smoky with thousands of seagulls, which was odd, like they were lost, and a pair of gloves my dad gave me that had little rubber bumps on them for grip. I liked the way he rubbed his forehead with the back of his wrist.

We talked a bit about eyebrows and their purpose. Then other hair topics. He said if he kept losing hair he'd have a forehead he could show movies on.

Like a drive-in? I asked him.

He said yeah, he'd stand out in a field and get paid.

You could sit, I said.

I'd have to sit, he agreed.

In your lawn chair, I added.

Yes, Nomi, in my lawn chair, he said. He knows I have an irrational hatred of his lawn chair. We saw a little red cowboy boot sticking out of a heap of badly organized garbage that did not make sense and my dad said to me whoah, remember Misty? Misty was a palomino I used to barrel-race in rodeos before I accepted boys and drugs into my heart.

That horse could turn on a dime, said my dad.

Yeah, I said. Powerful hindquarters.

You used to take those corners like Mario Andretti, he said, staring off dreamily at acres of decomposing trash.

Well, I said, it was fun. My dad used to shout, take it home Nomi! on the final stretch of the race. Remember when you'd yell, take it home Nomi! I asked him. He looked at me.

I did say that, didn't I? I nodded. Was that wrong?

No, no, it was funny, I said. I remembered him leaning up against the log fence of the corral in his suit and tie and jacket. The only person in town formally dressed for a rodeo. A kid had come up to him once and asked him if he was one of those clowns that distract the bull while the cowboy escapes.

He nodded and stared at the boot. Should it be there? I asked him. He shook his head but didn't move the boot. I knew he wanted to move it more than anything. He was working really hard to appear normal, for my sake.

Let's move it, I said.

Oh . . . no, he said. He waved off the idea.

Yeah, c'mon, I said. I picked up the little boot.

Where to? I asked.

Oh, really, he said. He tried to act dismissive.

No, c'mon, I said. Where should it go? He stared at me for a few seconds and smiled.

Fine, he said. I'll indulge you by allowing myself to be indulged. He took the boot and we walked about a hundred yards to a different section of the dump that included broken wagons, Hula Hoops, bent and rusted-out pogo sticks, cracked-up Footsies, headless dolls and some other assorted brightly coloured broken plastic stuff. Ray put the little boot in the middle of it and said, good. We walked back to where we'd been. The dump was kind of like a department store for Ray, but even more like a holy cemetery where he could organize abandoned dreams and wrecked things into families, in a way, that stayed together.

Twenty

We got home to find a bullet hole in the middle of our picture window. Who would shoot our house, I asked Ray. He stood in the grass staring at the hole and shaking his head.

The cop came and said it was going around—kids, BB guns . . . summer holidays around the corner. Any enemies? he asked Ray who shook his head yet again and then said well, there's a boy I'm keeping back next year. The cop nodded and said there you go, could be.

Ray thanked him and we went inside and sat on the couch.

Who're you keeping back? I asked him.

The cop's kid, he said. I read the paper while he stared at the hole in the window through his large square glasses. After a while I got up and made him a TV dinner and he said mmmm . . . my compliments to the chef in the type of upbeat manner that made me simultaneously want to curl up in his lap and cuff him in the head.

When negative experiences such as having one's house shot at occur in my dad's life he tends to come alive. His confusion lifts. Pieces of life's puzzle fuse into meaning, like the continents before that colossal rift. It's entirely logical to him that his house has been shot at and when he's able to spend a minute or two in a world that makes sense he appears almost happy. And when he gets happy he does decisive things like this time he went over to the bulletin board in the kitchen and took down the city bus arrival schedule that we've had up there since Tash left and before the bus depot itself closed down. He put it in the garbage can under the sink. Phew. Done. Goodbye past.

But then I imagined him on a day when shitty things weren't happening and he'd be feeling his usual mystified self and go to the dump and there he would see that little piece of paper with the schedule on it and it would bring him to his knees. Just destroy him for a minute or two, and he'd probably pick it up and wipe whatever seagull crap there was on it and straighten it out with the side of his hand and bring it back to the kitchen bulletin board and *arrange* it on there so you'd know it was the centrepiece of his life.

But for now, he was tripping 'cause our house had been shot at and things were as they should be, as he had suspected they had been all along, so he could relax and get rid of stuff that was keeping him down. He kept on saying corny things even while bits of glass dropped onto the living-room carpet and I glared at him stupidly. I don't know why. It's an act. It's a thing we do when something strange has happened and we don't know what to say about it. It's like we play these conventional roles of idiot dad and rebellious teenager even though we're way beyond that—we're more like two mental patients just getting through another day. It's like he's trying to dynamite his way through a mountain of so-called teenage contempt by saying goofy things knowingly in the hope that I'll grant him mercy for identifying his own shortcomings before I can. It's just an old sitcom script we fall back on. We have no idea how to act.

Bye, I said.

Have fun, he said. Be good.

Gotta make up your mind, I answered back, because he expected me to.

After Tash left, my mom's church singing got quieter and my dad's got a little louder. I developed insomnia. Nightmares of Tash screaming while she burned, a hand reaching out for help, my name on her lips, her face melting while the screaming echoed on and on and on. I'd wake up at night to find Ray gone, out on one of his nocturnal missions, so named by Tash before she took off, and my mom lying on the couch in the living room, reading.

She'd make room for me beside her and I'd talk to her about Tash and how I was so afraid she was going to go to hell. Isn't she? I'd ask my mom. There were pauses. I don't know what I wanted her to say. Either one, yes or no, was problematic. Isn't she? I'd ask.

My mom said: That's not for us to say, Nomi.

But isn't she? I'd ask.

Well, said my mom. It won't come to that, I'm sure.

But it could come to that, right? I asked her. That Tash would go to hell? That she'd be right there in the middle of hell, all alone and burning to death forever while Satan laughed and God cried and we were in heaven together without her?

Well, said my mom. I really don't—and I'd usually cut her off with wild demands like: Tell me the truth! Until she'd say what she always said: The truth is I don't know, Nomi. Which left me with nothing. And that it was a bad thing. At least I felt that way at the time.

Oh, the shit was coming down. Things were falling apart. Our family was on the skids, and the truth was *I don't know.* My mom started getting twitchy around the house. Slamming things and asking me if I was okay, when all I'd be doing was sitting there and peeling a banana or something. She quit her job at the library, but kept going to church.

Then she got this other job cleaning the leg wound of Sheridan Klippenstein's grandma, a very old woman who lived alone and refused to move into the Rest Haven. Sometimes, if there was nothing else to do, I'd go with her. She changed the dressings on Mrs. Klippenstein's leg and I sat on the couch and watched.

Mrs. Klippenstein's left leg was a thing of dark beauty. Large and shiny purple, with scales. She had an open sore, just below the knee, that would never heal. It oozed night and day, like Vesuvius, and her life revolved around its maintenance. My mom liked to help and really seemed to enjoy working with gauze and tape.

Sometimes I stood beside her and held things for her while she dressed Mrs. Klippenstein's sore. I would stare at the top of Mrs. Klippenstein's head, intrigued by a milky swirl of white scalp where her hair had fallen out. I could see tiny follicles that looked like goosebumps.

Her English wasn't very good. One time I told her she was lucky she didn't have to go to school (we'd been discussing my assignments) and she grabbed my arm and said I'll eat your heart out. She said things like slice me open a bun and throw me down the stairs a face cloth.

Trudie and I would try not to laugh.

Mrs. Klippenstein would force me to eat Scotch Mints and then tell me stories about her childhood in Russia, the golden dream of home. She told me her father owned three hundred chickens and that they had one hundred and eighty-six trees on their property. They also had an eagle that her father had bought one day from the black market. The eagle had a wingspan of eleven and a half feet. It would fight with dogs and men and they kept it tethered to a post in the yard.

Never marry a man out of pity, Nomi, she told me. Her husband had been excommunicated for something and afterwards, like a lot of the ghost people, had lived in a little shack next to the main house while Mrs. Klippenstein took care of the children and the farm. He became The Swearing Man.

I vaguely remembered him from when I was a little kid. He rode his bike around town, in a suit and tie, and swore. Eventually, he died. When he was a young man he had been kind and just. He taught his children to stand on each other's shoulders and form a human pyramid. He had a wonderful singing voice, was quick to laugh, especially at his own foibles, and never took offence. Those are all Mrs. Klippenstein's words. I loved the way she described him.

She told me that every night she lay down next to him and whispered in his ear: You are almost perfect.

I can't remember why he was excommunicated and I never asked. Maybe he took the fall for someone in his family. That happens. My mom did other things for Mrs. Klippenstein too, sometimes. Errands, housework, a load of laundry now and again. She spent a lot of time there. I guess it was distracting.

During that time, The Mouth came by to pray with us, and my dad began to spend his evenings sitting in the yellow lawn chair and staring at the highway, or down in the basement with his isotope material, finding comfort in the stability that's created from decay.

What we have feared has come to pass, said The Mouth.

What? What? I'd ask my mom, after he left. What are we fearing? What has happened?

One day my mother told me that Tash had become an atheist. My mom had known about it long before Tash had actually left town. Apparently they'd talked about it at

length. The Mouth had only recently heard about it—
through the grapevine.

Oh my God, I whispered. My mom said Nomi, you don't
know what an atheist is. She told me Tash had stopped
believing in God. No, I whispered. Yes, said my mom. I
couldn't fathom it. I didn't get it. That fucking library card,
man. Almost every night I'd crawl into bed with my mother
even though I was already thirteen years old and she'd whisper
to my dad: Nomi's here, honey, go sleep in Tash's room. And
he'd get up and lumber out of the room, leaving a nice warm
hole in the bed for me to curl up in. We didn't have to talk
about it any more. There was nothing to talk about.

I might move to Montreal, said Travis. I asked him what he
meant by that. We were sitting on Abe's Hill staring at the city
lights.

Nothing, he said. Just that I might move to Montreal.

But why? I asked. When?

In the fall, he said, if I can make enough money.

Well, have fun, I said. Write. He said I could come with
him but he didn't know what he was talking about. Right? he
said, poking me in the side with his guitar.

No, I said, wrong.

C'mon, he said, why not? Montreal's cool. I'll play for
money in the metro and you can pose naked for art classes and
stuff and we'll find a really cheap flat, eat bread and cheese.

Did you say flat? I asked him. He nodded. Just for that
I'm not going with you, I said. I got up and walked down the
hill except halfway down I tripped and fell and just for the hell
of it rolled all the way down to the gravelly bottom and lay
there in a clump while Travis sat on the top going Nomi? Don't
be that way!

When I got home my dad was in his goddamn lawn chair in front of the bullet hole doing some kind of watercolour painting. Is that all you're gonna do? I asked him. Sit in the dark and paint?

Where's Travis? he asked.

Who cares, I said.

Should we go for an ice cream? was all I heard before I slammed the door and walked into the kitchen for a couple of my sister's expired Valium.

I noticed that the dining-room table was missing. I went back outside to ask my dad where it was.

I sold it, he said. We never used it anyway. I also sold the freezer in the garage. While I was emptying the contents I found that stray cat of Tash's and thought you and I could bury it in the backyard.

Blackula? I asked.

Yeah, he said, wrapped up in some kind of cape. A red velvet cape. Kind of shocking, he said.

She was gonna bury it when the ground thawed, I told him.

Well, said my dad, she must have forgotten about it. We should do it tonight probably before it starts to decompose.

The evening was getting better and better. My dad dug a hole and I tried to make a stupid wooden cross but I was so strung out I could barely understand what I was doing. It was like my hands were moving around with wood in them like I was a drummer or something and a hammer lay on the ground next to me and next to the hammer was a little jam jar of nails but other than that I didn't have a clue. Eventually I just gave up and lay in the grass watching my dad dig.

I'll put a concrete slab on top of it so animals don't get at him, he said.

Yeah, I said, but more like yeeeaaaaahhhhh.

Or maybe we should cremate him first? asked my dad and I said naaaaahhhhhh. I was trying to pull myself up with a branch that was about fifty feet in the air. Finally I gave up and lay there, spreadeagled like a wheel. It was really dark outside and I thought how white my dad's shirt was. He'd tucked his tie in between the buttons.

Tired? he asked.

No, just lazy, I said. Travis had taught me the importance of denying fatigue. He was always telling me not to yawn. My dad suggested that my phosphates might need replenishing. Phosphates, I thought to myself. Phosphates.

Dad, I said, why aren't trains allowed here again?

What? he said.

No trains here? I said.

Neither one of us knew what I was talking about. But then after a minute or two my dad said: Oh, the train. Yes. The elders thought it would bring with it worldly influences.

With it worldly influences? I asked.

My dad looked up from his digging and said: It would make it easier to come and go. Especially go.

Oooooohhhhhh, I said. Don't let me die out here, dude, I said, and my dad went: No, no. He smiled at me. I could make his teeth out in the dark. I wanted to lie there forever.

I said: I want to lie here forever and my dad said no, no, that's Blackula's job now, heh, heh.

Everything felt really, really nice. The grass, the dark sky and stars and my dad smiling and wearing his white, white shirt and cracking awful jokes that weren't even jokes, and the smell of the fresh dirt and some faraway stubble fire.

What are the *blue* fields again? I asked him.

Blue? he said. That would be alfalfa.

Yeaaaahhhhh, I said. Affafa, alfffa, alfafafa.

Alfalfa! said my dad.

Okaaaaaayyyy, I said.

And still the night wasn't over. My dad left me lying in the grass next to Blackula and told me I needed to work on my rest, an idea I kept repeating over and over in my mind because I thought it was interesting, anachronistically.

I watched the sky turn purple and listened to the late-night sound of doors closing. Fluffy white things were floating around and I spent a long time trying to catch one in my hand. I felt the bumps on my head. I examined the various plates of my skull. I need a razor for my bangs, I thought. I crawled slowly through the grass towards the back door. Its brown sections reminded me of a Jersey Milk bar.

Travis liked straight bangs but Travis was going to Montreal. I liked the way my bangs looked razored. I put on Tash's Thelonius Monk record quietly and stared at myself in the mirror. I could hear my dad snoring. I turned down the volume and waited for him to stop breathing.

I'd forgotten how to count. I remembered my grandpa telling me he was so old they didn't have numbers when he was a kid.

I put on Tash's baby-blue kangaroo jacket and tied the hood around my razored head. I walked out the front door, past the bullet hole and down the driveway, across the number twelve, through my neighbour's yard, into their clothesline, down First Street, up Friesen, and onto Main. I sat down on the sparkly granite of the cenotaph next to the post office and read the names of people who had died four million years ago and then I heard my name being called.

Nomi, said Tash. I like what you've done to your hair. But who said you could wear my jacket?

This piece of shit? I asked. You left it behind. It's mine now.

It looked better on me, she said. You gotta boyfriend now, eh?

Yeah. Are you still with Ian?

No, I left him in Flagstaff. Prick.

Oh, yeah.

Yeah.

Is he sweet? she asked.

Who? I said.

Your boyfriend.

Sort of, I guess. Yeah.

That's why you're all alone out here? she asked.

You're here, though, I told her. Right?

God. Not only was I incapable of having an articulate conversation, I couldn't even imagine one.

When I got home I sat on the floor of the garage and tied the hood as tightly as I could around my face, leaving an opening only large enough to accommodate a Sweet Cap. It was a good night. Maybe someday I could be a photographer, I thought. And then, unpredictably, a corner of the garage roof collapsed.

TWENTY-ONE

~

School the next day. I fell asleep in math. And geography. The principal invited me into his office.

I decided not to say a word. I picked a spot on the wall to stare at the way they tell you to when you're in labour. Clearly these are not the best years of your life, he said to me.

I felt almost drunk with gratitude when he said that. I felt as though he had entered my mind and, like a weapons inspector, had thoroughly assessed the situation with a cool, slick professionalism and was, even as we spoke, formulating some kind of counteraction. It was a type of understanding. I thought he was going to rescue me. But that's where it ended.

At lunch Travis came to pick me up. Then left again all pissed off when the first thing I said to him was: Tell me you're not wearing a poncho. He spun out of the gravel and a tiny stone hit my binder. I wondered if I might have been killed if it hadn't been for the binder. Other kids were sitting in the grass eating their lunches and I had to walk past them to get back into the school. Time to find another boyfriend, said this primate, Gordo. I'll take yours, I said. Fuck you, bitch, he screamed. You'll get over it, I said. I fell asleep in American History. But it was the kind of non-committal sleep that allowed my memory to function, only in the role of a dream. I could hear people talking about Crazy Horse and Wounded Knee but all I could see and smell and touch was Trudie.

I remember walking through the town at night, barefoot and in my pyjamas, holding my mother's hand. Tash had left and I had woken up screaming, yet again, and Trudie said she couldn't take it any more. And my dad was standing in the doorway of my room begging her not to do it. May I please have the keys to the car, she asked him. May I? Please? And he said no, Trudie, don't go there. Please don't go there. And then the next thing I remember is walking down the quiet street in my pyjamas. And walking up the front path of my uncle's house and my mom banging away on the door until my aunt finally came and opened it and asked my mom if she was insane, like her daughter, meaning Tash, not me, and my mom said don't you ever speak that way about my daughter again. And then The Mouth was there and my mom asked me to sit in the grass but it was wet and I said no. Trudie, said The Mouth, what's going on here? What are you doing? And then she told him to apologize to me. She said tell Nomi you're sorry. She kept pointing at me and I just stared at the white pillars in front of The Mouth's house until my vision blurred. Ask her to forgive you, Trudie said. You've scared the shit right out of her, Hans. Tell her you're sorry. Tell her! Tell her it's not true. Tell her they are stories. You know nothing about love, nothing. You know nothing about anything at all and I hate you so much.

The Mouth stood there, right in the centre of the pillars, with his eyes closed and his head tilted up to the sky. She just went on and on. Now tell Nomi you're sorry and ask her to forgive you. Right now, Hans. You will not go back inside without apologizing.

Then Trudie was quiet for one or two seconds and I could hear crickets and I thought, now we'll go home. But then she said: No? No? No? You won't apologize? That's good. That's good. Because you know what? I will never forgive you. Nomi will never forgive you. It would bring you too much joy, wouldn't it, you smug monster, you . . . ask away. Apologize. Forget it. Forget it! I wanted to tell Trudie I would forgive him, that she was wrong, and then The Mouth told his wife to go into the house and phone my dad. Tell that man to come and get his wife, he said. He told my mom his heart wept for her. Then he went into his house. I sat on the curb waiting for my dad while my mom threw rocks at her brother's house and screamed profanities that I had never heard before.

After school Travis came back without the poncho and apologized. I told him he was full of shit sometimes and he said yeah he knew that but I could give niceness a whirl.

You're the kind of guy who in a simple robbery would panic and pull the trigger and end up wrecking a whole bunch of lives including your own, I told him.

Are you ever gonna take that hood off? he asked. We drove out of town in silence towards a different town called Anola.

I wanted to ask him if he was planning to truss me up and kill me in the bushes but I was too pissed off to open my mouth. We kept driving. Travis was singing with the radio . . . and I was breathing in dust from the gravel road until we got to this even smaller dirt road and we followed that for a while and then he pulled into this clearing in the bush that had a log cabin in the middle of it. He parked by the cabin and looked at me.

So? I said.

It's my parents' snowmobile pad. It's got a fireplace.

Great, I said. Fires are good.

And a bed and shit, said Travis.

Ohhhhh, I said. We both stared at the cabin. I guess this is where we'll come when . . . yeah. It's good? I took his hand and said yeah, it's pretty nice.

He asked me if I'd want to take my hood off and I said no thanks, I liked it that way. I told him I thought the chemicals had probably successfully tricked my body. He glanced in the general direction of my barren uterus and nodded. We sat there staring at the cabin holding hands and wondering and trying to find something good on the radio.

We drove back to town slowly. I leaned against his shoulder and stuck my feet out the window, and we shared my last cigarette. He called me baby. Here, baby, he said when he passed the cigarette over my head. Wouldn't it be so great if we could just keep driving and driving? I asked. He kissed my hair. He said yeah, someday we would. The Cars were playing on the radio. Everything was so nice. The air was a perfect temperature and smelled so good. All I could see was blue sky and smoke. Then he had to go and lay a carpet with his dad.

Everything my mother did after that night when she stoned her brother's house and called him really bad names seemed mysterious and troubling. I think now I'd call it grief. It's hard to grieve in a town where everything that happens is God's will. It's hard to know what to do with your emptiness when you're not supposed to have emptiness. Trudie started going for long walks at night. During the day, at home, she'd still do things like housework and cooking but she almost entirely stopped speaking. I came home from wherever one afternoon to find her and my dad standing in the middle of the kitchen in each other's arms with tears streaming down their faces.

What's wrong? I asked. And they said nothing is wrong and smiled and told me not to worry about a single thing. The kids at school had been talking to me about Trudie, wondering if she was a vampire or completely insane or what.

Why does she walk around like that at night, they'd ask.

I'd shrug. How the hell would I know, I'd say.

One day there was no supper and I got mad. What a spoiled little shit, eh? Anyway, I told her: Mom, we have to eat every day. And she said to me you know you're absolutely right and then she went over to the calendar and wrote the word EAT in every square, every day of every week of every month. There, she said when she was finished. That should help. When my dad came home from school he looked at the calendar, stared at it for five or ten minutes, quietly flipping the pages of the months, and then went and sat down beside my mom on the couch and took her hand and stared with her, catatonically, out the picture window at the world of sky and highway.

Somehow I managed to find the time to wander aimlessly around town and stare at stuff with a new expression I'd been working on that suggested a complex combination of hostility and hopelessness mingled with sad longing and redemptive love.

If I had a magic wand I would walk down Main Street and go *ting*—you're now CBGBs. *Ting*—you're an angry street vendor. *Ting*—you're Lou Reed. Hey Nomi. Hey Lou. Tour with me. You got it, man.

The Mouth had put up a new sign in front of the church. YOU THINK IT'S HOT HERE . . . GOD. I stopped and stared at the sign. I couldn't believe it. This was an entirely new approach. It wasn't even a verse. It was supposed to be funny. It was The Mouth making threats and using God as a dummy. The man was insane. My new expression fell apart entirely and

I stood there with my mouth open and my hand on my heart. It could have been the heat or the pot or the excitement of being with Travis or overtiredness or the effects of my body thinking it was pregnant when it wasn't but I started to cry and couldn't stop. Why couldn't the sign say: And you shall be like a spring whose waters fail not. Why not offer some goddamn encouragement?

I got up and walked around to the side of the church where The Mouth had his office and banged on the door. I kicked the door and then I threw rocks at the window.

I screamed: Let me in! Let me in right now! I guess he wasn't there. Or if he was, he was too busy with damnation work to see me. I walked back to the sign and kicked the shit out of it so that by the time I was finished black letters lay randomly on the ground next to twisted pieces of plastic. I sat on the curb breathing heavily and stared at the two cars that passed in a time span of at least fifteen minutes. How much for a blow job? one of the occupants inquired. A man with a six-inch reinforced heel on one of his shoes walked past me very, very slowly and asked me in the mother tongue if I was waiting for a parade. I shook my head and smiled. He patted my hair and said: And she being desolate shall sit upon the ground. I watched him disappear into Jesus' arms at the end of Main Street.

A tall girl, about twelve, and a short boy, about ten, walked up to me and asked me if I'd wrecked the sign.

I did, yeah, I said.

Why? they asked. The girl put her elbow on the boy's head. I shrugged.

Will you get in trouble? asked the boy.

I doubt it, I said. I asked them where they were going. The girl said to buy a box of chocolates. For him, she said, pointing at the boy. For being my faithful armrest all year. The boy smiled from under the girl's elbow.

That's handy, I said.

I know, said the girl. I get so tired of standing.

They promised they wouldn't tell anybody that I had wrecked the sign and I thanked them and watched as they too walked towards our man from Nazareth.

I missed Lids. Aimless isn't quite so aimless when you're doing nothing with a friend. I walked through a little park next to the Rest Haven and noticed a pup tent set up under a tree. I went up to it and said hello and a woman poked her head out of the flap. Oh sorry, I said. I was just curious about the tent. We're waiting for a home, she said. Oh, okay, I said. Sorry. Yesterday we found a twenty-dollar bill and we used it to buy food and soap. Right on, I said. We know we'll be provided for, she said. I smiled and nodded. Where are you from? Paraguay, said the woman. The Gran Chaco. Wow, I said. Do you know Doft? I asked. We know we'll be provided for, said the woman, again. I nodded. Well, have fun, I said. She thanked me and closed the flap.

I walked on to the hospital, taking Reimer Avenue past the Kids Korner where I used to work at trying to stay awake, and then the morgue tunnel. I took the elevator up to the main floor and went to Lids's room. Her parents were there and so was Dr. Hunter and a nurse.

Lids was lying in her bed looking scared and helpless and her face was glowing, almost flickering.

Oh, Naomi, said Lids's mom. We're having a bit of a discussion here. Would it be possible for you to come back another time?

Sure, yeah, I said.

Lids and I exchanged one very brief look and no smiles. I went into the hallway and asked the nurse, the nice one behind the desk, what was going on. She shook her head and said she didn't know. Some type of conference, maybe. Possibly related to Lids's having been stranded that afternoon.

What do you mean, stranded? I asked. The nurse told me that Lids had suddenly decided to get up and go for a walk but had only made it to the corner of Barkman and Lumber before collapsing on the sidewalk. Somebody saw her from their kitchen window and called the cop and he went over there to help her but she wouldn't let him touch her because it hurt too much. Then her parents came and so did Dr. Hunter but she wouldn't let anybody touch her. She just lay there on the sidewalk, moaning.

Then how did she get back here? I asked the nurse. Her parents finally just picked her up and put her in the back seat of the car, she said.

Is she feeling better now? I asked the nurse. Well, yes, in a way, said the nurse. We've given her a sedative and some toast.

Lids had been *wrestled into the back seat of a car.* Her parents had wanted to take her home but Lids had insisted on coming back to the hospital, said the nurse.

That's because at home they treat her with prayer and tomato juice, I told her.

Well, said the nurse, it's really not that much different here. We don't know what to do, to be perfectly honest.

I know that feeling, I said.

The nurse gave me a finger of her Kit Kat bar and told me she'd tell Lids that I'd be back soon.

I walked out of the town, past the parka factory, towards the lagoon. I'd never been there before. I had to climb a chain-link fence to get inside. There were four Olympic-sized pools containing the town's raw waste. It didn't look bad. It didn't smell bad either. If you could get past the idea of it, it was kind of pretty. The sun was in a position that made everything soft orange, like the inside of a cantaloupe. This is where it all began, I thought. Were it not for this strangely beautiful cesspool of unfiltered crap I would not be here. I just sat for a while. It occurred to me that Tash may have been bullshitting me when she said this was the place where Dad had asked Mom to marry him. Nobody else came. I tried psychically to prevent seagulls from landing in the pools. Eventually I got up and climbed back over the chain-link fence.

I stood in the lobby of the bank with my face against the cool granite, soaking up the air conditioning. Someone opened the door and I heard a familiar voice in the distance. Cast a cold eye on life, on death. Horseman, pass by. Only my dad would quote the words on Yeats's grave to a fundamentalist bank teller in a floral print dress. I didn't know the context. I saw her nodding and smiling and my dad standing solemnly on the other side of the counter like he was waiting for directions to the body. That's right, I heard him say. I'm fond of certain carbons. I couldn't hear what the teller was saying. She must have been a former student of his. Yes, he said morosely, I recall . . . the type of carbon where atoms are joined in a hollow structure . . . oh yes. He looked up and I waved.

We walked home together. He told me that for a second he'd smelled horse manure while standing in a parking lot that afternoon and he had thought of me. Yeah? I asked him. Yes, he said, only in the sense that you used to ride horses. Neither of us had much to say after that. When we got home there was a man there fixing the corner of the garage roof that had collapsed.

Well, asked my dad, is it doable? The man rattled off something in the language of our isolated people and my dad said something back to him, in kind. He shifted back to English and began to call out encouraging words to the man. He offered to bring him a glass of water. I went inside and watched my dad watch the man. I wanted to tell him not to, because it was embarrassing. I mean, why would you watch a man fix your roof.

Twenty-two

~

Tash had a summer job at thirteen, babysitting Trudie's mother so Grandma wouldn't get wasted on vanilla, burn down her apartment, get kicked out and have to live with us.

Tash told me it was The Mouth's fault that his mother drank. And regret, she said. For the way things could have been. I had the feeling she was quoting somebody, or would one day become a rock poetess, a term I'd recently seen on a scrap of city newspaper that the wind had carried to our town. For the way things could have been. We would sit in the crabapple tree outside Grandma's and watch her door to make sure she didn't take off on one of her wobbly odysseys to the Economy Foods baking goods aisle.

It was pretty good money for Tash and she gave me a dime for The Trampoline House every once in a while when I kept her company. One time we were sitting in the tree and she told me she had this thing about sneezing. That whenever she lay down in her bed to think about boys she'd immediately sneeze twice. After a while she got really nervous about it because she was convinced our parents would know what the sneezes meant. Heavy, I said. I just sneeze when I stand in the sun. She told me that's cause I was ten. Three years from then my sneezes would become a manifestation of different types of feelings of warmth and happiness.

Other things happened in that tree. She showed me how to hyperventilate. She showed me how to kill a person by punching their nose bone into their brain. We threw crabapples at cars. And she got her first period. We were wearing new bathing suits. Wow, lucky duck, I'd said because she looked so sad and she'd said yeah, merry Christmas to you too.

Travis taught me how to walk today. I have to roll and bob more, use my whole body. It's kind of a druggy walk. Travis prefers to call it *insouciant.* Then we promenaded over to the RK Ranch which is just past one of the dirt fields at the end of Main Street and stared at these giant horses with hairy ankles and eyes the size of nectarines. They were the horses that pulled tourists around the fake village in wagons.

It started to rain so we went into this little tack room in the barn and sat on saddles that were draped over boards. Travis turned on the floor heater and said I could put my wet shirt on it to dry so I did and after five minutes we smelled something strange and we looked over at my shirt and it had totally melted away.

He gave me his T-shirt to wear. I scrunched up the bottom of it and stuck it through the neck hole.

When the rain stopped we went outside and tried walking along the fence without falling off. I liked activities where the main theme was just not to fall down. I love being with you, I told Travis and he said I smelled nice, like his baseball glove. Which he never uses any more. I thought of what Mrs. Klippenstein had told her husband when they were both young and healthy, before he became The Swearing Man. You are almost perfect, she told him.

You are almost perfect, I told Travis.

I've got pimples on my ass, he said. We went back to his house and made iced tea and frozen sausage things and lay on the cool concrete of his basement-bedroom floor listening to Lou Reed in the dark and in between the songs the far-off screams of little Mennonite children at play.

Everything was wrecked when his parents came home and we'd fallen asleep and the candle had burned down and the record was going around and around and his mom was up at the top of the stairs switching the lights off and on as a signal to us that our world had come to an end and I had to get out of her son's room and leave.

We walked up the stairs into the shiny bright living room rubbing our eyes and going oh man, what time is it, and stuff like that and his mom looked at Travis and told him his dad needed him to install some carpet somewhere and that he should squeeze his pimples and I wondered which ones she meant.

Can I give her a ride home? he asked.

And his mom said I think she knows how to walk and I said yeah, I do. I just learned today. I went through their front door and set off this awful chimey thing that just went on and on. I could hear it halfway down the street.

When I got to my driveway my neighbour came out all pissed off with her screaming son on her hip. There were bubbles coming out of the kid's mouth and my neighbour said he'd just eaten two of her Max Factor bath beads that she'd been saving for her anniversary night.

That's too bad, I said.

My neighbour told me to just wait until I had kids.

And then what? I asked.

Well, then you'll know true misery, she said. *Oh, then?*

———

My dad was at the kitchen table looking at his hands. You weren't in school today? he asked.

Depends what you mean by school, I said. (Oh ho, clever. God, I'm a jerk.)

They say you're failing grade twelve, he said.

No, they have it turned around, I said. (I'm making myself nauseous.) I went to my room, slammed the door shut and fired up a Sweet Cap. I took a marker and made a word bubble coming out of Christina's mouth. FUCK YOUUUUUUUU! she said to that ugly old house off in the distance. I put on *Broken English* as loud as it would go without blowing the speakers and then stared at myself in my dresser mirror while I sat cross-legged on the bed inhaling carcinogens. I stared out the window and waved at a few RVs.

The tourists are coming in droves now to see how simple life can really be in Shitville. Travis has a job at the museum taking care of goats and sweeping out the windmill and erasing all the bad stuff tourist kids write on the blackboard in the fake one-room schoolhouse. He told me he wrote the word OBEY in huge letters across the length of the entire blackboard as a joke and The Mouth saw it and said he liked it. The Mouth is the grand vizier of the museum. Everything in this town, the school, the church, the museum, the chicken plant, is connected to everything else, like the sewers of Paris. There's no separation of Church and State, just of reality and understanding, and The Mouth is behind the wheel of it all.

Sometimes Travis has to go sit behind a rope in the authentic replica housebarn pretending to be the husband of a fake pioneer girl in a long skirt and bonnet who rocks a Cabbage Patch doll in a cradle. He sits there reading the Bible with a candle. They're supposed to smile at each other periodically.

The girl's name is Adeline Ratzlaff and she once brought brass knuckles to school to beat the shit out of another girl for stealing her look which as far as I can remember was tight Great Scott jeans, Greb Kodiaks, tube top, Fawcett hair, and tons of base. Same as everyone else. Here comes Menno Girl. Travis has informed me that he wants to start a shunning booth for the American tourists. Like a kissing booth, he said, only—yeah, yeah, I told him, I think I get it.

When my record stopped I heard the garage door open and then the car back out of the driveway and take off down the highway, probably going to America for coffee. I stretched out on my bed and stared at Christina. There were many things left not to do today. I went into the kitchen for a look in the fridge. I sat at the table and drew on a piece of paper. My dad had written something on it:

Qualifications of a leader/elder.
Personal—v.2,3
Family—v.4,5
Church—v.5,6
World—v.7

I wondered how our lives might change if my dad became a world leader.

I turned the paper over and studied a chart titled "Satan Cast Down." There were different categories linked together with arrows and verses. Rapture, saved dead, unsaved dead, millennium, bottomless pit, lake of fire, beast and false prophet, new heaven, new earth. I tried to follow the complicated system of arrows and timelines. I gave up and turned the piece of paper over and put it back on the table where my dad had left it. I returned to my bedroom.

——

I lay in my bed and tried to fight my evening face ache by methodically relaxing every single muscle in my body. It didn't work. I felt like Frankenstein, like I had bolts in my forehead and a giant chin I could barely move. I decided to get up and go for a walk down the number twelve to the museum to see if Travis could get a break and hang out with me for a while. I put on my strappy Jesus sandals and my cut-offs and a pink halter top. Then I put on a ton of eye make-up and pulled my hair back into a really tight ponytail so I looked like a badly aging Hungarian gymnast.

I left a note for my dad: Don't you think we should fix the window? I'll go to school tomorrow. Who was Samuel Champlain again? xoxo nomi. I liked to ask my dad questions about Canadian history because it made him happy to talk about it.

Travis and his fake wife were smoking a joint behind the sod hut and laughing as though they were enjoying themselves.

What are you doing? I asked.

We're on break, said the girl.

I wasn't talking to you, I said.

Nomi, relax, said Travis. Toke? He held his breath and passed me the roach. He started coughing and then he asked me what was with the eye make-up.

Can we go for a walk? I asked. He said sure and got up and said later to the girl. We walked off towards the windmill and he took my hand and said don't be mad.

You're not having some weird thing with her are you? I asked.

God, no, he said. We were on a break. What do you expect?

I was stumped. *Expect?* Are you really going to Montreal? I asked him. Fuck, I don't know, he said. I want to but I also want to be with you and I need money to go and my parents would freak out. I don't know. It's complicated.

Yeah, I said. We walked into the little barn where the goats live and he introduced me to them. We sat in a pile of hay and chucked black pellets of food into their pail.

Do you have to go back? I asked.

Yeah, he said, soon.

Please don't be happy with that girl, I said.

He said okay, he wouldn't be.

He told me I looked like Alice Cooper. We got up and he put his arms around my waist and held me like we were a long-time couple with my head on his collarbone and his chin on my head.

I went to the general store and bought a long stick of orange candy from a woman in a black dress. She said she hadn't seen me in church lately. I know, I said. I'm sorry. And I was sorry.

When she looked at me she saw a child surrounded by flames, screaming. And that must have been hard for her.

I didn't want to leave right away. I liked stores, the way people came and went and looked at things. I asked her how her day was going and she said it was almost over. She was tired. I nodded and smiled again. And it's so hot in here, I said. Oh, I have a fan behind the counter. She pointed at it.

That's not authentic, is it? I asked. She smiled shyly.

I mean I don't think it's a sin or anything, I said.

Oh goodness, I hope not, she said. We both laughed a little.

Nomi, she said. May I make a suggestion? I said of course she could. May I suggest you start with Matthew? she asked.

That's probably a good idea, I said. Thank you. She seemed so happy then. I felt good about sticking around and talking to her. I wanted what she had. I wanted to know what it really felt like to think you were saving someone's life.

How's your dad? she asked. How's school?

They're doing carbons, I said. And thermodynamics. His beloved Second Law. She shook her head.

He's hooked on extremely unstable carbons, I said.

Ohhhh, she said.

And entropy.

Is that right? she asked.

Yup, I said.

Wow, that's interesting, she said.

In a way, I said. We nodded together in kindly clued-out unison.

May I pray for you? she asked.

Of course, I said. I thanked her and said goodbye.

I walked down Kokomo Road to the pits and waded into the water. I floated around in all my clothes sucking on my candy with my eyes shut. I left when I heard some cars pull up and guys get out and start smashing things and girls with them saying no, don't, no, don't. I didn't feel like going home so I went to Abe's Hill and sat on top of the toboggan shelter making designs on my legs with the navy-blue water dripping from my cut-offs and waiting for the city lights to come on.

When I was five my favourite book had no words, only colours. The first page was black—that's what my heart looked like without Jesus in it. The second page was red. That was Jesus' blood washing over me and saving me, somehow, and the third page was white which meant my new clean heart and the fourth page was gold which was the colour of the streets in heaven

where I'd live forever and ever and ever and ever and ever and
ever and ever and ever and ever and ever and ever and ever and
ever. In Sunday school our teacher would hold up the pages of
the book and point at each one with her long index finger that
poked out from a sleeve that she'd stuff used Kleenex into and
we'd recite in this dirge-like monotone the meaning of all the
colours. Then it was felt-board time. We were not allowed to
put anyone but the felt Jesus onto the old rugged cross, and we
could not do voices for the characters because it always ended
in Jesus leaping from the cross and drop-kicking the bad guys.

One day, at home, I scratched a mosquito bite until it
bled and I held it against the page of Jesus' blood and his was
orangey in comparison, which spooked me. I took a pin and
poked the tips of all my fingers trying, with increasing
desperation, to find a shade that matched the blood of Jesus.
No dice, my blood was wrong. Tash found the book in the
bathroom garbage covered in bloody fingerprints and made this
huge deal out of it because I wouldn't tell her what I'd done.

Twenty-three

~

They threw my mother out. Gave her the old heave-ho. The term is *excommunicated*. She was excommunicated, said my dad.

Ah, I said. I nodded. I'd heard that story before.

That's pretty much that, he said. The townspeople were expected to rally around the church and cut her off in their own special way. There were different methods. Silence was popular.

The Mouth and the other elders and the deacons and lay people had met for a good seven or eight minutes before they decided that Trudie was history.

I don't know how she felt about it. I never had the chance to ask her. I have this vague picture in my head of my mother sitting on my bed and looking at me. I think her hand was on my arm and she was wearing a black turtleneck sweater and she was just staring at me. I think she was smiling the same kind of real smile that Tash had smiled just before she left. It's a scary smile. It's a smile that means there is nothing left to lose. That you are free, according to Janis Joplin. I looked right at her for a couple of seconds but it was dark and I don't know if she noticed. She moved her hand up and down my arm, slowly, and then I heard her begin to cry very softly and I buried my face deep into my pillow because I didn't want to hear her cry. And then I felt her hand on my head and the next thing I knew she had closed my door quietly and was gone.

I hadn't known then that she had left for good. But in the morning my dad was standing in the middle of the living room, looking out the big picture window at the highway, and he didn't move all day. And he didn't speak and he didn't eat. He just stood there in his dark suit with his necktie all done up and everything and his hands in his pockets, moving his change around. That was the only sound all day, the sound of coins clanking against each other.

I know that after my mom was gone my grandma's drinking got worse. She made up her own wild tales. My dad told me that she had told him once that she'd been entombed in concrete for several days and managed to survive. She told him that when The Mouth was born she'd been so happy. He was the most beautiful baby, she said, but he took everything so literally. I could never engage him in whimsy.

Well, said my dad. What else could he say? I honestly don't think he hates The Mouth. Mr. Quiring said that ideologies were to blame for most of the world's problems, not individuals. What could The Mouth do but throw his sister out? What a colossally ridiculous mess.

Then one day, maybe a month or two after Trudie left, I was walking around downtown and I saw Mrs. Klippenstein sitting in front of the Rest Haven in a wheelchair with a blanket over her legs and a red wool toque on her head. I asked her if she was visiting and she said no, she lived there now, her kids had finally won the argument.

I remembered Trudie racing around the house, getting ready to go to Mrs. Klippenstein's. Almost every other day, after supper, she'd throw her gauze and tape and ointment into her kit, clap her hands and say all right, I'm off! See you later! Where'd she been going if Mrs. Klippenstein was living at the Rest Haven and not alone in her house needing medical care?

How long have you been here? I asked Mrs. Klippenstein. She shook her head. Then she gripped the metal bars of her wheelchair and stared off into the distance.

Take me Lord, make me new, she said. I asked again and she did the same thing. Take me Lord, make me new. Take me Lord, make me new. I eventually walked away.

Trudie was gone. My dad and I were alone. We did our best to live—you know, we ate, we slept, he worked, I went to school. I started doing all the laundry. Sorting it into colours, breaking it down into loads, washing, drying, folding, and putting it away. I decided to use my mom's drawer for some of his stuff, for his socks and underwear and handkerchiefs. So first of all I emptied the drawer of her things including that passport with her photo, the one where she thinks her eyes are hazel, and the letters from Mr. Quiring.

I stared into houses on my way home from the museum. I ran through sprinklers. Dogs barked. I sat on the curb outside Vinny's Pizza and waved to Bert every single time he drove past as though it were the first time and he were my best friend and I hadn't seen him in two years. When I got to my place I found my dad in his lawn chair, asleep, with a photo album in his lap. I went into the garage and started the car for a second to see the mileage. He'd driven almost three hundred miles since after school when I slammed the door. I went back to the lawn chair and took the photo album off his lap and brought it to his room and put it back in the top drawer of his bedside table. I took a blanket out and wrapped it around his legs and took his glasses off and brought them inside and put them on the kitchen table. There was a little note that said: You know who Samuel Champlain is. One other question, I wrote back. Why didn't she take me with her? I lifted his glasses up to the kitchen light and then I breathed on them and wiped them with the bottom of my halter top and put them back on the table. I poured some soap into the dishwasher and started it and then I went to bed.

Really big thunderstorm at night that made some of the manhole covers on Main Street pop up like champagne corks, my dad said. You just said *champagne corks,* I said. I thought champagne was on my dad's list of things not to say because of the connotations of celebration. One of the manhole lids had smashed a hole through the Darnell's Bakery display window and created a little pink river of jelly and powder. There was a soaked wedding cake upside down near the curb. The windmill got hit by lightning and one of the giant blades started to burn and then flew off into the night sky. The animals at the museum were going nuts. My dad saw it all. He woke up around three in his lawn chair soaked in rain, got up, and drove around town watching things smash and burn all night. I mean, was that fun or what? I asked him. He looked at me like he knew me from somewhere, but where?

I slept through the whole thing dreaming that I had a ton of chest hair.

When I woke up my dad had one buttock perched, barely, on the end of my bed. His arms were folded, his legs were crossed and he was staring at the floor.

Oh you're awake, he said.

What are you doing here? I asked.

I just wanted to say something, he said.

Say it then, I said, and he told me about the storm. I listened and nodded and then he said don't be too surprised if things are a little different when you get up. And then he left. I waited for a minute and then I got up and walked into the living room and found out that the couch and love seat and coffee table weren't there any more. I went into the hallway and saw my dad's Thursday shoes and they had little cards on them with writing as a reminder of what he was supposed to do the next day. I picked one up and it said: Develop new life strategy. Fridays clearly were big days for him. The phone rang and I answered it and it was him and he said I should really try to make an effort to go to school. He said he knew it didn't mean anything to me and that he didn't blame me or anything but that grade twelve was something I might want in the future.

What a funny word, I thought, *future*.

I said okay. I would. I asked him why he was getting rid of the furniture and he said he liked empty spaces because you can imagine what might go in them someday.

We were quiet for a long, long time. Then I told him I wasn't going anywhere. That I'd never leave him. And he said well . . . and then nothing else.

Champagne corks, eh? I said. He said it was wild. He told me he had a library meeting after school and I said I'd have a really super-nice meal ready for him when he got home and we could watch TV together in the evening and go for ice cream later on. We said goodbye.

I looked down at the table and saw his note. He'd answered my question, sort of. She didn't take you with her because you were sleeping when she left.

Finally. Hmmm. I guess he meant that I had stopped
believing in hell and was no longer having nightmares. Maybe.
Hard to say. I think I knew another part of the answer which
was that she knew he needed me more than she did. I'm pretty
sure she left town for his sake. It would have killed him to
choose between her or the church. The only decision he'd ever
made without her help was to wear a suit and tie every day of
his life. How could he stand up and publicly denounce a
woman he loved more than anything in the world. And how
could he turn away from the church that could, someday,
forgive his wife and secure their future together in paradise, for
all time. He was stuck in the middle of a story with no good
ending. He had the same disease I had.

I smoked a Cap and listened to "Down by the River" over and
over while I got ready for school. I thought about all the things
my dad liked to eat. I heard my mother say Nomi, there is
always the possibility of forgiveness. Remember that. And I
heard Tash saying oh my god. After she left I got a job at Kids
Korner, the town daycare. My first job there was to hang out
and play with the three- and four-year-olds but I got moved to
babies after Mrs. Groening, the daycare director, caught us
dancing to the Beatles with big pink hearts taped to our cheeks
and foreheads. The next thing I knew I was sitting in the dark
nursery while four or five babies in cribs had their afternoon
naps. I couldn't read because it was too dark. It was clinically
impossible not to fall asleep, especially after I'd suffered so long
from insomnia. I tried all sorts of things to stay awake.
Thinking. Humming. Amphetamines. Nothing worked.
Eventually I was caught fast asleep in the rocking chair and
fired. The older kids gave me a going-away card. It said thank
you for teaching us how to play toilet tag. No mention of the

fact that I tried to teach them how to shake their Menno booties. I miss kids. The way they react to everything like they're alive.

In the morning the two grade twelve classes had a baseball tournament. I didn't have a glove so they put me in centre field four hundred miles away from the action and after about twenty minutes of walking around in a tight circle I decided to stand perfectly still with my hands on my hips and my legs spread wide apart and just not move the entire time. I could hear the far-off muffled whoops and cheers of the game and see tiny figures running around the bases occasionally. When it was our turn to bat Mr. Quiring yelled Nomi! Come in! and I'd sprint back to the dugout as fast as I could. I decided to do that all day. I would either speed-run or not move at all.

When it was my turn to bat I ran to the plate and then stood there frozen with the bat on my shoulder and the pitcher threw me four balls for a walk. Mr. Quiring kept saying to the batters: Leave one go by. When the ump said take your base! I dropped the bat and bolted like hell for first. Then when I got there I froze in the type of primed position that indicated my readiness to take off to second. I wondered if I could spend my entire life in two gears, neutral and fourth. I was so tired of shuffling. Martin Schultz was playing first base and he asked me if I was retarded.

In the afternoon we went swimming at St. Malo, past the closed-down drive-in and the dump. There was a dam that was covered in green slime and perfect for sliding headfirst into the water. A group of girls from my homeroom were sitting on the sand crying and hugging and when I sprinted over to ask them what was wrong they said, this is the end. I'm sorry, I said. I sat perfectly still except for lighting a Sweet Cap. Tina asked me if I was trying out for Up With People in the fall. Then we had hot dogs and popsicles and chips and the confident boys snapped towels at the pretty girls and the other kids stared at them or played Frisbee. Len brought me home in his Vauxhall. He asked me if I wanted to see what it was like to ride in the trunk and I said yes I do. He opened it up but it was full of shit he was too lazy to move around so I sat perfectly still in the front seat and then bolted from his car to my house when he dropped me off. When I got inside the phone was ringing. It was Sheri from the yearbook committee. She was wondering if it was okay if they wrote under my picture: Do do do do do do do do. I asked if that was the theme from *The Twilight Zone* and she said yeah. I asked how the readers would know and she said, They'll know.

And then I went into the empty living room and sat on the floor away from the shattered window. I closed my eyes and saw nothing but I heard her voice, serious but not, at the same time.

Tash: Do you know what a hard-on is?
Me: Of course.
Tash: That's all you need to know.
Me: Get out.
Tash: Nomi, world. World, Nomi.

Twenty-four

~

It was time to make Ray's birthday dinner. It wasn't much of anything but it was very elegant in its nothingness. Paper-thin crêpes with a fine syrupy drizzle, and cantaloupe. I dimmed the lights and closed the curtains and lit a couple of scented candles and put on Tash's record of Keith Jarrett playing a live concert somewhere in Sweden.

I gave my dad a green ceramic frog that goes on the outdoor sprinkler tap and some goofy-looking socks for his golf clubs and a bag of Glad Garbage Bags for the dump and a new shirt from Schlitzking Clothing that had a special section in the front pocket for a pen. Then I brought out a cake I'd made called One Two Three Four Cake with a bunch of candles on it and a sparkler in the middle. Sorry, I said, I couldn't afford forty-three. But I sang. And the whole time he had the sweetest smile on his face and he kept rolling his shirt sleeves farther and farther up his arms and then when I was finished singing he blew out the candles and I said no girlfriends, and he said nope and then I took the cake back to the counter and cut us both giant pieces.

It was the same cake my mom had baked for me when I suffered my first major disappointment, at the age of four. My grandpa, my mom's dad, had died and I missed him a lot so one

197

day I decided to write him a letter in heaven, something like: Dear Grandpa. I hope you are having fun. I am having fun. I miss you. I love you. Please write me back when you get this. And then on a very windy day I took it outside and stood on the back steps and threw it up into the wind so that it could be carried up to my gramps in the sky. I watched it blow around for a while and then sure enough, the wind took it straight up to God. Every day I'd sit on those stupid steps for hours waiting for my grandpa to drop me a letter. And then one day I went outside and there it was sitting in the middle of the yard and I was really excited and happy and grabbed it and went running inside and showed it to my mom and she read it to me. Grandpa was fine and feeling good and missing me too. He said he'd have a place all ready for me to live in when I got there but that wouldn't be for a long, long time so I should just forget about it and have fun with other kids and run around and play and not worry. Or words to that effect.

About a week later my mom and I were getting out of the car and I saw a scrunched-up piece of paper wedged against the fence by our driveway and I ran over to it and picked it up and smoothed it out and realized it was my letter to my grandpa. How can this be here? I asked my mom. It's supposed to be in heaven. That means he didn't get it, did he? I started to cry and my mom took my hand and we went inside and sat down at the kitchen table and she told me that she had written that letter supposedly from my grandpa because she couldn't bear to see me so sad and hopeful at the same time. She told me it was impossible to send a letter to heaven because the wind does not go there. Heaven is always calm, with no wind. She said other stuff but I didn't really understand it. I understood there was no wind in heaven. That's partly why I love the wind that blows around in this town. It makes me feel like I'm in the world. And then she and I baked a One Two Three Four Cake together and during that time I stopped crying and feeling sad and even had a little fun especially when we surprised Tash and my dad with the cake when they got home from school.

My dad said thank you very, very much Nomi, this is quite a surprise. And I said you're very, very welcome. Happy birthday, Dad. And then he took off his old shirt and put on the new one and I gave him a pen from the drawer to put in the special pocket and he said look at that.

We ate our cake and smiled at each other while Keith Jarrett played and moaned and when I asked him if he wanted another piece he said no thank you, then I will have eaten to superfluity. Afterwards we carried the TV outside and plugged it into the outlet near the garage and sat in lawn chairs watching a baseball game in Detroit while the sun set without us noticing. We had one of our usual discussions about that particular phenomenon.

Hey Dad, it's dark, did you notice the sun setting? No, did you? No. Weird. Very. He told me it had been a super birthday, just super. He said I spoiled him.

After the game my dad went to bed and I called Travis and he came to pick me up in the truck. I helped him paint the goat barn red.

We were getting so much paint on our clothes that we decided to take them off. I let him paint weird hieroglyphic things all over my body with a big fat exterior brush and I put a target on his ass. Then we put plastic down on the front seat of his dad's truck and drove to The Golden Comb's place and hosed ourselves off with purple gas. Travis chased me around for a while with a lighter, flicking it and trying to set me on fire.

We drove to the pits and rinsed the purple gas off in the water which made it beautiful and we floated around in gassy rainbows for hours talking about stuff and lighting the gas with Travis's lighter so it was like we were in hell. Rainbow pools of fire in the pits, the smell of smoking stubble, the hot wind, dying chickens, the night, my childhood.

How do you remember a town that's not supposed to exist in the world?

Went home. Came down. Got sad. There was a note on the kitchen table. Nomi: Any plans for after graduation? That's how we communicated large, vague ideas. On paper that can burn up in less than one second. I stared at the words for an exorbitantly long time.

Then I wrote. Dear Dad: I intend to become a model of courage and dignity.

I went into the bathroom, puked, passed out in my bed, and briefly died, until the sun rose once again reminding me of renewed hope and promise and other abiding things. I needed to find something large and dark to put in my window or I would slowly die of fatigue.

I sat down on my French horn on the corner of Second and Kroeker and lit a Sweet Cap and wondered why I hadn't practised more. The French horn, when played well, is the most beautiful instrument in the world, according to Tash. That was the reason why I picked it. She chose the flute because she dug the way the case looked like it could also contain a sawed-off shotgun. She used to play "Oh Shenandoah" in her room with her blinds down, burning cones of incense in a teacup. I'd lie in bed and listen to the funny way she had of breathing while she played.

It was so hot I could see the heat. I could feel my internal organs warming up. I wondered if I could boil in my own blood. I heard the second bell but I couldn't move. I was moulded to my French horn case like the Ken doll is to his underwear. I leaned over and fell off my case hoping that the hard impact with the concrete would encourage some kind of re-entry into the world but all it did was hurt me.

A woman came out of an aluminum house and asked me in the language of our people if I was all right and I thought about the question for a while and then said *yo, yo, fane, schmack,* and a few other words I could remember from talking with my grandma on the rare occasions when she was sober and we were not guarding her from the crabapple tree. *Zeia gute, danke,* I said, waving.

The woman frowned. *Yo?* she asked.

Oba yo! I said. She went inside and slammed the door while I rose to my hands and knees and prayed for a cloud, one cloud. I'd plant a church somewhere in Africa for one fucking cloud. Why do you hate me? I cried out, yeah, *cried out,* to the sun. I heard a locking kind of click coming from the door vicinity of the aluminum house.

Dialogue with school secretary regarding my fifty-dollar deposit for the French horn:

—They said I'd get the fifty bucks when I returned the instrument.

—We issue cheques upon graduation, taking into account overdue library books, things like that.

—What if I don't graduate?

—Then I suppose you won't get your deposit back.

—But what does one have to do with the other?

—I don't know, but that's our policy.

—But it doesn't make any sense. Here's the French horn so fifty bucks please.

—I'm sorry.

—Give it to me. Please?

—I can't. I'm sorry.

—Please? I don't understand. I got here. I walked . . . it shouldn't . . . oh God, please?

—I can't. Our policy is . . .

—I know, I know, but I need that money. I got here . . . you have no idea . . . of . . . just please?

—No, I'm sorry and I'd suggest you get to your first class. You're already twenty minutes late.

—Oh sorry, I know, okay . . . sorry.

—You can leave that French horn, Nomi.

—No, I'm taking it.

—But the school policy is . . .

—No, no, that's okay, I'm taking it.

—I'm afraid you'll have to leave it here in the office.

—Don't be afraid.

—Nomi!

—Shhhhh . . .

—Nomi!

I don't remember much after that except that I picked some purple flowers in the ditch along the number twelve with the intention of trading them for drugs. When I woke up I was lying on my own couch. Except that my couch was in The Golden Comb's trailer. I still had the flowers in my hand.

Should we put those in water, asked The Comb. I handed them to him and he walked over to the kitchen. He was wearing his Tiger Claw School of Kung Fu T-shirt. The trailer was pretty much one room with sections.

Do you mind if I ask you something? I said. Where'd you get this couch? The Comb told me he'd bought it off my dad in the middle of the night a few days ago. He was sitting on it in the front yard like at three or four in the morning with a suit and tie on like he was waiting for me or something, said The Comb.

I said yeah and nodded and then Eldon said barley sandwich? Old socks? And I said cool, thank you, Eldon. He said donesville and headed for the fridge.

The Comb sat in a La-Z-Boy folding laundry and nodding moodily to *The Dark Side of the Moon*. I said: I was gonna get the deposit on that thing and, like fifty bucks, for shit . . . and then, but they said no, so.

Oh yeah, said The Comb. So, no dough?

Kind of yeah, no, I said. I kind of got those . . . flowers there for . . . I picked them and . . . hoped. This is not a smooth transaction, I thought to myself. The Comb closed his eyes and grooved for a while. I looked over at the worn-out shiny part of the sofa cushion where my dad had put his head when he napped. Where he had dreamed away the darkness. Eldon came back with my beer and pretended to open it with his eye.

That's so fu— . . . that's . . . wow, I said, smiling up at him like he was Santa Claus. Then he sat down in a different La-Z-Boy chair and I drank my beer and tried to keep flies from landing on the opening of the bottle and stared at that part of the sofa that my dad had worn in with his head.

So! said The Comb, finally. What are we gonna do, Nomi? I smiled and shrugged and then Eldon came up with the idea of strip Scrabble but I said noooooo thanks.

Ordinary Scrabble? he asked.

I'm pretty bad with uh . . . words, I said. The Comb said that Eldon kept track of his scores and studied words every evening.

That's freaky, I said and Eldon said why is that freaky, why is that freaky?

And The Comb said whoah, Silver, she means it's interesting.

Then Eldon looked over at my French horn and said we could keep that in exchange, what's it worth?

Nothing, I said. It's really pretty useless. I rest on it sometimes. We all stared at it for a few seconds and then The Comb asked me how desperate I was.

Well quite severely so I guess, I said.

So we keep that baby, he said, and you go away happy. Happy? Eldon was firing up a shiny blue blowtorch and The Comb was stroking the lid of an old Sucrets tin.

Well? asked Eldon.

I was studying that word in my head, I said.

What word? he asked.

Happy, I said.

Are you mocking me? he asked. The Comb lifted his hand and glared at Eldon and said give it up, man.

You know how it is when you say a word over and over and over in your head? They looked at me. I put my hand on the sofa cushion and felt its warmth and worn-away feeling. I'll just take my French horn now and go, I said. No offence or anything. I mean you guys are the best, thanks for the beer and sitting here inside, it's so . . . round . . . and shady. Whew. I smiled and mimed like I was wiping sweat off my forehead. Bye guys, I said. Nice couch. And closed the screen door really, really softly.

———

I sat on the church steps and stared at the cars on Main Street. I got up and walked over to The Trampoline House for a few minutes of uninterrupted jumping. I sat in a wooden swing set in Travis's backyard. My French horn was becoming intolerably heavy. I walked home down the highway, six inches away from the speeding semis carrying loads of doped-up livestock. When I got to my house I found my dad at the kitchen table looking at a pile of coupons that all advertised half-price fabric softener.

I guess whole stacks of papers that all say the same thing really interest you, eh? I said. He looked up and smiled and lifted his hand like a traffic cop.

How goes the battle? he asked. That was one of his favourite questions. I tilted my head and smiled grimly. Not yet time for the white flag I hope, he said.

Hell no, captain, I said. He didn't like the word *hell* but he kind of liked the word *captain* although he probably associated it with the word *mutiny.*

They called, he said. You have your driver's test tomorrow at six o'clock at the arena.

I'll need the car then, I said. Don't sell it.

What's for supper? he asked. Things starting with *J? K?*

I went into the garage to get some stuff from the freezer but then remembered that the freezer was gone. There was a three-by-six-foot rectangle of clean garage floor where it had once been. I went back inside and sat down across from my dad and said: What are you doing?

He said, we don't need such a large freezer. He blinked from behind the glass. His eyes were so green and pretty.

Dad, I said, do you even know what fabric softener is? He looked at his stack of coupons and sighed. We need . . . he didn't finish. We sat together quietly staring at the coupons as if they were showing signs of coming out of a long coma.

Finally I said we should do something fun tonight and he said how about the Demolition Derby.

It was nice leaning up against the fence with him at the old fairgrounds watching cars smash the shit out of each other and then come back for more, smoke puffing out around their hoods and doors missing. My dad was the only person at the fairgrounds wearing a suit and tie, of course. During the intermission we walked over to the ditch by the highway to watch some boys do jumps with their mini-bikes. And we counted cars with American plates—twenty-seven. On their way to watch The Mouth read Revelations by candlelight in the fake church while the people of the real town sat in a field of dirt cheering on collisions.

Afterwards he let me practise my driving. I drove around and around the outskirts of town on Townline Road and Garson and back up the number twelve to Kokomo Road, like I was a real *thorough* or possibly forgetful dog marking my territory. My dad asked me what those fires were in the bushes off behind Suicide Hill and I told him: kids. Kids hanging out. Staying out of the wind, drinking beer, pairing off, and hoping to have a little fun before that endless swim-a-thon in the Lake of Fire. My dad asked me please not to *schput*—an old word meaning don't make fun of eternal damnation and other religion-based themes.

I didn't want to go home. I couldn't get my hands to turn the steering wheel towards home. So I just kept driving around and around the same roads and my dad kept staring out the window like he'd never seen any of it before.

TWENTY-FIVE

Me and Travis sat on top of the monkey bars at Ash Park in the moonlight swinging our legs and slamming back warm Baby Duck. We tried to hang upside down and drink but it didn't work very well and I dropped the bottle from laughing too hard and it broke and Travis used a piece of it to carve half an *N* for Nomi into his arm before it started hurting too much and he asked if he could stop.

After that we walked slowly around talking about stuff until we found a shopping cart and he lifted me up and put me inside and pushed me all the way to the RK Ranch. We went into the barn and gave each other haircuts with this horse razor we found on a shelf in the tack room and then made out soporifically in some hay in an empty stall until we heard one of the ranch guys drive up (he was whistling "We Are the Champions") and we ran out the back door laughing our heads off because it was getting light outside and we could see how awful our hair looked.

We ran all the way to Main Street and climbed up to the top of the fire escape of the feed mill which was the highest place in town and kissed like crazy hoping some early morning farmer out in his field would see us silhouetted against the rising sun and feel excited knowing happiness was a possibility even in a town with no bar and no train.

Mist was coming off the Rat River and the fields around the town were blue and yellow and the little trees in all the yards were pink and purple and the heat was about ready to start shimmering and everything was so quiet and beautiful like a secret Shangri-La. It was the outdoor version of waking up to your mom making breakfast and your dad sitting confidently at the table with no plan to sell it and your sister saying something like Nomi, I've never really noticed before but you have nice teeth.

Used Tash's Lady Schick to finally reveal my entire head to the whole fuckin' world and found my old fish-hook scar again. I put in all my earrings, threw on a ton of mascara and eyeliner, and my cut-offs and a bikini top and my giant police boots and rode my bike to school.

Mr. Quiring told me he was still waiting for my written assignments. I . . . yeah . . . I will, I said.

You seem to have forgotten the school's make-up and jewellery policy, he told me.

No . . . I said. I just . . . I didn't forget.

So you're flouting the policy intentionally? he asked.

No . . . I said . . . what? I mean . . . what?

Should you be seeing the guidance counsellor, Nomi? he asked.

Should you? I said. I'd reverted to age nine. I was sitting on the floor in front of my locker. I turned my cheek to feel the cool green metal.

Mr. Quiring grabbed my chin and said look at me, are you having a nervous breakdown? I told him not to touch me and he told me to get out.

I have to graduate, I told him. He said that wasn't his problem which struck me as an honest thing for him to say.

——

One day, when I was nine years old, I got up early and went for a walk around town. I wore a thin white cotton T-shirt, navy-blue polyester pants meant to resemble real denim, and North Star runners with no socks. I walked around and around and I felt so good. I felt happier than I had ever felt in my entire life, perfectly content and absolutely carefree.

When I got to school I told my teacher I was on cloud nine. I told her I was so happy I thought I could fly. I told her I felt so great I wanted to dance like Fred Astaire.

She said life was not a dream. And dancing was a sin. Now get off it and sit back down. It was the first time in my life that I had been aware of my own existence. It was the first time in my life I had realized that I was alive. And if I was alive, then I could die, and I mean forever. Forever dead. Not heaven, not eternal life on some other plane . . . just darkness, curtain, scene. Permanently. And that was the key to my new religion, I figured. That's why life was so fucking great.

I want that day back. I want to be nine again and be told, Nomi: someday you'll be gone, you'll be dust, and then even less than dust. Nothing. There's no other place to be. This world is good enough for you because it has to be. Go ahead and love it. (Menno was wrong.)

Rolled a giant spool of purple hydro cable up and down William Avenue for old times' sake. I went to my dad's school and tapped on his classroom window. He didn't hear me at first but I could hear his voice through the screen. He was talking about his class doing some kind of performance, maybe choral or poetry or something like that. He was sitting on his desk which was crowded with containers of lilacs the kids had picked for him.

There's something I need to tell you, I heard him say to the class. And I'll say this even though it might hurt, he continued.

I thought he was going to tell his kids they were all hopeless monotones, that they couldn't carry a tune in a paper bag or some such thing. I saw him grimace and fold his arms across his chest, hating himself for being the bearer of bad news.

It's a good idea to smile periodically at the audience, he said. His grimace didn't fade, not even slightly, and he appeared to be looking at the floor, embarrassed.

I should have empathized with his suffering but I started to laugh and that's when he heard me and looked up. He came outside and stood in the shade with me beside a stucco wall. His sleeves were rolled up and his tie was stuck between his buttons.

Whatcha doing? I asked him.

What I do, he said.

Same old thing, eh? He said yup.

And you? he said. I shrugged.

I see the idea of attending school today left you . . . cold?

Yeah, I agreed. It did kind of. He nodded and stared off at the parking lot. He told me he'd better go back inside or it'd be a zoo in there. I could see some of his kids staring at us through the window. I waved and they got shy and ducked.

They're so cute, I told my dad. They're good kids, he said. Then we said goodbye and he went back in.

I went home and tried to read *The Screwtape Letters*. I tried to make another list of ways to self-improve. I got as far as: Pretend you've already died and things will matter less. I lay in my bed and tried to relax to a degree that would allow me to levitate. I fell asleep.

When I woke up I went into the living room and discovered the body of an old woman lying on the floor next to the stereo and Ray standing at the kitchen sink staring out the window with a glass of water in his hand. Oh, he said, shhh. He opened the back door and gently pulled me outside into the yard. I found her wandering around the halls at school, he said. She's completely disoriented. He told me that she was an adjudicator from the city and that she was here to give marks to all the choral and poetry groups. I think it's the heat, he said.

I asked him why he brought her home and he said that she needed to rest. A couch would have been good for that, I said. He nodded. He'd forgotten about the couch not being here any more.

I'll make her some tea, he said. She can have it when she wakes up.

I asked him if his class had performed yet.

Tomorrow, he said.

I went back into the house quietly to have a peek at the woman but she wasn't in the living room. I heard the toilet flush and the bathroom door open and then the woman came walking down the hall and into the living room.

Hello, I said.

She smiled and shook her head and said oh boy, that was . . . She wore a turquoise woollen skirt and jacket ensemble. I think she was about seventy years old. Ray came in and asked her how she was doing and she said much better and he introduced her to me, her name was Edwina McGillivray, and then the three of us stood there smiling at each other until I offered to make the tea and Ray suggested they go outside and sit on the front step and get some air, it was cooler now, and after that he could drive her back to the school.

I brought the tea outside and sat in the grass next to Ray and Edwina. Ray had given her his yellow lawn chair and he was sitting on the step next to her like a little kid. She could have reached out and patted him on the head.

So, she said, is it just the two of you? Ray and I looked at each other and I nodded and he said well, yes, for the time being I suppose it is.

Mrs. McGillivray nodded politely and sipped her tea. Ray swatted at a wasp that was flying around her cup and saucer.

Now, she said, what did you say your last name was? Nickel, said Ray. Ray Nickel.

Nickel, Nickel, said Mrs. McGillivray. Why does that sound so familiar? Ray smiled and I shrugged. Mrs. McGillivray shifted a bit in the lawn chair and looked down at Ray. Would you happen to know a Trudie Nickel? she asked.

Ray cleared his throat and said yes, yes he did. In fact, she was his wife. Her mother, he said, waving in my direction. I nodded to confirm that fact and stared at Ray who was looking up at the sky with what seemed like awe but might have been panic.

How do you know Trudie? I asked her.

Well, I don't really know her, said Mrs. McGillivray. She sang. Didn't she?

Did she sing . . . I guess, I said. I mean . . .

Yes, said Ray. Yes, she sang. Yup.

But, I mean did she sing, I asked him, or did she . . .

She sang, said Ray.

She sang? I said.

Yes, said Mrs. McGillivray, oh did she sing! I saw her perform oh what was it now . . . my goodness, that was long ago . . . a musical at Pantages Playhouse on . . .

What? I asked.

Ray said oh, that was a very long time ago. That was . . . yes, well, that was . . . she was very young. Can I get you more tea?

Was it *West Side Story*? asked Mrs. McGillivray.

Ray stood up. It could have been, yes, very likely.

Tea? Please, said Mrs. McGillivray.

So you saw her perform in a musical? I said.

Yes, she was delightful, said Mrs. McGillivray. Just a real live wire.

Ray went into the house.

Well, but . . . I said.

Oh, she was talented, said Mrs. McGillivray. Her voice . . . she sighed and laughed. I smiled and then wondered if I would ever have another afternoon as interesting as this one. Mrs. McGillivray whispered: Do you mind me asking where she is?

We . . . I said. She . . . you know, they . . .

Mrs. McGillivray nodded and said she understood.

Ray came back out with some more tea and began to talk about the migration of the monarch butterfly, because one had just landed on Mrs. McGillivray's turquoise skirt. He talked loudly, and with very few pauses. None, in fact. And then Mrs. McGillivray felt that it was time she got back to the school for the evening performances.

Do you feel all right, now? Ray asked her.

Oh yes, she said, I'm much better now, thank you. Much better.

Do you mind cleaning this up? he asked me. And then took Mrs. McGillivray's left arm and hustled her down the sidewalk and into the car.

I got my bike out of the garage and rode to the museum to tell Travis everything was cool. I whispered it to him in the doorway of the house so his wife wouldn't hear me. He was so sweet. He rubbed my bald head and said my scar added character and he said he'd finish the *N* on his arm that night.

We walked over to this outdoor clay oven where they baked old-timey bread and Travis lifted me up so I was sitting on it and I put my legs around his waist and he rubbed his face against my chest. He let his suspenders drop off his shoulders and his black felt hat fall to the ground.

After that we did some stupid racing where he runs backwards and I run forwards and he still wins. His wife came out of the house holding on to the Cabbage Patch doll and told Travis to get his ass back in there.

Don't, I said. Leave her. He smiled. Hey, I said, do you know any songs from *West Side Story*?

He said no and told me he had to go and he'd pick me up around eight. I wandered over to the windmill to watch these Dutch guys work on the new blade. They waved and I blew them kisses and laughed and tried to act sexy in the dirt by lying on my side with a blade of grass in my mouth. Then this weird thing happened.

I remembered my car-washing job at Dyck Dodge. Mr. Quiring had told me that I had to start making plans that I stuck to, so I decided right there on the spot that I would never go back to my job, ever. It felt good.

I got up and waved goodbye to the windmill guys and walked over to the forge and sat on the hitching post in front of it swinging my legs and smoking a Cap. I had missed six or seven Saturdays of washing cars and nobody had bothered to tell me. I guess the job was officially over.

An American male teenager came walking up to me and said hello. I smiled.

Do you speak English? he asked.

Yes, I said.

Are you a Mennonite girl? he asked me.

I said yeah. He nodded and smiled and asked me if I had an extra cigarette. We sat on the hitching post together and smoked. I asked him if he was here with his parents and he said yeah.

What's good here? he said. I asked him if he had checked out the threshing and flailing demonstration. He said no.

He asked me if I knew where he could score and I gave him directions to the Silver Bullet. I asked him how he felt about being an American and he shrugged and said he never thought about it. I asked him what he did in America and he said nothing really. I liked him. Then his parents came walking up to us and said they were happy they'd found him.

Hello there, they said to me. I said hi. The father asked me if I was a local girl or a tourist.

Local girl, I said.

He nodded and his wife smiled and their son hopped off the hitching rail and told me it was nice meeting me.

Likewise, I said. They walked away and the boy was a few steps behind his parents and he turned around and shrugged helplessly. I nodded and smiled and then waved goodbye. When I had finished my cigarette I got up and wandered over to the big barn. I watched as several older men in overalls slaughtered a giant pig that they'd strung up from some kind of authentic wooden thing. The men were scooping out the insides of the pig and chucking what they found into large white pails.

I heard a tourist saying to her kid: Stand back, hold my hand, I said hold my hand.

The men's feet were making red tracks all over the gravel but I guess a little blood helps to keep the dust down sometimes.

The tourist was pulling her kid away from the slime that was moving towards their shoes and the kid was screaming let go of me, let go of me. I gave myself an assignment: Ride my bike no hands from one end of town to the other end of town with no stopping and if cars come, tough.

———

It didn't work at all. A lot of the trees had green worms hanging from them and I had to use my hands to steer effectively around them. I went home to worry about the evening. Time passed. I lay in bed. I changed my clothes. I played my music. I charted the majestic arc of my life and practised my smile.

In a way I think it might have gone better if I hadn't been bald, drunk, depressed and jealous. And if, when Travis whispered in my ear move with me, I hadn't said: To Montreal? When he meant no, now, here, my body. And if afterwards he hadn't given me an old mini-golf scorecard to wipe the blood off my legs and I hadn't started crying in the truck on the way home and slammed it into reverse for no good reason going fifty miles per hour.

Twenty-six

Somewhere around four in the morning my clock radio was still playing and I heard my dad pull up into the driveway so I got up and went out and asked him why he drove around so much at night and he told me. He said: I work during the day.

I poached him an egg. We sat at the table, him in his new suit and me with my knees up and my T-shirt stretched over them and he said: You don't want to spend the rest of your life here do you?

And I said: You mean here? Or here—and I swooped my arms around a little to indicate a much larger space, kind of sphere-like.

Hmmmm, my dad said.

I put my bald head on my knees and closed my eyes, saw nothing, and said Dad, I'm so damn tired. And in spite of his not liking the word *damn* he did reach out and trace my fish-hook scar really gently with his finger and he said he remembered that day.

The four of us been out in a boat on Falcon Lake. It was my mom's idea to go there and rent a little nine-horsepower boat and take some food with us and go to an island off at one end of the lake and have a picnic. My mom wore a matching shorts and shirt set that had large blue-and-yellow paisleys all over it with her bathing suit underneath it and her white Keds and my dad wore his bathing-suit trunks and a dress shirt buttoned up but with no tie and brown socks and shoes.

Tash and I were so excited and my dad kept giving us turns steering the boat but every time we did that we all had to move around and we came close to tipping a hundred times which we all thought was hilarious, especially my mom.

When we got to the island she put all the food on a blanket and while she was doing that my dad and Tash and I went fishing off a big rock that jutted out near where we were planning to eat. My dad was trying to show Tash how to snap the rod so the line went backwards and then forwards into the water and he said to me oh Nomi go and get the bait from the cooler, and so while I was walking away from Tash and my dad to get the bait she snapped her rod and the line went backwards and the hook on the end of it landed in my head.

There was a lot of screaming and bleeding and Tash felt awful and my mom and dad calmed us all down and removed the hook and washed out my giant gash with lake water and wrapped a tea towel around my head so I looked like an Egyptian goddess.

Then we all ate the food but while we were doing that we noticed storm clouds moving across the sky and the lake starting to get really choppy and my dad decided to check on the boat and then five minutes later he came back and told us it wasn't there any more. My mom started laughing and Tash said we were the Swiss Family Robinson now too.

I was happy to be stranded on an island with my family and a towel around my head and my only worry was that the boat was a rental and we'd have to pay for it because we'd lost it. I worried about things like that along with the constant threat of hell.

Do we have flares, my dad asked, which made my mom almost die laughing.

Oops, she said, I forgot to pack the flares.

It was warm and we had food and bug spray and even some blankets and we were together. My dad kept saying stupid things on purpose to make my mom laugh and Tash and I wandered around the edge of the island picking up rocks and things and talking about how we'd survive on the island for the rest of our lives and then have a movie made about us.

And then it started raining and we all went running and screeching into the trees and held the picnic blanket over our heads and when it stopped for a while my dad went out and tried to build a fire for us to roast marshmallows, which didn't work very well so we decided to go swimming because we were all wet anyway and we played tag in the warm water right beside the island and Tash and I saw my mom wrap her legs around my dad's waist and kiss him and he looked shy and confused and hilarious without his glasses on.

After that my dad was able to make a fire with bits of a newspaper we had brought along for kindling and we roasted the marshmallows and watched the sun go down. And then out of the blue our boat bobbed back into view, right before our very eyes, about a hundred yards from the shore, and we were all quiet and disappointed. Finally my mom said well honey, I guess you should swim out to it and bring it back. And so he did. And my mom and my sister and I sat on the beach together near the fire watching him swimming out into the lake and rescuing our boat.

Hey, Ray, I said. Would you like another egg?

He said no thanks and smiled.

You didn't tell me Mom was in a musical, I said.

True, said Ray. I should have. She was probably as old as you are now.

Did you see her? I asked. He said yes. He said she was amazing.

Hans took her in for the audition, he said. Out of the blue and she got the part.

Hans? I asked. The Mouth!

It was different then, said Ray. More . . . less . . . He lifted his hands and let them drop again.

Hey, how'd your class do in the festival?

The kids were wonderful, he said. Flawless. He stood up and said he was going to bed.

So what mark did Mrs. McGillivray give you? I asked.

Forty-nine percent, he said.

What? What the hell? I reached out and tugged on the back of his suit jacket. Why would she do that? You made her tea! You kept the wasp away from her!

Ray put his hand on the wall phone, just let it rest there against the black receiver. I don't know, he said. I really don't . . . I can't figure it out. The kids were on top of their game, giving 110 percent, like I said . . . flawless, just flawless.

Ray removed his hand from the phone and left the kitchen. I got up and followed him down the dark hallway. The kids, I said. They must be . . .

Devastated, he said. And closed his bedroom door.

In the morning I pulled one of my dad's abandoned notes to himself from out of the kitchen-sink garbage bag. Inquire re: lung capacity.

The phone rang. I said hello and my dad was at the other end. Don't worry, he said, we're not being bombed.

It's okay, Dad, I said. I understand what thunder is.

Ah . . . he said. Do you? I mean in scientific terms?

I know it can't kill me, I said.

Not directly, he said.

I read page three of the front section of the newspaper and learned that the once-pristine peaks of various mountain ranges around the world are now littered with trash, I told him.

Yes, he said.

You cut it out and left it lying on the counter beside the toaster, I said.

I'm sorry, he said. That's unlike me.

Should I ask where the kitchen table and four ugly matching chairs are? I said.

He said no. Then he said yes, he meant of course I could. I wondered for how many seconds he could hold his breath while being awake.

I don't really care, I said. I heard him exhale. Please don't say thank you, I thought.

Lightning on the other hand, he said.

Yes, I know, I said.

We hung up. And then he phoned back.

Oh hi, Nomi? he asked, as though there were an entirely real possibility that I'd left the house in two seconds and been replaced by a complete stranger who didn't live in our house but who sounded like me.

Dad, is that you? I asked.

Uh, yes, he said. Had he been momentarily unsure?

You forgot your driver's test, he said. I moaned and he waited.

They phoned and I told them you were unwell.

We use the word *sick* now, Dad, I said.

I rescheduled your appointment for this afternoon at 4:30, he said. I'll meet you there with the car. That should provide enough time to get from school to the arena.

Generally though, Dad, I said, I stay late at school working on extra projects, theorems, vivisections.

Yes, he said, I know. I've heard all about it. In fact, I meant that it would give *me* enough time to get from school to the arena.

When I was ten Tash took me swimming in the pits and we had this little dinghy with a rope around it and we were diving off it and after this one dive I got my foot stuck in the rope and I couldn't get it out and I thought I was going to drown and Tash hadn't noticed until the last possible second when all my air was gone and then I felt her hand on my foot and the rope being moved and I burst to the surface and then into tears. Later that day I realized that I could have died and I decided it was time to create some type of legacy so I asked my dad what people would sooner remember, the things I said or the things I didn't say. His response was: Forgive me, but what people?

Aced the test. My dad stood outside the arena waiting for me and when I came back I told him I'd made it and he said right on twice, loudly. And then he said aha! as though he'd discovered something. He also said, when I sped up to pass a car, there you go, now you're cooking with propane. At a stop sign I turned and looked at him and said wait a minute, are you smiling? What's wrong? And he sucked in his cheeks the way Tash used to and maybe still did and then looked out the window at the seriously ugly little buildings lining Main Street like a mouthful of rotten teeth.

We had minestrone soup and minute steak for dinner.

I'd forgotten we were on *M* tonight, he said. We were sitting on the floor in the living room. My dad had taped a large piece of cardboard over the bullet hole that said DO NOT SHAKE CONTENTS on it. He asked me to describe my block and I told him I needed a triggering point, a climax and a conclusion.

To graduate, he said.

That's what they say, I said.

Hmmm, said my dad. He stirred his soup and stared at it. I got up and went into the kitchen to look at the clock.

You're missing *Hymn Sing,* I told him.

Is that right? he asked. Do you mind? He pointed at his soup.

Go ahead, I said. He took his bowl and went downstairs. I finished eating and then I cleaned up and went outside to stare at the neighbour's wash line while I smoked a Cap and tried not to think about the obvious fact that Travis hadn't called since I'd botched yet another common human activity that even animals seemed to be able to do instinctively. I should practise the walk, I thought. I should grow my hair back.

I went back inside and phoned him and his mom said he was doing a job in Lowe Farm. Lowe Farm, I said. How far from here is that? She thought about twenty miles. Where in Lowe Farm? I asked. Well, at someone's house, she said. A customer's house. Are there many houses in Lowe Farm? I asked. Maybe twenty or thirty, she said. It's near the border. Near the border! I said. Lowe Farm is near the border? Yes, she said, between Morris and St. Jean. Well! I said, if it's near the border I should go there. But he's working, she said. I could help, I said. For nothing. You wouldn't have to pay me. I'll drive. I have my licence. I just got it today.

There was something wrong with me, I knew that much. I wanted to talk to Travis really badly. I wanted to hear him say he loved me and to really believe it.

She told me she thought he wouldn't need my help. What do you mean? I asked. What's the address in Lowe Farm, do you know? She said she knew, but she didn't think it was a good idea for me to go there. Not a good idea? I said. It is so a good idea. I'm going. I don't care if you won't tell me where he is. I'll just drive around until I find him. She began to say something else but I hung up on her. I could hear the choir in the basement singing I'm coming home, I'm coming home, to live my wasted life anew, For mother's prayers have followed me, have followed me, the whole world through.

I'm taking the car! I yelled over the music, and left before Ray had the chance to not know how to respond.

I drove all over Lowe Farm. There wasn't much to it. I didn't see the truck anywhere. I drove to St. Jean and Morris and checked them both out. I drove down every single street. I drove back to Travis's house and rang his doorbell. His mom came to the door in a bathrobe.

I'm sorry but I have this feeling you're lying to me, I said. Is Travis here?

She said he wasn't and then his dad came to the door with a newspaper and asked her what the problem was.

Nomi's wondering where Travis is, she said.

He's doing a job for me, said his dad.

You see, Nomi, I wasn't lying, said his mom.

No, he's not, I said. I drove all over fuckin' Lowe Farm and I didn't see him anywhere.

Please, Nomi, said his mom.

We'll tell him you were by, said his dad.

No, no, no, don't, I said. He'll think I'm pathetic.

No, he won't, said his mom. He cares about you. Oh God, this was extreme. His mother was being compassionate and Travis *cared* for me. I didn't want Travis to care for me. I wanted him to shove me up against the stucco wall of the boarded-up bus depot and tell me if he couldn't have me he'd kill himself.

Nomi, said his mom, it's quite late, honey.

Oh, yeah, I said. I looked at the sky.

I'm . . . you know I think I might have forgotten something in his room. I heard Tash say: Nomi, you're sad, man. Get a grip. Walk away. What have I taught you? And I thought: You taught me that some people can leave and some can't and those who can will always be infinitely cooler than those who can't and I'm one of the ones who can't because you're one of the ones who did and there's this old guy in a wool suit sitting in an empty house who has no one but me now thank you very, very, very much.

What did you forget? his dad said.

Oh, I said, it was . . . I'm not sure, but . . . I think um . . . like, a bracelet.

You can't remember what you forgot in his room? asked his mom. She whispered something to his dad and his dad went back into the house and she stepped outside and put her arm around my shoulder.

Nomi, she said, you're young and you've got your whole life ahead of you. In five years you won't remember any of this. His dad came back and said he couldn't find a bracelet and then his mom asked me if I'd like to go look myself so I went inside and went downstairs to his room and stood there for a few seconds looking at things and saying goodbye to Soul, the rodent. I took a guitar pick off his crate and put it in my pocket and went back upstairs. Any luck? asked his dad and I shook my head and whispered none.

———

I cry when I'm angry and then I just go to sleep sometimes for a long time and when I wake up it's usually better. It's like waking up out of a dream even if I can't remember the dream. I spelled Travis's name with cigarettes, all laid out nicely in the grass in his backyard, behind the bushes and next to the wooden swing. I stared at them for a long time and then smoked the *T* and left the rest, hoping Ravis would understand.

Twenty-seven

~

I was in four places last night. The Kyro Motor Inn and the hospital and the Silver Bullet and the blue field out behind the dump. It was like being in the middle of the ocean because the sun was just coming up and making the dew on it sparkle and seagulls from the dump were flying around and making a little noise so when I sat on the hood of the car it was like being on the deck of a cruise ship and I could see water for miles and miles and miles. I had this strange feeling.

It was the same feeling you get when you've spent a lot of time with a friend or relatives or someone and you're kind of sick of them and want to be alone again but then the time comes for them to leave and suddenly more than anything you don't want them to go and you act really nice again and run around doing things for them but you know that time is running out and then when they're gone you're kind of relieved but also sad that you hadn't been a better friend and you tell yourself next time for sure I'll be a better friend. And you kind of want to call them up and apologize for being a jerk but at the same time you don't want to start something stupid and you hope the feeling will just go away and that nobody hates you.

Just an hour or so before I sat down on the car hood, I was in the hospital looking for Lids, but she wasn't in her room

and her stuff wasn't either and I wondered if maybe the Rapture
had happened and I wandered up and down the halls looking
for a nurse or somebody who could tell me where my friend was
and then I spotted the orderly guy Lids and I had known from
school, the one who'd wiped up the apple juice I'd thrown, and
I went up to him and asked him if he knew where Lids was and
he said she'd been moved to Eden.

What? I said. What?

Eden, he said.

What the hell is Eden? I whispered. I'd started whispering
for some reason. It's that place, you know, on the other side of
the river, a few miles from here . . . *was he being cryptic?*

Eden, I said. She's gone to Eden? He nodded.

I'm not sure, he said, but I think her parents gave Dr.
Hunter permission to . . . He touched his head with all ten of
his fingers and said *zzzzzzz*.

I don't know what you're . . . I said.

Shock therapy, he said. So she can judge things better, like
. . . better judgment. I don't know, he added. All I know is she
went to Eden, that mental institute out . . . somewhere west of
here. He had to go swab a patch of corridor.

I walked back towards the front door of the hospital and
a nurse behind the counter asked me if there was something
she could help me with. I walked up to the counter and
whispered that I thought I was dying and she asked me how
old I was and I said sixteen and she said that was silly, I was as
healthy as an ox.

Is there nothing you can do? I'd asked. I remember
attempting to roll a joint right there in the hospital, trying to
get my stupid papers out of the cardboard thing and not being
able to. I kept tearing them, one by one, going shit, shit, shit.

What seems to be the problem she asked me and I said it
seems my face is the problem. I get these face aches. I get so

aahhhh . . . I just want to, you know, rip my head off, or just, shit, shit, shit, like fuckin' annihilate . . . everything. I don't know. I mean, not annihilate but . . . These papers are driving me . . . ohhh. I mean I wonder if some kind of painkiller, like Aspirin, or morphine, or . . . surgery. I don't know. An X-ray. But I think I'm gonna die, you know? Did you hear me? I feel that way. I feel halfway there.

You're sixteen, she said, that's a wonderful time in a girl's life. Go home and make yourself a cup of tea and try to relax.

Yeah? I said.

Yes, she said, just lie down on your bed and close your eyes.

But I do so much of that and it doesn't . . . okay I will, I said. If I still have a bed. The furniture keeps. Can I . . . I pointed at some files behind her head. Do you have sample kits or you know . . . sample . . . no? Okay, you said tea, right? And lying down, closing my eyes. Sorry, but did you just say the world is my oyster? She nodded. Okay, thank you. I'm sorry for bothering you so late at night and stuff, you don't have any matches on you, do you? Mine keep . . . I think . . . it's pretty windy outside now, isn't it? I mean, do you know where Eden is?

She shook her head and began to type something.

So then I went to the blue field and sat in the dark watching the car lighter pop out about a hundred times and holding it close to my hands for warmth. I slept . . . that long sleep I was talking about . . . and woke up on a cruise ship.

But before that, before the hospital and the field, sometime, I set a truck on fire in the parking lot of the Kyro Motor Inn, parked *hastily* outside room number six. They must have found a sitter for the Cabbage Patch doll. It was just a tiny corner of a rolled-up carpet sticking out of the end of the truck, but it went poof, fireball, really fast.

I drove off and picked up a Mountain Dew and rolling papers at the Mac's and Gloria asked me what I was still doing in town. I'm . . . I don't know, I said.

I thought you were leaving for the city, she said.

I am, I said. I mean I can't really.

But I thought you'd already gone. You came and said goodbye, right?

Yeah, but . . . I just . . . I wanted this, I said, pointing at the can of pop. So . . . thanks. I'm sorry for saying goodbye and not leaving. She said it was okay.

Did you cut your hair for the summer? she asked.

Yeah, I said. I mean no. But I like it, she said. I said thanks and just stood there with my head tilted way over so it was almost resting on my shoulder as though my shoulder was somebody else's shoulder or should have been.

What were those rules again? I asked her.

No hugging and no picking flowers, she said. Yeaaaahhhhh, I said. I wanted to hang out with her until her shift was over and then we'd go back to her rec room and feed the fish and listen to some records and trade clothes and watch TV. But another customer came in and I slowly swivelled around to stare at him like he had no fucking business walking into that store and then Gloria had to find some mayonnaise for him so I eventually straightened my head and walked out.

I walked all the way to my grandma's old house and knocked on the door. I didn't know what I would say to whoever opened it. I thought of: Hello, I'm sorry to bother you. But that might have left an awkward and ambiguous silence if I had nothing further prepared. Nobody answered my knock so I opened the door and went inside and up the stairs to the little bedroom with the slanted ceiling that had belonged to Trudie when she was a kid. There was a messy bed in it and a wooden crate and a yellow dresser and a bookshelf with what seemed like a thousand Hardy Boys books. Little piles of clothes on the floor. A few posters of hockey players and one of Jesus.

I lay down on the floor and closed my eyes and tried to imagine Trudie dreaming of musicals in the city. I saw her flying through the air, catapulted from my cousin's motorcycle, Tash and me screaming in the grass.

My hand accidentally grazed the small flannel pant leg of a pair of pyjamas. What is my problem, I whispered. I got up to leave and noticed a small class picture on the boy's bookshelf. I wondered which one he was, if I could find clothing in his bedroom that would match his outfit in the photo, and then I saw Ray, standing proud and tall, smiling, at the end of the back row. Mr. Nickel, Grade Six Teacher. The kid beside him was looking up at him with a sidelong glance and laughing. No doubt Ray had made a cheesy crack seconds before the shutterbug had snapped the shot. For a minute I stared at the picture and considered taking it with me.

I took the cornfield path behind the cemetery to The Golden Comb's place because I thought there'd be a chance I would get lost. I passed a wooden sign that said SLOW: HORSE CROSSING and for a second I thought hey Travis would like that for his room. And then I thought oh, right. And suddenly it seemed that the very best experience the world had to offer me was in Travis's room, lying face down on the cool concrete, listening to him play "Fire and Rain" or anything at all on his guitar, maybe lifting my head slightly, smiling, saying wow, crazy. Or maybe not saying anything, just taking his hand and putting it on my heart, and he would know everything there was to know about me.

The Comb opened his screen door. Eldon was in the living room playing air guitar with The Kinks and I smiled and held out my hands.

I'm broke, I said. The Comb nodded slowly and asked me why I was there then.

I don't know, I said. He gave me one of his cigarettes and I handed him my can of Mountain Dew. He said it was okay, I could keep it. I sat down on the floor by his front door and held the can against my cheek.

Tired? asked The Comb.

No, no . . . I said.

Watch out, he said. Your hair's gonna . . . I moved the cigarette away from my head and nodded.

Thank you, I said. My favourite song was starting but Eldon took it off and put on The Commodores and started slow-dancing with himself. The Comb sat down beside me on the floor.

Hi, I said. You like sitting too? He said yeah and then he kissed my shoulder really softly and I put my head back and closed my eyes. Don't cry, he said. C'mon now, don't cry. He kissed me some more and while he was doing that he took something out of his pocket and put it in mine and then he stood up and held out his hand and I took it and he put my cigarette into a plant and we went into his bedroom and closed the door.

I woke up on the hood of the car in the middle of a pretty blue field. The Comb told me I gave it up real sweet, and I said oh my God, the car, I forgot it at the Mac's. He gave me a ride to my car and said check your pocket. The key was still in the ignition and I got in and drove around for a long time trying to find something good on the radio and a place to get high, so I guess that's where I ended up. I still had my can of Mountain Dew but it was empty. It was clear to me I'd found myself a home. I could live in the car, walk into town for supplies. I could pick up American radio stations that sometimes played real music late at night. I'd sleep during the day. Get a night job doing . . . something. I'd have my dad over for dinner and we could eat sitting on the hood of the car watching the sun drown and then throw the leftovers of our dinner overboard to the seagulls. I was thinking about that when Jesus Christ came walking across the water in a suit and tie carrying two cardboard cups of takeout coffee.

He put the cups down on the hood and took off his jacket and put it around my shoulders. The shiny smooth lining felt nice on my bare skin. Then he reached around and took two muffins out of the inside pocket where he always kept his church bulletin, folded twice, like he was planning to kill flies with it later on.

We're on *M,* right? he said.

No, I said, *N.* It's the next day.

I don't have anything starting with *N,* he said.

I stared at the muffin.

Is that a nut? I asked.

It's a nut muffin, he agreed.

I'm not looking forward to tomorrow, I said.

No, he agreed again. We did some staring off into the distance.

But Nomi, he said. There is the flip side to that.

The dump looks like an island, doesn't it? I said. A clean island. I mean, it's super tidy. You're the world's best dump cleaner.

We're cleaning up the banks of the Rat today, he said.

Who is? I asked.

My students and I.

I looked at him. Yeah? I said. He puckered his lips and nodded slowly like the dipping bird I bought him.

Did you know that fear is something you can actually smell? I asked. The sun was sparkling off his head. He took off his glasses and breathed on them and then wiped them off with a handkerchief that he struggled for about five minutes to get out of his pocket because of his sitting position. He held them up, squinted at them, put them back on and stared at me. A clearer me.

Is that better? I asked. How many fingers? I held up three.

That's for unconsciousness, he said.

We sat quietly, listening.

You can do anything, he said. I knew it wasn't true. I knew he was saying, really, that he felt as though *he* could do nothing for me any more. But that also wasn't true.

What's the flip side, Dad? I asked him.

To what? he asked.

Before, I said, you said there was a flip side to not looking forward to tomorrow.

Oh, he said. Faith.

Faith is the flip side? I asked.

I think it is, he said. That tomorrow will be better. That sounds simplistic to you, doesn't it? he asked.

Yeah, I said. It does kind of.

Well, he said, there you go. I think my dad might have been giving me a triggering point, but I'm not sure.

The Mouth and his silent wife came to our place for coffee and he spoke loudly, in echoes. Or maybe it just sounded that way because our house was empty and could barely absorb anything louder than a whisper. They stood in the front entrance next to my dad's shoes and notes and my dad and I sat on the kitchen counter, on either side of the sink, listening.

It's been determined, said The Mouth.

What has? asked my dad.

Nomi's excommunication, said The Mouth.

I looked at him and whispered yikes, shit.

Based on what criteria? asked my dad.

Lack of attendance, said The Mouth. And other various . . . we can't have church members setting fires . . . and . . . He glanced at me briefly. I hadn't changed out of my cut-offs and bikini top. I was still wearing my police boots and I had streaks of dirt all over my legs. I smiled and nodded.

We understand, said my dad.

You know, said The Mouth. He cleared his throat. Some of your neighbours are wondering what's going on, just in terms of . . . there's a cross in your backyard, and your front window . . . it's shattered, isn't it?

Yes, said my dad. I nodded. And . . . The Mouth looked around and shook his head. You have no furniture?

We're . . . said my dad. He looked at me.

We're cleaning up, I said. My dad nodded.

I see, said The Mouth. He smiled sympathetically.

Rather thoroughly, he said. I'm sorry Nomi.

Oh, that's okay, I said. I'm . . . there's . . . no, no. I waved my hand around. I smiled at my Aunt Gonad. The corners of her lips twitched slightly, like she was involuntarily coming to.

More coffee? I asked. The Mouth said no, they had to attend a ribbon-cutting event in honour of the new blade on the windmill at the village museum.

Oh, said my dad, that was quick.

Yes, said The Mouth, we're thrilled.

I can imagine, said my dad. Let's hope lightning doesn't strike twice in the same place, he said.

That's right, said The Mouth. The windmill adds so much to the tourist's experience of genuinely understanding how we once lived.

Exactly, said my dad. I nodded.

Those were the days, I said. I turned the tap on.

Water? I asked.

No thank you, said The Mouth.

I leaned over and drank from the tap. I stayed there, eventually soaking my entire head, until I heard the front door open and close.

And all our righteousnesses are as filthy rags, and we all do fade as a leaf and our iniquities, like the wind, have taken us away. That was my dad speaking. Intoning morbidly.

Is that a verse? I asked. Or did you just . . . I waved my arms around in the air.

Nomi, would I just . . . he imitated me, waving his arms. It's a verse. I shook my head and got some drops of water on his glasses.

Sorry, I said.

Not at all, he said. I'd given him another opportunity to clean them.

Here, said my dad. He handed me a tablecloth to dry my hair and wipe my make-up off.

So what's . . . your lung capacity? I asked.

Oh that, he said. Your face is grey now, he said. From rubbing your make-up. I looked at my reflection in the fat blade of our only remaining knife. I found a clean corner on the tablecloth and rubbed some more.

Should we . . . I'll cook something delicious tonight. I've got a new system.

He nodded. Systems are good, he said. One needs a system of some sort.

And laundry, I said. Where are we at? I'll get that done tonight, don't worry. I thought about laundry. I ran downstairs and checked to make sure we had a washer and a dryer. When I came back up my dad was putting on his shoes.

May I? he asked. He held his hand out. I took the car keys out of my pocket and gave them to him. I thought he might have wanted to say something else because he stopped at the door and turned around to look at me.

Forget something? I asked. His glasses were very clean. Our eyes met and seemed to fuse, briefly, and then he left.

I pulled the tablecloth over my face and walked to my room without bumping into a thing because there was nothing to bump into, except something big and hard in the middle of my room. I took the tablecloth off my head and saw my French horn. I sat on my bed and took it out of its case. I blew into it a few times. I turned to face *Christina's World* and blew as hard as I could. FUCK YOUUUUUUUU! she said. I opened my eyes and stared at myself in my dresser mirror. He was right. My face was grey. My head was bristly now. I held the French horn to my mouth. That's better, I thought. Brass obliterated my face. I opened my case and found some of my old band music. And then I packed it all back up and took it with me to Abe's Hill.

I sat in the toboggan hut and propped up my lighter on the bench next to the sheet of music so I could almost see the notes and taught myself how to play "All Through the Night."

I liked the way the flame lit up the gold shiny metal of the horn. I stared at the lights of the city. And then I plowed my way through it over and over and over until it became not beautiful, but in a way almost bearable.

I imagined Tash lying in her bed with her window open thinking hey, that's Nomi on her French horn, the most beautiful instrument in the world when played properly. I tried to smoke a Sweet Cap afterwards but my lips were too numb to hold on properly so I just held it between my fingers and watched it burn away.

Twenty-eight

~

I have a car, a Custom 500 Ford four-door, plenty of legroom. He'd taken it to the car wash before he disappeared and left it gleaming in the sunshine on the driveway.

How did he leave? Walk? Hitchhike? How do you leave a town with no train, no bus, no car?

I also have a French horn I plan on learning how to play, an Akai stereo and my records, Tash's stuff, and an official looking note saying the house is mine.

All my dad left with was his new suit, his dipping bird, and the bible he'd had since he was a kid. He laid out all the information in a note he left on the kitchen table. How to deal with the sale of the house, how to change the oil in the car, not to get a basement apartment if I could help it, and to list my number with my first initial only. *N*, he wrote (in case I'd forgotten?), looking forward to that delicious meal you promised. I'll give you a year or two or five to develop your system. In the meantime, we have work to do. Remember the affirmative words of Jesus, Nomi. *Lo, I am with you always.*

He left me a verse from Isaiah, the prophet of redemption: For ye shall go out with joy, and be led forth with peace: the mountains and the hills shall break forth before you singing, and all the trees of the field shall clap their hands.

I doubted that. But I liked it. I liked the way it sounded and the way it made me feel.

That *N* was nice. That mysterious fullness. I looked at it for a long, long time. I think he'd been *aware* of writing it when he wrote it. I think he might have slowed down when he wrote it, looked at it and smiled. It was what I had. It was a very loving *N*. He hadn't needed to write it. I knew my first initial.

He'd written a PS too, another verse. And remember, when you are leaving, to brush the dust from your feet as a testimony against them.

Against whom, I wondered. Against what?

I sat in his yellow lawn chair for a while, staring at the highway, waiting, in case he'd change his mind. He was going to use his enormous lung capacity to climb mountains and clean the garbage off the top of them for a couple of years and I'd use mine to learn how to play the French horn properly. And if none of that worked out, we'd just breathe.

There was something else too. I'd just been ex-communicated, shunned, banished, exiled, whatever you want to call it. If Ray wanted to keep his faith and stay in town . . . yeah, I'd have been a ghost to him, a kid he loved but couldn't acknowledge. And it was comforting, in a fragile, loss-filled kind of way, to know that Ray had decided to keep the love alive in his imagination, and leave. That's what people around here are forced to do if they aren't strong enough to live without some kind of faith or strong enough to make a stand and change an entire system or overthrow a church. And who of us are that strong anyway? Not the Nickels, that's for sure.

This weird thing happened to me while I waited for what I knew was not going to happen. I stared at stuff for a while and then I slowly started filling the car with my things trying not to make too much noise because it was still really early and people were sleeping and then the neighbour kid came out of her house in her summer nightgown and asked me if she could watch while I loaded the car and I said sure. She told me she was a sleepy snake. She asked if she could feel my head. She put her finger on her cheek and said she had a good idea.

Yeah? I said. Gonna clean your room? She said noooooo.

Gonna drink your milk? I asked. Noooooooo, she said. She started humming softly and dancing around the car in her little white nightie.

I have an idea, I have a good idea, she said, finger on her cheek the whole time. I dragged it out for a long time until I had loaded everything and was ready to go.

Come here, freak, I said. I spun her for a really long time in the front yard telling her shhhhhh whenever she shrieked or laughed. And after ten or fifteen minutes of spinning we both fell down on the wet grass and everything, the sky, the sun, the clouds, the branches overhead were swirling around and making me feel like throwing up so I closed my eyes and that's when the odd thing happened. I started to see things in my town clearly, the pits, the fire on the water, Travis's green hands playing his guitar, him whispering in my ear move with me, and the trampoline, and the old fairgrounds and the stuff written on the rodeo announcers' booth and the lagoon and the cemetery, and the toboggan hut and the RK Ranch and the giant horses and my windowless school and my desk and American tourists and The Mouth and Main Street and the picnic table at the Sunset Diner, and Sheridan Klippenstein and everything, everything in town, the whole of East Village, and it didn't seem so awful to me any more in that instant that I knew I'd probably never see it again except for every time I closed my eyes and then I saw my dad in his suit standing in front of the mirror at Schlitzking Clothing and his green eyes blinking behind his large glasses and a smile just beginning to form.

I thought about Menno Simons and what kind of childhood he must have had to want to lead people into a barren place to wait out the Rapture and block out the world and make them really believe that looking straight through a person like she wasn't there, a person they'd loved like crazy all their lives, was the right thing to do. I thought about Lids in Eden having her brain electrified and I thought about that little piece of newspaper that had floated down into our town from some other place that had on it the words *for the way things could have been.* Which is what I'm calling my assignment. It's got a nice ring to it even though it kind of reminds me of a Barbra Streisand song. I've put my name in the top right corner and I'll be leaving it on your front porch. I'm assuming you'll mark it INCOMPLETE, the word circled in red. I don't need it back, Mr. Quiring, don't worry. Feed it to the chickens. And please be kind to Lids.

It looks like I'm still trying to impress you with my story, as though it matters. I'm like a terminal patient still dreaming of the day I climb Everest. There's a part of me that needs your approval and I don't know why. Maybe it comes from being a teacher's kid. Or maybe I just wanted you to think I was as creative as my sister. And maybe there's a chance you'll ask me to read my story to the class.

There were so many times I wanted to talk to you, but what could I say. Because in a whole bunch of perversely complicated ways I can understand your attraction to Trudie and hers to you but in another whole set of perversely complicated ways, I can't. Where's that guidance counsellor when I need her, eh?

You provided my family with an ending. You took to heart your own advice. You practised what you preached in class. Every story must have a beginning, middle and end. I've enclosed, with my "Flight of Our People" assignment, a copy of an excerpt from the last letter you wrote to your sad, sweet Trudie. Except that in this letter you don't call her your sad, sweet Trudie any more. You don't include any formal salutation at all. Seems a little harsh considering the "bottomless depths" of passion you originally felt. But things change. Stories unfold. Narrative arc and all that. You just begin.

> I will tell Hans that you kept the key to Mrs.
> Klippenstein's empty house and let yourself and several
> local men in, at night, to engage in adulterous activity.
> Whatever you say to refute my statements will not be
> believed, trust me.
>   You have a reputation in this town as being
> crazy, by which I mean demented, and your words are
> worthless. Will you reconsider?

Were you expecting her to take you back after calling her a nutcase and threatening to turn her over to The Mouth? You don't think flowers would have been more effective?

I have a theory, though: It was grief that drew my mom to you and love that pulled her back. Love for Ray. And for me and for Tash. And for the perfect idea, at least, of us being together again. There are so many perfect ideas in this town. But love, like a mushroom high compared with the buzz from cheap weed, outlasts grief. It does. Love is everything. It *is* the greatest of these. And I think that we all use whatever is in our power, whatever is within our reach, to attempt to keep alive the love we've felt. So, in a way, the only difference between you and me is that you reached out and used the church—there it was as it always has been, what a tradition—and I stayed at home, in bed, and closed my eyes.

Life being what it is, one dreams not of revenge. One just dreams. I could smell that hot June wind again—it was starting up for another day, blowing warm sweet promises, getting ready to break the hearts of all the Mennos in East Village one more time.

And that's when the neighbour kid rolled over in the grass and put her arm around me and rubbed my bald head and I whispered thank you. I meant thank you to Ray for, in the midst of his own multitude of crap and bewilderment, knowing one true thing. That I would never have left him and that if I were ever to get out of that town, he would have to leave first. That's two things, I heard him say. And the neighbour kid said you're welcome, because she was a polite kid and thought I was talking to her. She was a good kid. We were all good kids. Amen. And then it was time for me to leave and for her to go home.

The idea of my mom leaving town to spare my dad the pain of having to choose between the church or her, knowing it would kill him, was the story I liked the best. The other possible ending to the story of my mom's shunning was that it opened a door for her, a way out of this place, which raised the possibility that my mother had never really loved my father, or that she had loved him years ago but had since stopped loving him, or that she loved him but not more than the idea of being free. That it was just a convenient excuse. That could be the truth. I don't know.

Did she have a thing with you because she was angry with Ray for keeping her in a town that she knew would inevitably break up her family? Did she live every day with the conundrum of wanting to raise her kids to be free and independent and of knowing that that's just the kind of kid a town like this chews up and spits out every day like happy hour? The Mouth had suggested once that my mother might have killed herself out of guilt and regret. I think it was the ending he most enjoyed. The typically grim outcome that made sense to him.

Let's be realistic, he said, which had made even my dad laugh out loud. But it did make me wonder. If she had planned to travel far away from this place why had she left her passport behind in the top drawer of her and my dad's dresser? Was her body at the bottom of the Rat River, her hazel eyes wide open, staring in eternal mock horror at the flailing limbs of fifteen-year-olds being forced underwater in baptism by her brother, The Mouth? Or was she alive and well and selling Amway or something in some tourist town on the Eastern Seaboard? Or maybe she had finally managed to get to Israel and was working as a courier in Tel Aviv?

Had my dad really gone to pick garbage off mountains or was he also at the bottom of the Rat—no, I preferred the first story, the one about sacrifice and pain, because it presented opportunities, of being reunited, of being happy again, somewhere in the real world, our family, and because it was about everlasting love and that's what I like to believe in. The stories that I have told myself are bleeding into a dream, finally, that is slowly coming true. I've learned, from living in this town, that stories are what matter, and that if we can believe them, I mean really believe them, we have a chance at redemption. East

Village has given me the faith to believe in the possibility of a happy family reunion someday. Is it wrong to trust in a beautiful lie if it helps you get through life.

I put my leather bracelet between the doors of Clayton's mom's house and got back into the car. I knew she would find other ways of keeping Clayton alive in her imagination. I lit a Cap, pulled the seat up a little closer to the wheel, found a half-decent song on the radio, and drove.

That sounds good, right? Actually I haven't dropped off the bracelet yet but I will. Soon. I'm pretty sure of that. I've got the car. All I have to do is sell the house. Good solid unfurnished bungalow. Perfect for families. Going cheap. Truthfully, this story ends with me still sitting on the floor of my room wondering who I'll become if I leave this town and remembering when I was a little kid and how I loved to fall asleep in my bed breathing in the smell of freshly cut grass and listening to the voices of my sister and my mother talking and laughing in the kitchen and the sounds of my dad poking around in the yard, making things beautiful right outside my bedroom window.

ACKNOWLEDGMENTS

Hearty thanks to Michael Schellenberg and his all-star editing abilities that combine a Zenlike calm with heat-seeking missile precision and to Carolyn Swayze for gently reminding me that writers write and to Paul Tough for reading earlier versions and to Cheryl Cohen for shepherding a thousand details to safety and of course, as ever, to NCR for guarding all the exits.

Also by Miriam Toews

ff

All My Puny Sorrows

Shortlisted for the Folio Prize

Elf and Yoli are two smart, loving sisters. Elf is a world-renowned pianist, glamorous, wealthy, happily married: she wants to die. Yoli is divorced, broke, sleeping with the wrong men: she desperately wants to keep her older sister alive. When Elf's latest suicide attempt leaves her hospitalised weeks before her highly anticipated world tour, Yoli is forced to confront the impossible question of whether it is better to let a loved one go.

'To write fiction out of personal events of such magnitude is hard, almost unbearably so, but the result is a novel that reaches beyond the limits of itself.' Sophie Elmhirst, *Financial Times*

'From its arresting opening sentence to its heart-catching last line, it is jaunty, matter-of-fact and full of zest and verve . . . Reads as if it has been wrenched from her heart.' *Sunday Times* Summer Reads 'Top Choice'

'I can think of no precedent for the darkly fizzing tragicomic *jeu d'esprit* that is [*All My Puny Sorrows*] . . . I laughed aloud even as tears rose in my eyes.' Stevie Davies, *Guardian*

ff
A Boy of Good Breeding

Hosea Funk is the Mayor of Algren, a tiny town in Canada. For most of his adult life, Hosea has believed he is the biological son of John Baert, the prime minister. When he receives a letter from Baert, informing him that Algren is in the running for the prize of Canada's smallest town, an accolade that would be awarded by the prime minister himself, Hosea's task becomes clear: if he can keep the population of Algren down to 1,500, he will win the prize and finally be reunited with his real father.

The return of Knute and her daugher Summer Feelin' to their home town therefore is not welcome news to Hosea. And his girlfriend Lorna's endless requests to move in with him – which would tip the scales well over the magic number – have to be negotiated carefully. And what with all the multiple births these days and so many people living a long time, the obstacles to Hosea's goal are stacking up . . .

'Binds you in a spell so good humoured you never want to leave.'
The Times

'Seriously funny, rather brilliantly structured and full of characters who speak the same laconic language as Garrison Keillor's in Lake Wobegon.' *Independent*

ff

The Flying Troutmans

Hattie, living in Paris, has just been dumped by her boyfriend when she receives a phone call from her eleven-year-old niece. Hattie's sister Min is having a particularly dark episode and Thebes asks Hattie to come and look after her and her brother Logan. By the time Hattie arrives back in Canada, Min is on her way to the psychiatric ward. Suddenly responsible for two children, she realises that she is out of her depth and hatches a plan to find their long-lost father. With only the most tenuous lead, she piles Logan and Thebes into the family van and heads south.

At once hilarious and heart-rending, *The Flying Troutmans* tells the story of a fractured family on the verge of spinning off its axles and a road trip that just might keep them together.

'I absolutely loved it . . . One of the most original, fresh, funny and heartbreaking books I've read in a long time.' Jane Fallon

'With wit, warmth and a firm pinch of absurdity, Toews has produced a grittily sparkling cocktail of a novel.' *Spectator*